Murder at Town Meeting

Wes Blauss

W0009135

Murder At Town Meeting © 2019 by Wes Blauss. All rights reserved. This book or any portion thereof may not be reproduced or used in any manner whatsoever without the express written permission of the publisher except for the use of brief quotations in a book review.

ISBN (Print): 978-1-54396-114-0
ISBN (eBook): 978-1-54396-115-7

In loving memory of

Louise Buckley, John Dias,
Henry Howland, Carol McCormack,
Mary Puleio, Mike Regan, Frank Romano, Barry Ross,
Della Snow, Ed Spinney, Patty Stearns,
Elizabeth Waterman,
and all the wonderful people in the 1970s
who made Town Meetings so entertaining!

"A town should be judged less by what it says in public than what it tolerates in private."

--- Gottlieb Thurgood,
Community in Conundrum, 2001

OCTOBER 4, 1976,
SPECIAL TOWN MEETING

7:31 PM

I'm sitting in the non-voters' section at Town Meeting. I'm sixteen so I have to wait two years before I get to sit down on the floor with everyone else. You used to have to be 21 to vote, but that changed back in 1971 because of Vietnam. Sparky Manx says, if you're old enough to fight, you're old enough to vote. So they lowered the voting age. It took a lot of kids dying and a lot of kids holding signs to make that happen. I was only eleven so I didn't get to vote or die or hold signs. I didn't even know what a Vietnam was until last year in history class. My parents went on a big march in D.C., back in '69, but they didn't take me with them. I thought they were in the Macy's Thanksgiving Day Parade or something, just without balloons. I was little and they didn't want to scar me. They said I should wait till I was older.

Seems like life is all about waiting to get scarred.

Anyway, it's Monday, October 4, 1976, 7:31 P.M., and I'm here at the Special Town Meeting for the Town of South Quagmire (just north of East Quagmire). I'm recording this for our school newspaper, *The Quagmire Quarterly* which, to the best of my knowledge, has never come out more than twice in one year. I'm a junior. I got assigned to write about this special Town Meeting because our school has an article on the warrant, Article Four.

We're waiting for a quorum, which is one hundred people. That's the least amount of people you need to vote. I count 97.

Actually, it's Birnam just counted 97. Birnam's my brother. He also wants me to say that today is exactly two hundred years and three months after the signing of the Declaration of Independence, which is not exactly true if you want to talk about who signed the Declaration of Independence when, but I'm not arguing. All men are not created equal. Birnam is brilliant with numbers. He's not so good at other stuff, but we all have our own strengths and weaknesses. There are two cops standing behind us, Officer Farrell and I don't know the other guy's name. They are giving me the eye. I think I will take my tape recorder and move.

7:34 PM

I'm sitting in the sound booth at the back of the middle school auditorium balcony. It's really just a big box with a glass window and a couple of consoles for running lights and microphones. I asked Mr. Carroll, who's sitting in the non-voters' section because he lives in one of the Bridgewaters, I forget which one, and he said I could. He's school superintendent. He's cool. I haven't been in here since eighth grade when we did the spring talent show. Arianna, she was my girlfriend at the time, until my parents interfered, we ran six lights and two mikes, nothing compared to what we got at the high school. We popped a circuit breaker and messed up the order on two songs. No big deal.

We made out fine.

'Made out' being the operative word.

'Words,' Birnam says. Birnam's very particular. He came in here with me. There was no chance I could ditch him.

Arianna's sitting in the non-voters' section with her friend Karen Pina. She hasn't noticed I moved in here yet. She's sixteen too, seventeen in November. Karen's eighteen already and she's a registered voter, but she says she doesn't want to sit down on the floor with old white men.

It's funny being back in the middle school. It's a lot smaller than I remembered. The stage is especially small. I was on it for *Pirates of Penzance* in the eighth grade. I got to play a pirate but didn't get a solo because my voice was breaking. I got to marry Arianna, who was a daughter of the Major General. Birnam was a policeman for about the first week of rehearsal and then he dropped out. The stress was too much for him. He was in the sixth grade, but he was supposed to be in the fifth. He's got double-promoted twice, which is why now he's a sophomore when he's only supposed to be in eighth grade. He's very smart, and we'll leave it at that.

Arianna's just turned around and is trying to figure out where I disappeared to. So, that's good. We had a rough summer, but maybe things will get better now. (Birnam, quit punching me.) The high school did the play *South Pacific* last winter, and I got to play Lieutenant Cable and she was my girlfriend, Liat, who is supposed to be Tonkinese, which is kind of like Chinese. Arianna got cast because she has beautiful skin color. She's Cape Verdean, which is not black, but is a kind of black, except people from Cape Verde, which are some islands off the coast of Africa, are Portuguese, not really black, which is not the same as white but not black either. It's a little tricky, and we got in trouble because I was supposed to fall in love with her in the play, but I also fell in love with her back-stage. Actually, I've been in love with her since *Pirates*, so last year I invited her to the Sophomore Swing, which is a dress-up dance in the spring, and she said yes, but then my mother told me we couldn't go to a dance together because my dad talked to her dad, and they decided it wasn't a good thing, so we had to break up, and she ended up going with Jimmy Gomes, who's Cape Verdean too, and he's only a freshman. Well, sophomore now.

It was kind of like in the play where Lieutenant Cable loves Liat but can't marry her because she isn't white.

I'm white, so it was a problem for my parents, which is funny because my parents packed me and Birnam in their Jeep Cherokee and we did Woodstock when I was nine. and my parents are the biggest hippies on the planet, love, peace, and rock-and-roll, and you'd never guess they are prejudiced. They were stoned and naked the whole time. I guess they didn't think that would scar me. No one knew it was gonna be such a big thing back then. Just some concert in a field that got way out of control. But I don't remember black people at Woodstock except maybe Jimmi Hendrix onstage a little, so I don't know. I was only nine and wasn't paying attention to those things.

Only a few black people live in South Quagmire, but a lot of the people who live here are Cape Verdean. They came to work on the cranberry bogs. Arianna's grandfather came here when he was ten. He left his home and his parents and came here with his older brother. He's been here ever since, and now he's on the School Committee. So Arianna and I have been together in school since first grade and we've been friends since eighth grade when we got married onstage, which our drama teacher, who is really just the elementary school music teacher, Mrs. Lewis, called color-blind casting.

I think she is not as prejudiced as my mother.

My father, I don't know. They wouldn't say what he talked about with Arianna's dad, and he wouldn't tell me either.

My father's name is Charles Wood, but everyone calls him Chuck. Chuck Wood, get it? Some people call him Woodchuck Wood just to be funny. He doesn't like it. He works at the cranberry company as a maintenance foreman. Runs a forklift, keeps the refrigeration units from breaking down. My mother's name is Gladys, but she changed it to Cher when she married Dad. Cher Wood. Like in Robin Hood, right? Or because she's a big fan of Sonny and Cher, I don't know. My brother Birnam is three years younger than me. My brother Woodstock just turned six. My parents say he was conceived at Woodstock, but Birnam says, "Do the math!" and Birnam is usually right about these things. My name is Petrified.

My parents spend a lot of time under the influence of drugs.

Anyway, it's our country's Bicentennial year, and our town of South Quagmire's been through a lot... (Huh, what? Yes, thanks, Birnam) ... one-hundred-twenty-eight years' worth of Town Meetings. We broke away from East Quagmire and formed our own town in 1848. We had our hundred-and-twenty-eighth annual Town Meeting in March which I didn't go to. Karen Pina did, and said it was boring as hell and lasted three nights. But I did get to ride in the ladder truck in the big parade on the Fourth of July and a girl went streaking down the middle of the street. After she went by, Sparky Manx almost drove off the road and killed a bunch of Girl Scouts. They had to jump over the stone wall that borders the cemetery to escape getting run over, and the high school band never did find the right key again, and the trumpets all went sharp for 'The Star-Spangled Banner.'

She was hot.

She wasn't from around here.

She was someone's cousin from Detroit.

Chief Dobbs just walked in.

That makes 98.

He went right over and started talking to Miss Makepeace. Everyone's placing bets he won't make it past Article One before he has a tantrum and storms out. Chief Dobbs has a really bad temper. He's our town's fire chief and you don't want to make him mad. Whew, boy, does he get mad. The adults are placing bets with Nigel Brate, he's the town bookie and also a selectman, and he owns the packy, that Chief Dobbs won't make it to the end of the meeting. This is illegal, but the police chief won't deal with it if he wants his raise to be radioact—der, stupid, stupid... retro... retroactive... I keep messing that up… in his next contract, which comes up in June, so everyone's getting in on the act. People go to Brate's Liquor Emporium to buy booze and cigarettes and bet on dogs, horses, football, that kind of stuff, but Town Meeting time he runs a pool on stuff like what article will Chief Dobbs storm out on and how many times will Miss Ottick say she was born in this town. My parents are betting Article Six for Chief Dobbs and four times for Miss Ottick, that's the younger one, Miss Edie, except they won't put money on it because they hate Brate. He's part of the military-industrial complex, which has something to do with a bunch of helicopters he keeps stashed over in East Quagmire. Anyway, Dad says Chief Dobbs has to get through Article Three at least because there's a lot of money involved in Little Quagmire Swamp, but then he'll go mental over the ambulance. It should be interesting.

C'mon, c'mon, people.

What's wrong with people, they can't even show up for Town Meeting? Miss DeBarros, she's Arianna's aunt, she was my history teacher last year, she says Town Meeting is the purest form of democracy, but how's democracy supposed to work if people don't show up to vote? It's now 7:39 and we need two more people to have a quorum so we can start the meeting.

I don't see Little Anthony. If he was here, we'd have our quorum. Almost. It's funny Arianna is here but not her father. She's still looking around for me.

Now she sees me. She's waving.

I'm waving back.

She's looking at me funny. Maybe she remembers the last time we were in here together.

Nothing much else is going on, so I guess I'll keep talking.

Chief Dobbs is looking very emotional at Miss Makepeace. She's hot. He's probably emotional about her driveway or how the police chief burned rubber in her driveway. Chief Dobbs hates the police chief. Sparky Manx says it was him laying her driveway started the whole thing. Chief Dobbs called it a driveway fit for a goddess. He laid it, then he bragged about it for weeks and made all the firefighters go over and look at it, but they could only stand on it in their stocking feet. When it rains she supposedly can see her reflection in it. She's the town's executive secretary. She got promoted from the Board of Health because she's so healthy.

Yeah, right.

Chief Dobbs likes laying asphalt among other things, that's what Sparky Manx says. Sparky's thirty-eight and knows about laying driveways and other things, even though she's never been married, so I don't know what it is she could know about other things.

Miss Makepeace has a coffee pot in her office at Town Hall, and in the mornings in summer she comes over to the fire station carrying coffee mugs she made herself. Chief Dobbs gets the biggest mug because he's the fire chief. He carries a Colt .45 M1911 in his holster and he shoots rats with it, but his aim sucks. Also, he laid her driveway. "Black silk," she said, and she winked at him when she said it, like the rest of us wouldn't get what 'black silk' was about, although maybe Reverend Jake, who's a call fireman and an EMT and a minister at the black Baptist Church, didn't get it. I don't know what ministers get and what they don't. His mug has a cross on it, an actual silver cross stuck right in the clay, though maybe it's stainless steel. She put it there herself. Biff Larson's mug is shaped like a fire hose nozzle. Little Anthony's is stenciled with a fire truck. Little Anthony is Arianna's dad and another call fireman.

He's the best. They all live together down on Hancock Street, him and Arianna and Miss DeBarros. There was an older brother too, but he drowned a long time ago when he was still a kid. That's what Article Four is about, a memorial to him, sort of. Sparky Manx, who's one of two full-time firemen in town, or, I guess, she's a fire-woman, but can't be lieutenant chief because they don't let girls be lieutenants, she says it was pretty tragic. Her mug has a real spark plug inlaid, and I even got one too Miss Makepeace made for me special. It says 'Aryan Youth,' which is kind of a joke, because I'm blonde, six-foot-one, and the corners of her mouth turn up in the nicest way whenever she calls me that. She's dressed sharp tonight and is really pretty, which is why Chief Dobbs is getting all emotional right now. Her smile can draw sweat from a cactus. Sparky has a cactus, and I've seen it happen. Her fingernails come in colors on the outskirts of the rainbow, red and violet, purple, mauve, and they're in constant motion, touching us, patting our shoulders, ruffling our hair. Tonight they're red, sort of a cranberry vermilion. I can see them from all the way here at the back of the hall, and she's onstage behind the selectmen.

It was a good summer except for the part about me and Arianna and her dad and the break-up. Chief Dobbs was in love. He was so pleased with her driveway no buildings burned down. That's love. Miss Makepeace did his laundry. That's love too, I guess. I got to drink coffee with the guys at the station… even though Sparky's a girl… and I loved being with Arianna's dad, because he was nice to me when he had every right to be pissed. He used to call us Aryan and Arianna as a joke. There are times I wish I had him for a father instead of the one I have. No one makes fun of him. Miss Makepeace, who only arrived in town two years ago, she likes him too. She respects him. Actually, she pretty much respects all of us. She asked us all kinds of questions about people and how the place worked. We were happy to tell her everything we knew. I was just a sophomore and figured life would go on like that forever.

But Chief Dobbs is an arsonist.

At first I thought an arsonist was someone who collected weapons, like his Colt .45 M1911, which he uses for target practice on stray dogs, but his aim sucks, but later my mother told me it was a person who plays with matches.

When Chief Dobbs decided the town needed a new fire station five years ago, the old one burnt down. At night. Most of the call firefighters were at the Second Congo attending their weekly AA meeting. By the time they made it through the twelve steps and heard the alarm, which was delayed by a tripped circuit breaker, the blaze was out of control. Chief Dobbs said it was faulty wiring. No one reported the empty canisters of kerosene in the dumpster. Sparky says we should just keep quiet about it.

So Town Meeting 1972 voted for a new fire station.

It's huge. It has eight bays. We only have two trucks, but Chief Dobbs likes to talk about the day when we have a whole fleet of vehicles. People call the firehouse Tubby's Palace. The Ottick sisters, who are old, call it Tubby's Phallus. My mother laughed for two days when she heard me call it that. I thought a phallus was something with eight bays. I didn't know it was another word for 'dick.' 'Phallus' was not on our seventh-grade spelling lists.

She said we shouldn't call him 'Tubby' though. It's rude.

The town's old library, which was empty since the new library slash senior center opened next door to Brate's Liquor Emporium, needed a new roof, and before Town Meeting could vote money to fix it, the library went up in flames one Sunday morning while the call firefighters were sleeping off a retirement party for Harry Dane, the lieutenant chief. There were no books in it anyway, just some old Hardy Boy mysteries I'd already read. Nothing was left but the brick foundation and melted bits of Tiffany glass.

"Don't remove the bricks," Chief Dobbs told my mother when she showed up with a wheelbarrow. "They may be needed as evidence."

But he never discovered any evidence, and the empty canisters of kerosene in the underbrush are buried under a blanket of poison ivy today. My mother turned the melted Tiffany tidbits into hand-crafted jewelry. My mother's very artsy-fartsy.

And after there was no more need for roof repairs to the library, money became available for the new ladder truck.

Old lady Ottick or I should say, Miss Katherine Ottick, the older sister... she's sitting up onstage... is the richest person in town, and also a selectman, and she was mad. She came right down to the fire station and told us so while we were sitting in our lounge chairs, getting tan, although Little Anthony and Reverend Jake are plenty tan already. "What possible use could a community of eight thousand souls find for a ladder truck?" she yelled. There wasn't a building in town over two stories. She was going to march right over to Town Hall and demand a rebate on her taxes in protest of this "flagrant misuse of municipal funds."

That's when she decided to run for selectman, and she won because no one else ran.

But then her sister's cat spent a day and part of two nights in a catalpa tree and the ladder truck made its first official call-of-duty. I got to ride in the cab with Little Anthony. It was awesome. I was thirteen, and Arianna and I weren't a couple yet. Unfortunately, the cat scratched Chief Dobbs and he shot it dead with his Colt. His aim is OK at close range.

Which only made the Ottick sisters madder. They said they would sue the pants off Chief Dobbs, or get him fired, but luckily Miss Kay really hated the cat... It was Miss Edie's cat... so she was too cheap to hire a lawyer.

Miss Edie says Miss Kay will never understand. She wasn't born in this town. You gotta be born in a place to really understand it. If the ladder truck had been around six years ago, the fire tower wouldn't have burned down. That happened when Chief Dobbs got mad at the county fire marshal who squealed on him after Chief Dobbs set fire to End Zone Island.

The fire marshal had new binoculars.

I don't understand why setting fire to End Zone Island should bother anyone but the Ottick sisters. Chief Dobbs has been losing control of campfires on End Zone Island since high school. That's what Sparky says. So has every cool kid for thirty years, and a few who aren't cool, but want to be.

Twenty years ago, Chief Dobbs, whose real name is Tobias, and kids called him Toby then because he wasn't fat in high school, was wicked cool and also, according to Sparky, wicked hot, except Sparky didn't think he was hot, he was an underclassman, but other kids did. He was the star running back for the Quagmire Quarrymen and he celebrated winning football games with his team and the cheerleaders out on End Zone Island. The campfires always got out of the stone circles and torched the place, scaring game birds and forcing half-naked drunk teenagers into the water. Today's coolest kids... also some 'wannabes' who end up pantsed and vomiting... carry the tradition on.

Proudly.

At least, that's what Sparky Manx says. I don't play football and I'm not cool, so I wouldn't know. You can't be cool and come from the family I come from.

I have a hard time seeing how the kid in those old black-and-white, but mostly brown, photos in the fire station can be the same guy who laid Miss Makepeace's driveway. Chief Dobbs is still tall, but he's old and bald and his belly's huge, which is why people call him Tubby behind his back. Am I going to look like that when I'm thirty-six? He isn't anything like the football hero who supposedly had all the cheerleaders lifting their pompoms for him, but for old times' sake he still goes out and sets fire to the swamp. Thanks to the Surplus War Property Administration, the South Quagmire Fire Department has a flame thrower. The rule is, use it or lose it.

Chief Dobbs likes using it.

He needs End Zone Island to burn, that's what Sparky says, and he wants to turn Little Quagmire Swamp into a wasteland because TouchDown Realty has plans for developing it.

That's what Article Three is about.

The swamp is owned by four different people. My parents have about sixty acres on the east side where we grow marijuana because both of them suffer chronic conditions that require homeopathic medicines like herbs, weed, tobacco, and alcohol. I am perfectly healthy. That's how I knew I was adopted a few years before I knew I wasn't.

A private school for bad boys owns, like, a thousand acres in the southwest corner and the sound of semi-automatic weapons keeps our waterfowl freaked. Three of the boys are in the back row in the non-voters' section. They're all dressed in camo and probably packing heat. The two cops are keeping an eye on them. I hope this glass is bullet-proof.

But the biggest part belongs to Miss Ottick, the selectman… woman. She's the daughter of the man who invented cranberry juice freeze-pops, and she plans to sell her piece to TouchDown Realty if Article Three fails because the town's new sewer system means some of it's developable.

I don't want Article Three to fail. I'm with my parents on that one.

It's 7:54.

Here comes the town moderator, Tim Drummond.

Mr. Drummond is Chief Dobbs's best friend. He played linebacker in high school. They both played for the Quagmire Quarrymen, which kids from other towns call the Quagmire Queerymen when they want to pick fights. Now the two of them are part of TouchDown Realty and in it for the money. That's what Sparky says, and also Miss Kay's younger sister Miss Edie, and my father too. If the swamp is worthless, they can get it cheap, and Chief Dobbs knows someone in the state and can get around wetland restrictions.

So there's a chance people will vote against Article Three, against buying the swamp, because of the money. Also, everyone's afraid Chief Dobbs will come around some night and burn their houses down. I know everyone in town (well, except Miss Kay) is careful to keep on his good side. He has a lot of kerosene stored behind the station and no one is taking any chances.

I don't know where Little Anthony is. If he were here we'd have our quorum.

Arianna is talking to Karen Pina. Karen's Cape Verdean too, but she's also very nice, except she smokes and she's a senior.

It is now 7:55 P.M.

I was five-foot-six when I was twelve-years-old, five-foot-nine when I graduated middle school, and my mother said I would be one of those kids who's tall in middle school and then suddenly stops growing, but she was wrong. I spent seventh grade wearing floods because I was taller than every boy in my class and all but two girls. My pants couldn't keep up with me, and my sneakers too, but this was good because everyone had to look up to me. I didn't get bullied, which in South Quagmire happens to kids who aren't athletic or wear floods or have a name that makes people think of logs and fossils.

My teachers call me PT. That helps.

I'm not athletic, or at least not athletically-minded. My gym teacher wanted me to play basketball and football because of my size, but my parents said no and I swore to hate them forever, but I didn't really much care about missing out. My jump shot sucks and I don't like getting hit.

I like ducks. I'm a bog boy.

I like frogs, toads, painted turtles, dragonflies, red-winged blackbirds, black-bottomed newts, but more than anything else, ducks. Miss Makepeace says all Aryan Youth share an affinity with nature. She may be right. She's right about a lot of things.

Besides the half-acre of marijuana my parents cultivate in the middle of a woodlot, the rest of our property is mostly a small cranberry bog and the reservoir that irrigates it. Ducks love our pond, which is far enough away from the school for wayward boys (I think its real name is the South Quagmire Military Academy) and also the Rod and Gun Club so gunshots are more an annoyance than a threat. My mother grows corn to hide the marijuana plants, and since no one in our family likes corn, I get to use it as duck food. I lure the ducks onto our property and then I draw them. We have mallards, mergansers, wood ducks (a family favorite), and one fall we had a pair of goldeneyes that spent a week. I skipped school for three days to hang out with them and wore twenty-two black crayons down to the nub. My teacher was pretty upset with me missing classes, but later, when he saw my drawings, he was OK with it. He said I was artistic, and that we were lucky. We live in a landscape crazy littered with moraines and kettle ponds and eskers from the Ice Age. Our town boasts the best interrupted drainage system in New England. That's why the ducks keep coming back. In middle school, when I wasn't in school or at the fire station, I had migratory birds to keep me company and, when they were flying off to faraway places I might never see, I had my family to make me wish I could go with them.

It's now 7:57, and that loony-tune with the oxygen tank and his wife, or girlfriend, or whatever-she-is in the wheelchair, just rolled in. Theobald Doppelmeier, how's that for a name? I dunno what her name is, just Mrs. Doppelmeier, I guess, but not necessarily. Mr. Doppelmeier has gone through women like he was a rock star or something, that's what Sparky says. He was a quarterback in high school, but Sparky says his offensive line was weak and he got hit in the head too many times, and now he lives in some kind of imaginary BINGO game, whatever that means, and his skin is blue. He drives a Corolla Wagon, or mostly he keeps it parked between the post office and the Dunkin Donuts dumpster in the handicapped spot, and Jasper Lovell, who drives the mail truck when Bill Early's sick, even though he's only sixteen and doesn't have his license, only his permit, and stayed back twice which makes him the world's biggest sophomore, not to mention the dumbest tight end on the football team, he's backed into it so many times the thing looks like it's been through a world war, but Mr. and Mrs. Doppelmeier never make it around the car and probably haven't seen the rear door in years so they don't even know it's no longer operable, or, if they have seen it, it hasn't registered on them yet.

Anyway, does this make a-hundred-and-one registered voters? Do we have a quorum finally? Birnam says we have a quorum. The town moderator, Mr. Drummond, is going up onstage to the podium, so I guess we have a quorum. He's going over to the Town Treasurer. They're too far away to tell for sure, but it looks like they're angry. This could go on for a while. The Town Treasurer is part of TD Realty too. My parents hate TD Realty. They don't care anything about the land, just about selling it and making money.

Birnam is pointing at his watch and getting frustrated. He's obsessive-compulsive about things.

This is taking way too long. I have an English paper due tomorrow I haven't even started yet. C'mon, people.

Now the Town Treasurer... Mrs. Épée, something like that... is yelling at the moderator. She looks mean. Now she's yelling at Mrs. Drummond. Mrs. Drummond's the Town Clerk.

"I am going to the bathroom and, Tara, don't try to follow me!!!"

God, she's loud. I can hear her right through the glass.

She's marching off the stage. Waving a bunch of papers around. She is one big woman. I hear hippos are the most dangerous animals in Africa. Mrs. Drummond is looking at her like, I don't know, frightened or confused. She is *not* following her to the bathroom. Why would she? Get a hippo in the bathroom, there's no room for anyone else.

Birnam is breathing heavy. This is not a good sign.

Birnam's the best brother a kid could have, and also the worst. He's three years younger than me, double-promoted twice. He's six-foot-tall and a-hundred-ninety pounds and still growing. He towers over our father, has shoulders like a gorilla, which he gets from our grandfather on my mother's side, and is a phenomenal mathematician. Birnam can tell you what day of the week February 8, 2095, will fall on, and he'll be right. Not that I ever have a clue he's right, but you just know he is. He can give you the answer in under five seconds. (Tuesday. Thanks, Birnam.) Once he explained to me how easy it is to calculate, but he lost me after the first sentence. I'm good at math but nothing special. He's crazy good. Great with numbers, not so hot with people. Eye contact is almost impossible for him. He talks to walls and windshields.

He's talking to his watch right now.

Everyone bullies him. He's too big for physical abuse, only the occasional bump or shove in the school corridor. He never pushes back or protests because protest needs eye contact, but his classmates, who are, like, two or more years older, say the meanest things, and never let him join in any reindeer games. The cool kids are vicious. The uncool kids steer way clear of him for fear of being bullied by association.

It's 7:59, and the moderator is talking to the Town Clerk, who happens to be his wife. Karen Pina's interning for Mrs. Drummond this semester in the Town Clerk's office. She says it's boring as hell. I mean, the work, not Mrs. Drummond. Well, yeah, maybe Mrs. Drummond too. Now Chief Dobbs has gone up onstage and joined them. None of them look happy. I should not have put off writing that English paper. There goes my grade-point average. People are starting to get antsy in the voters' section. You can hear the grumbling even back here.

I don't think people in a small town are mean at the core. I think it's something that comes out when you get it no one in a small town is important in the big world, and we'll never amount to anything that's gonna be remembered in history. You can be the prettiest girl in the junior class, but a few hours with a Hollywood magazine and you sorta understand you'll never be famous. You can be the biggest football player on the team, Homecoming King, but if you're still in town by the time you're twenty, you know you'll never do anything that'll make the record books. Chief Dobbs had the attention of Miss Makepeace, but it didn't last more than a few weeks before the police chief came along and left rubber in her driveway, and then Chief Dobbs was yesterday's news in her eyes and everybody else's, just some tubby, bald guy with a cool gun who couldn't kill anything except by accident.

He can turn a swamp into scorched earth, drain it and develop it, make a million bucks if he's lucky, which we'll know after tonight. None of it means anything. Two towns over, nobody even knows his name, probably.

People want to be somebody, and to be somebody you gotta be smart, know stuff, sound important. What's to know in a small town? Gossip and stupid stuff and who's going out with whom. Not much else.

Keep your head down and stick to ducks, that's what I say, and maybe someday if you're lucky, someone it's OK to love.

I love Arianna DeBarros, and I love her dad, Little Anthony, too, and my brothers, even Birnam who keeps punching me, and is starting to hyperventilate.

I wish life was easier for us white boys.

Little Anthony still isn't here. Where is he? This is really weird.

Little Anthony isn't even little. He's maybe an inch shorter than me, thirty-one-years old, no, thirty-two last Friday. He's wicked muscular. You should see him when he takes his shirt off, which is all the time. He works out a lot. He had Arianna when he was, like, sixteen or something. (Birnam says, "Do the math!") He has brown eyes and black hair which he keeps short, and big hands for his size, and he smiles a lot. You can see where Arianna gets her good looks. Or it might be from her mother, but her mother ran away when Arianna was, like, a year old, so I don't know.

He's called Little Anthony because he wasn't the oldest kid in the family, and he had an older brother who drowned during high school when a bunch of them were diving in the quarry. Little Anthony lives with his sister who was my history teacher last year, Miss DeBarros. Georgina DeBarros. She's Arianna's aunt. Neither one of them are married, although Miss DeBarros is dating the biology teacher, Mr. Corr, *and* Reverend Jake at the black Baptist Church.

Both at the same time.

She is pretty hot for a teacher.

She's the one proposed Article Four to get a plaque in memory of their brother.

Their brother was handicapped which is why he drowned.

My brother is handicapped too. His disability is mental, not physical, but it means I have to keep him from getting hurt which is all the time. We know what it's like to be our brother's keeper. It isn't pretty. Little Anthony was there the day his brother dived into the quarry and never came up. They never found the body either. There are lots of bodies in the quarry, that's what Sparky Manx says.

The quarries are all closed now. Someday they'll be drained so people can build a golf course on top of them, and it'll be like opening up a graveyard.

It's 8:02.

At last, we're starting.

Moderator Drummond bangs his gavel, one, two...

He's fallen to the floor.

He's fainted.

People onstage are jumping up and knocking over chairs and crowding around him.

We may have lost the quorum.

Birnam says we have.

We may be here till midnight!

I should not have left off writing that English paper. It's due tomorrow. I thought we'd be out of here by 8:30. There's only nine articles, I mean...

Now I'm screwed.

8:04 PM

I'm supposed to say what?

I can't do this.

OK, OK.

OK. Sorry. It's… 8:04 PM.

The Town Moderator is on the floor. There's people all around him. I can't tell if he's unconscious or what. Sparky Manx is giving him CPR.

Miss Ottick, one of our selectmen, just kicked him in the head with her shoe, well, nudged, really, to see if he's alive.

Karen says it looked like a real kick to her.

PT and Birnam are counting down from a hundred. They do that whenever Birnam gets freaked out. I think he's freaked out right now because we lost the quorum. PT's given me the cassette recorder until he gets Birnam breathing back to regular again.

OK, OK. Sorry.

Yes, OK.

My name is Arianna Albertina DeBarros and my father is Anthony John DeBarros. He's an EMT. He's on the fire department. He's a call fireman.

My friend Karen Pina is with me in the sound booth. She's a senior. She plans to run for school committee next spring and then president of the United States.

There's a sound system in here and if I can remember how to turn it on, maybe we can hear what's going on onstage. You can't hear through the glass. Maybe the microphones *[unintelligible for five seconds]* using portable speakers, but maybe…

I forget.

I haven't been in this box for, like, three years, and then I did the lights, PT did sound.

Karen says she just heard someone shouting, "Pacemaker!"

Maybe Mr. Drummond has a pacemaker?

Karen doesn't know. Karen works for Mr. Drummond's wife, who's Town Clerk, in the Town Clerk's office. She's interning for Mrs. Drummond this semester. She says it's boring as anything.

OK, how do you turn this thing on?

I don't know where my father is. He should be here by now. He had to run back to the station to get the ambulance, just in case. I think 'just in case' is happening right now.

OK, OK. Sorry.

Chief Dobbs just head-butted Sparky Manx. Sparky fell off the stage. Now the chief's kneeling on top of Mr. Drummond and he's giving him CPR. He's very big. He might hurt him. I don't think it was a deliberate head-butt. They just accidentally bumped heads while the chief was trying to relieve Sparky.

Karen says it was definitely a head-butt.

Ten compressions, one breath. Chief Dobbs just threw something. I think it's a pack of cigarettes.

Karen says Mr. Drummond is a chain smoker. Karen's in the doorway and she definitely heard, "Pacemaker."

He had to [unintelligible for six seconds] can perform CPR.

PT and Birnam are down to fifty-four.

Fifty-three.

Fifty-two.

Fifty-one.

What?

Oh.

PT just asked if we've lost the quorum.

We may have.

Does the moderator count in the quorum?

Oh, no.

Birnam is gasping for breath. He's beating on his brother. He's melting down all over again. PT has some kind of cross-chest carry like in lifesaving going on. They're back to a hundred.

White boys are so emotional.

Sorry.

Karen said that, not me.

What? I don't know what brand. Why? Are you out? My father would know. He probably sold them to him.

Karen says she thinks the moderator doesn't count in the quorum, so maybe we haven't lost it. Anyway, Karen can go down in the voters' section. She's been a registered voter since March. She just doesn't want to sit with old white men.

I wish I remembered how to turn on the sound so we could hear what's going on. I think...

No.

No. Nothing.

Reverend Jake just came in with a whatever-you-call-those-rolling-stretcher-things. He's trying to get by Mrs. Saville. She's the funeral director. She's—

"Is he dead or is this another one of Tim's ploys for sympathy?!!"

Got it!

Volume.

Sorry, sorry.

That was Mrs. Saville. She's crowding the stage. Sparky's on the radio. I think maybe she's radioing my father about the ambulance.

Yes, Mrs. Drummond is saying she thinks it's his pacemaker.

Mrs. Saville has taken out a tape measure. It's black.

Chief Dobbs has quit CPR. They're rolling Mr. Drummond off the stage onto the...

Gurney, Karen says.

PT and Birnam are back at a hundred again.

PT's got him in a headlock so now PT's doing the counting and Birnam's—

Right, right, OK.

Sorry.

Reverend Jake and Sparky have got Mr. Drummond onto the gurney. Mrs. Saville is measuring him while they're rolling. How do you measure someone with a black tape measure?

Where's my father? We need the ambulance now.

Karen says it's too late for the ambulance. Mr. Drummond is definitely dead.

His wife is running after them. She's crying. The police chief has stopped her. Chief Crockett. He's making her turn around and go back to the stage. She's trying to fight him. He's holding her. He's pointing her back to the stage. She...

She's going back to the stage, but she's crying. She keeps looking back. She's watching them take Mr. Drummond out. Where are they taking him? There's no ambulance here.

Karen says the walk-in refrigerator.

That's gross. With tomorrow's school lunch?

The police chief has got the microphone:

"Ladies and gentlemen, a moment of silence please for one of South Quagmire (just north of East Quagmire's) finest citizens, Mr. Tim Drummond."

Volume.

Down.

Sorry.

Everyone is standing.

Seventy-seven.

Seventy-six.

Seventy-five.

"Thank you. We've got a quorum."

That was a very quick moment.

"We're not going to lose it now. You know Mr. Drummond would insist we continue, and maybe before we're done tonight, Mrs. Drummond can still sing 'The Star-Spangled Banner.' Won't that be nice?"

"No, no, I couldn't."

"Tradition, Mrs. Drummond. Tradition. And we don't want to lose the quorum, now do we? And remember, we never start the meeting until you've sung 'The Star-Spangled Banner,' but maybe we can save it till later when you feel better."

"No, no, I can't. Tim—they just took—he—"

"Your husband would expect nothing less from you, Mrs. Drummond. Breathe. Just breathe."

"I can't."

"Nineteen years, Tara. Nineteen years. Remember? Everyone's expecting you… We're looking forward—"

"I can't. Tim—Tim! Let me go. Please."

"Later."

Mrs. Drummond just went to go back to her seat and the police chief stopped her. She's crying. They're not letting her sit down. This is awful. I think everyone's scared because Chief Crockett has a gun on his belt. A man is standing up behind the selectmen. He's coming to talk to the police chief. They're talking. The police chief has his hand over the mike. Now the selectmen are all standing. They're all talking at once.

Karen says the man talking to the police chief is the town's lawyer.

Town Counsel. She doesn't know his name.

He's taking the mike. He's got a nice suit on. He's very small.

"Edgar Vade, Town Counsel. Apologies for the confusion. We've never lost a moderator this early in the proceedings before. (He's clearing his throat or something.) According to town by-law, in the event the moderator is incapacitated, his position will be assumed by the Town Clerk. The meeting will need to vote to elect Mrs. Drummond temporary moderator for the evening. Yes. What? Oh, yes, a simple majority."

Everyone's talking at once.

Oh, no, they can't do that. This is awful. Poor Mrs. Drummond. She's Town Clerk. She looks like she's going to faint. The police chief is holding her up. Oh. He's got her by the…

Oh, no.

I think it was an accident. Her...

Karen says that was no accident. He was copping a feel.

Karen said that, not me.

He's taken the mike from the lawyer. He's got her in one hand and the microphone in the other.

"I move that the town appoint Mrs. Drummond temporary moderator."

"Is there a second?"

That was Town Counsel. Nobody's seconding his motion. No one's...

"I second the motion!"

Oh, the Town Treasurer is back. She doesn't look happy.

Karen says she never looks happy.

"All those in favor, raise your hands."

The police chief's just...

Oh.

He's taking his gun out of his...

Holster.

PT says holster.

PT's down to twenty-one now.

Twenty.

Nineteen.

Birnam is breathing again.

Counting.

People are...

Well, some people are raising their hands. Karen says no one dares vote no. All the exits are blocked by policemen.

"All those opposed?"

No one's raising their hands.

I think it's the gun.

"Mrs. Drummond, take the gavel."

She isn't taking the gavel.

"Tara, take the damn gavel! You know you want it! Then you can sing your ridiculous song and everyone will be, so, "Oh, Tara, you sing so divinely," and "Oh, Tara, you're so talented," and "Doesn't she just have the best voice in town?" and "When she hits that high note I get goose bumps!" So take the gavel and let's get this show over with so we can all go home!"

That was the Town Treasurer. Wow, she is *very* unhappy.

Mrs. Drummond is taking the gavel. She looks shell-shocked.

She's looking around. Now she's talking to the police chief. He's tapping on the mike:

"Karen Pina? Is Karen Pina in the room?"

Karen, they're looking for you. Oh, this is so not good.

8:17 PM

OK, PT Wood again. I'm back. It's 8:17 PM. My brother's breathing. I think I've broken a rib. They called Karen down to sit in for Mrs. Drummond while she's the moderator, but there was some heated discussion we were not supposed to hear, and after a bit Old Miss Ottick, the selectman... I mean, selectwoman... thanked Karen for volunteering, which she hadn't, but said due to her age and inexperience it was better they ask someone to fill in who's been around longer, and, you'll never believe it, they dragged Theobald Doppelmeier up to the front and made him the substitute Town Clerk for the meeting because, I guess, he was Town Clerk for a couple of years in the sixties. They had to drag up his oxygen tank and everything, and his wife, or woman, whatever, in the wheelchair. This is ridiculous. They got him propped up like a rag doll. He's moving papers around like...

I dunno. Is that a squirrel?

I think he's got a stuffed squirrel or something. He's setting it on the table in front of him. What the heck? This guy is so wacked.

There's also a woman beside him who's talking into some rubbery-gray funnel thing Karen says is a dictamask, and she's dictating what she hears. Supposedly she'll write it all down later from tape. So that's good.

Karen's happy to be back. Too many old white men down there for her taste. A few of them look like they should've died years ago.

I guess maybe it was because she's too young, but I don't know. Reverend Jake got up and gave a prayer for Mr. Drummond, and a bunch of people didn't bow their heads.

Reverend Jake's black.

Also, Wampanoag Indian. I know, it's a little confusing.

No white people go to his church.

Mrs. Drummond just led us in the Pledge of Allegiance. She didn't seem to know all the words. Then, when everyone sat down she said something about not giving Mr. Drummond his B-12 shot this month and Mr. Doppelmeier started shouting, "B-12, B-12!" He actually thinks he's in a BINGO game! Sparky's right. This guy is messed. He definitely needs more oxygen. He looks even bluer than when he came in.

He's doing something with the squirrel. Sick! And are those nuts?

Now his wife looks like she's passed out in her wheelchair.

Mrs. Saville's tying a black armband around Mrs. Drummond's arm. This is really weird stuff. But at least maybe we can start now and I can get home before midnight and write that paper.

Mrs. Saville is helping her bang the gavel.

She's still standing.

This is good.

ARTICLE 1

———

"To see if the town will vote to transfer from Article 5, line B - 2, Postage, of the 1975 Annual Town Meeting, $6,700.00 to the Police Expense Account, for the purpose of paying that portion of the replacement costs of an equipped Police Cruiser not covered by an insurance recovery, or take any other action in relation thereto."

"Uh… Chief Crockett?"

"I move that the town transfer from Article 5, line B-2, Postage, of the 1975 Annual Town Meeting, $6,700 to the Police Expense Account, for the purpose of paying that portion of the replacement costs of an equipped Police Cruiser not covered by an insurance recovery."

"Is there a second?"

Mr. Doppelmeier's jumping up and down in his seat and shouting, "B-2! Beef Stew! Got it!"

Omigod, he really is wacked.

Chief Crockett says, "I believe that's a second."

Town Counsel whispers to Mrs. Drummond. She says:

"Is there a recommendation from the Finance Committee?"

The Finance Committee, oh, right.

OK, there's a bunch of people sitting at one of the tables onstage and they're all shaking their heads and looking not very helpful. One of them is standing up. She looks very stern. She's saying something about needing that money to mail out tax bills.

Birnam, quit punching.

Birnam, quit punching, for God's sake!

Birnam says there's eight-thousand-three-hundred-fifty-six people in town, or two-thousand-three-hundred-seventeen households...

Wait, what?

And that means...

Two dollars and eighty-nine cents per household...?

The woman at the table...she's saying something about state-municipal chain letters.

What the heck are state-municipal chain letters?

Oh, no, the hippo's getting up. Oh, boy. She does not look happy. She's coming over to Mrs. Drummond. I think the floor is shaking. She's grabbed the mike. Just hip-checked Mrs. Drummond... She's...

"Obviously, it is a waste of my time to explain the intricacies of state reimbursement to... hairdressers, storeowners, cops... but I shall read from a recent arrival from the State Treasurer's Office:

"Dear... So-and-so-and-so-on:

"On receipt of....

...

"Make twelve copies of this letter and mail it to twelve neighboring municipalities...

"Etc., etc.

...

"Enclose a check for two hundred dollars in each...

...

"Within two weeks you should begin receiving checks for two hundred dollars from other communities as your town moves to the top of the list...

"And so on...

"Receive up to twenty-five thousand dollars by Christmas...

"Don't break the chain!!!! One town did so and lost all state and federal funding a month later and was forced to hire a full-time town administrator.

"Yours truly,

"Etc.

"It should be obvious to all the algebra dropouts in front of me that high level finances require a great deal of postage, and I strongly urge, if you have even a shred of intelligence among you, which I very much doubt, to defeat this article.

"Thank you.

"I am going to the bathroom and, Tara, don't try to follow me!"

Wow, that was intense. And Arianna had the volume turned down to almost zero. Mrs. Drummond did *not* follow her to the bathroom. I wonder if the zombie filling in as Town Clerk got all that. His head's on the table and he's playing with his nuts. I couldn't keep up with her. She just left the stage and people look scared.

My parents hate her, I know that. She's, like, the main person in TouchDown Realty. If they get their hands on the swamp she'll probably kill all the ducks.

So anyway, the issue is, obviously, we need the police cruiser more than we need postage. It got wrecked in August because of the driveway. Everyone in town knows about it so I'm not spilling any secrets. It was parked in front of the hydrant in front of Miss Makepeace's house, right in the middle of the day, and Chief Dobbs got wind of it. He had the ladder truck out. He was polishing the gold ball on top of the Town Hall flagpole, and he went tearing over there and smashed into the cruiser, which he said was an accident, but nobody believes that. He says nobody gets to park in front of a hydrant, not even the police chief. But, of course, we all know he wouldn't want him parking in the driveway either.

So now we only have one cruiser, a '69 Chevy Caprice that looks like junk and doesn't start in the cold. We need a new cruiser. Chief Crockett's not gonna let us out of here tonight until we've voted yes. He's got all the doors blocked with cops. And no one's gonna vote against the police. Even my parents don't dare. No one's going anywhere until he's got that cruiser, not if it takes all night.

Postage doesn't stand a chance.

Oh, oh, here we go.

Chief Dobbs is up onstage and he's yelling at Chief Crockett. He's a lot taller than Chief Crockett, but Chief Crockett looks way more fit. Chief Crockett runs five miles a day and lifts weights, but Chief Dobbs's got at least five inches and a hundred pounds on him. This could be it, folks. Everybody's laying bets Chief Dobbs won't even make it to Article Two, and this could be it. He's turning red. Miss Makepeace is up now and she's trying to get between them. I don't think that will help. It can only make matters worse. Really, it's because of her the two of them hate each other so much.

Sparky always said that driveway was going to be big trouble.

Holy shit!

Chief Dobbs just threw a punch, and Chief Crockett dodged it and came back with an upper-cut to the jaw. People are scrambling from the stage. It's a madhouse down there! Chief Dobbs is holding his jaw. He's storming off stage. Jeez, he really is storming! Whoa! It's like a tornado, people are flying out of his way. This is crazy! He just knocked over Mrs. Doppelmeier's wheelchair with her in it. He's out the door. He slammed the door. The cop couldn't stop him.

Ouch, Birnam, cut it out!

What? Oh, shit! Have we lost the quorum?

Sorry, Arianna, sorry. I didn't mean 'shit.' I mean... I just got carried away.

What?

OK, sorry, Karen. I didn't think you'd... I mean...

Yes, I apologize.

Ouch, Birnam, I'm warning you...!

NOVEMBER 18, 2007

Abruptly, the recording ends. In 1976 you flip the cassette after an hour. I'm guessing the tape never got flipped. The recorder that Petrified Wood borrowed from the A.V. department at Quagmire Regional High School for his civics project is abandoned, then misplaced for thirty-one years, and only resurfaces this spring when our new town administrator, who we get with or without the help of state-municipal chain letters, starts cleaning out Town Hall basement and finds it in a closet. He brings it to my office, along with a bunch of other crap. There's a pile of water-stained books from God-knows-when that are completely illegible, leftovers from one of the many times the cellar flooded in heavy spring rains, and three umbrellas with Bicentennial logos printed on them, still in plastic wrappers. A big expanse of cloth turns out to be a muslin backdrop with a pastel forest scene, now moth-eaten and mildewed, that may have hung on Town Hall stage a century ago. And there's the tape recorder. I know it in an instant, QRHSAV magic-markered on the side. I recognize it as if it was yesterday. He asks if I think this stuff should be tossed, or would the Historical Society want any of it as memorabilia? I'm not listening. It all comes flooding back to me, Arianna and her dad, Petrified Wood, or rather, PT, trying to get his brother Birnam to breathe, Mrs. Drummond replacing her husband, the first casualty of the night. I blinked, and thirty-one years went by: college, a degree in business administration, two terms on the school committee, two marriages. I never did run for president. We just elected our first black president (well, half black), but I think we'll find the country's still as racist today as it was in 1976.

We just pretend otherwise.

I'm Town Clerk now. They wouldn't let me fill in that night Tim Drummond died and his wife had to take the gavel. Which reminds me. Out of respect for the dead I should follow the format laid out by my predecessor on tape that night.

My name is Karen Angelina Pina Cabral Wood. It's 9:15 AM, Sunday morning, November 18, 2007. I've finished my second cup of coffee and *The Boston Globe*. I've finished transcribing everything I could get off the cassette tape yesterday. A lot of it is garbled or inaudible.

Fortunately, I don't have to rely entirely on an antique tape or my aging memory to tell you the story. The oxygen-deprived Doppelmeier (fatally deprived, as it turned out) never did record anything we could decipher, but in those days the town employed an outside firm to dictate the proceedings into a dictamask, so we have a complete transcript of how events played out that night.

When the dust settled, eight people were taken out of the world, my family was reduced by three, and three white boys came into my life in a big way. Four of the dead belonged to TouchDown Realty, two were collateral damage, two more were... well, therein lies the tale. My Uncle Anthony DeBarros hanged himself in his jail cell. No one removed his belt. Tara Drummond lived four more years, then took her own life in Florida. Shortly before her death she claimed to have seen a ghost. No one believed her at the time.

That meeting changed everything. Most of the people in the hall are no longer with us. Christmas, 1979, one of the boys from the military academy shot and killed the head of school over a *Victoria's Secret* catalog. He went to prison, died there. Thus ended the school for bad boys, which most people in town felt uneasy about anyway. It was like a halfway house for juvenile delinquents. I think the NRA was a corporate sponsor. And then the Ottick sisters died of smoke inhalation when their house burnt down in 1981. The ladder truck might have saved them if the ladder hadn't gotten tangled in the power lines.

Arianna DeBarros and her Aunt Georgina stayed until the end of the school year, 1976-77, then moved to New Bedford. They came back a couple of times, when Reverend Jake was killed in a plane crash spraying cranberry bogs with Nigel Brate, and when my grandmother died twenty-three years ago, not since. Arianna never married. Last I knew, her aunt's still a school teacher in Fall River. Georgina must be close to retirement age.

PT Wood died two years ago of AIDS in Miami, and there was some argument about a final resting place. He's buried in Second Parish in the family plot under his own name. His brother Birnam insisted. It wasn't a given.

Now, thanks to the resurfacing of PT's cassette recording, and a chance discovery Birnam made last month in the Town Accountant's office, I can finish what my late brother-in-law started, then abandoned. Man, that boy could talk. Give him an audience and there was no stopping him. I half-expected him to sit up in his casket and implicate us all in his criminal history, topped off with heartfelt thanks to everyone who made it possible. Then again, he could be succinct when occasion demanded. Besides his given name and dates of birth and death, there's just one word and a punctuation mark on his stone:

"Live!"

And live he did, more lives than his own. But the events of that October evening stopped him in his tracks. Stopped us all in our tracks. Left us grappling for answers, for closure, for a happy ending. He never finished the story for the school newspaper. He made up his own ending instead. That English paper he was freaking out about, who knows? He graduated class valedictorian, so I'm guessing, yes.

As for the local papers, I actually saved that week's edition of *The Quagmire Express*, 'Death by Democracy', and have it somewhere. If I start spring cleaning, hopefully it'll show up. In the meantime, I've made copies of the official transcript in the Town vault at the taxpayers' expense and have them with me now. I haven't written an actual story since high school, just some slop about star-crossed lovers and how they overcome racial prejudice, like that ever happens, but it feels as if the Ghosts of Town Meetings Past or spirits from beyond the grave are giving me a sign, and while I don't believe in signs, or ghosts, or half of what PT left me in his will, well, PT and Birnam and I bear some responsibility for these restless spirits. They've done about all they can do, and I may be the only one standing who knows most of the story behind the story, me and Sparky Manx (of course), so, "Who does not take the risk does not taste."

I guess I'm taking the risk.

I guess you're choosing to bite.

MURDER AT TOWN MEETING:
THE TRUTH, MORE OR LESS

South Quagmire (just north of East Quagmire) is an unexceptional town.

It's unexceptional in 1976, it's unexceptional today.

Most of it is uninhabitable.

The southern half of the town is cedar swamp, home to red-wing blackbirds, snapping turtles, and the endangered black-bottomed newt, which may or not exist anymore. The Conservation Commission agent hasn't found one in six years. A purported bog beast, the Pleasant Street monster, is sometimes thrown in for good measure. This creature of indeterminate enormity is the invention of old-timers living on the perimeter. Cloaked in scraggly black hair and wreaking vengeance on two legs one night, four the next, it gets blamed for the occasional demise of a dog, a chicken or two, caged rabbits. Kids don't believe in it. Kids don't not believe in it. It adds a *frisson* of danger to the place.

That, and the great white sharks, which Rocky Mackiewicz claims swim upstream from Narragansett Bay and lurk in the shallows off End Zone Island in what is called an estuary. [1]

---

1   The movie *JAWS* came out the previous summer, 1975, and skinny-dipping in local ponds ended, especially at night. Whether or not we believe Rocky Mackiewicz, we're nervous about snapping turtles.

Today Little Quagmire Swamp is the property of Massachusetts Fish and Wildlife, and still teems with ducks, which should make PT rest comfortably, but back then it's privately owned. It goes on for miles south of the 'Cranberry Company,' Mr. Gabriel Ottick's conglomeration of rangy, railroad-straggling buildings of brick and tin, since torn down by his daughter Katherine, under the direction of Open Door Realty, Associates, to put in a subdivision of twenty houses. (They wanted seventy.) It's littered with hummocks and hillocks that are great for exploring if you have a canoe, aren't afraid of swamp monsters and sharks, and can find a weekend when Fire Chief Tobias Dobbs isn't exercising his flamethrower. My boyfriend at the time has a beat-up Old Town, and we spend afternoons and weekends stroking out of public view. I hate the bugs and the mud, and we won't even get into the leeches, but the lack of parental oversight is welcome. Dirt roads crisscross the expanse, threading their way through pine groves and skirting the cranberry bogs. Kids in town learn to drive on those back roads, starting about the age of ten. Hemlock and cedar trees bear the scars of their incursions. Most of the swamp is owned by our selectwoman at the time, Miss Katherine Ottick, and she doesn't mind our joyriding across her property. She posts No Trespassing signs which we are free to ignore. There's nothing we can harm except our cars and each other.

About six hundred acres though is owned by a military school for troubled boys, and they like to shoot the tires out from under us if we get too close. So, we don't get too close.

They're all white boys. They shoot white kids' tires too.

White kids stay west of the train tracks that bisect the four-thousand-plus acres. The rest of us drive mostly on the east side. We all steer clear of the South Quagmire Military Academy if we value our Firestones. Otherwise we'll have to call Big Pauly Silvio and get him to ratchet our Ford Impalas out of irrigation ditches with his tow truck. And once he gets his tires shot out too. Boy, that doesn't end well.

At sunset, when the wind's from the west, you can hear *Taps* coming over the water. Its distant, melancholy brass makes my hair stand on end, but in a mystical way. The music says that the dead are always with us: a prayer and a reminder in case we get complacent.

The inhabited part of town, about eight thousand of us living, hunkers on high ground, a series of low hills, glacial drumlins (PT explains in too much detail) on the great outwash plain that is southeastern Massachusetts. Three little rivers run through, Bim's Brook, Stump Brook, and the Shumatuscacant. They join in the swamp. Main Street crosses all three on minor bridges, fast decaying, and halfway along Main Street is town center. The buildings are mostly white clapboard, a smattering of brick facades, with open doors and plate glass to lure in 'Cranberry' employees and their paychecks after work. Town Hall squats, all cornices and quoins and bearing an odd resemblance to Bates Motel from Alfred Hitchcock's *Psycho*. There's also a bank, a diner called The Grub Pub (I work there waiting tables Wednesdays and Saturdays from 1975-1977), and the grocery store with its over-sized parking lot, rusty shopping carts scattered along the perimeter. Big Pauly's service station, Tubby's Phallus, and the new library slash senior center, they have the swamp in their back yards. So does Nigel Brate's Liquor Emporium, which is flanked by Bim's Brook on one side, Stump Brook on the other. Sometimes the creeks flood in spring and his postage stamp parking lot disappears underwater, so liquor sales require boots and waders and the drunks have to be fished out by the town's rescue boat. Bambi

Saville's Beauty Salon and Funeral Parlor is on Bridge Street (which has no bridge), abutting the Shumatuscacant (a name no one in town can remember, let alone pronounce). Religion's available on the side streets, two Protestant churches, (both white) and the Catholic Church (mixed race). Reverend Jake's black Baptist Church is farther south on East Hockomock between the lakes, and there's another small one, Eucharistic Eutheists or some such thing, with a congregation that prefers wine to grape juice, whoops and hollers weekends, and then burns itself out after a few years (without the help of Fire Chief Dobbs).

The two schools, elementary and middle, are near the Town Forest on Elm Street, the elms long lost to Dutch Elm Disease (another factoid PT is intent on sharing with us). The high school's on the town line with East Quagmire (just west of South Quagmire. Don't ask.). Most of us get bused, but you can always walk uphill both ways in the snow if you need to impress on future generations how easy kids have it today. [2]

The town is segregated, not by law or regulation, more by choice and opportunity. Self-segregated, for lack of welcome mat. It isn't *West Side Story*, the Sharks versus the Jets. We don't fight, we don't travel in gangs. People of color live in the southeastern corner, between the swamp and the Satucket River and the lakes, around the bogs. Whites live everywhere else. It's easier to maintain a public

---

[2] OK, you had to ask. Both towns are southeast of Quagmire, now Eire, which changed its name after the contentious three-way split in 1848. South Quagmire got the library and the bogs, East Quagmire the Town Hall, and Eire the best drinking-hole in the Taunton River Watershed.

peace and a private space when fewer elbows rub. Less chance of friction generating unwanted heat. [3]

We all go to school together. We're in classes together for twelve years, thirteen if you attend kindergarten. Kindergarten is private, only for those who can afford it. A few Cape Verdeans go to free preschool at the black Baptist Church, those whose parents are willing to let their four-year-olds hang out with Baptists. Most of us are Catholics because our parents and grandparents were Catholics back on the islands. Our little ones stay home. That's what aunts and grandmothers are for. We start school in first grade and get to see people outside our family, our neighborhood. They look lighter than us, but I don't think we attach meaning to that until later. And when we do, well, it doesn't seem like a big deal. We're young. We don't know history yet.

Every first of October, teachers take an official count of the students in their homerooms in order to obtain state educational funding. I remember my cousin Georgina telling me that she has to get numbers for how many Whites, Blacks, Hispanics, and Others are in her class. If she can't be certain by sight alone, she discreetly questions the child individually and asks his thoughts on the subject. As often as not, his thoughts are a bit vague. We're all Americans, after all. Race isn't much discussed around the dinner table. Homework, Aunt Mary's vertigo, say 'please' and 'thank you', can you believe the price of gas? I waited in line for an hour. Talk around the dinner table is pretty universal and not into skin color, but behind every family story in America, skin color dictates how the tale plays out.

Take Cape Verdeans.

---

3   In 1998, PT's 29-year-old brother Woodstock tells Birnam that a neighbor putting her house up for sale assures him she will "never sell to blacks… or Jews."

Cape Verdeans are a mixed bunch, owing to our combined European and African ancestry. We have the luxury of diverse racial heritage. Today the islands are claimed by Portugal, thanks to the fifteenth century's Henry the Navigator, a Portuguese prince remembered mainly for sponsoring exploration and conquest in the western Atlantic and giving the slave trade a royal boost, but Africans from Senegal and Gambia, wandering seafarers, found the archipelago long before. The islands are volcanic and not particularly hospitable. Visitors from the Gulf of Guinea come ashore, look around, choose not to settle in great numbers. The lovely beaches can't compensate for lack of arable farm land. Portuguese sailors, however, using the islands as lay-overs and watering-holes, enslave whom they can, intermingle as they might, and eventually go native as one does when separated from home by half an ocean. There isn't a lot for their slaves to do, little to cultivate, nothing to mine, salt, maybe, and bird poop for gunpowder, not much else, and sailors are not over-concerned with the complexion of their bed warmers. Thus, the blood of two continents flows equally in our veins. None of this do I learn in school. I doubt our teachers know or care. Certainly, I've never once heard Cape Verde mentioned in class, not in twelve years of public education. In geography we skip right over them and land on Madagascar instead. (Madagascar exports cloves. I've never forgotten!) Our teachers assume we're Black (Black came after Colored). They aren't much interested in shades of gray. The Irish, who are just moving into town from Southie and Dorchester, can tell the difference between Italians and Poles. The one Jewish family remains silent about Christmas decorations in the classrooms. The Swamp Yankees whose families have lived in town since before the Revolution consider the lot of us foreign interlopers whose greatest sin is not having been born in town. But to the teachers, and to us, They all look White and We don't. And while Blacks, Native Americans (a couple of vestigial Wampanoags who somehow managed not to get killed off by Pilgrims), and Hispanics are in the minority (we also have a handful of mixed Asians from Korea and the Philippines), there are enough of Us so I never feel overwhelmed by Them. The Ku Klux Klan hasn't held meetings at the local Grange in forty years. We go home after school, kick back to *The Jackson Five* and *Diana Ross and the Supremes*, don't much socialize with Them, unless you play on sports teams, and few of Us do. The few who do aren't allowed in the Athletic Association. That's Whites Only. (Its members don't have much use for women either.) [4]

Which leads us to this story. It begins, as do all good American stories, with football. Isn't every beginning about football? Race may inform the final score but, even back then, football kicks off the game.

Little Anthony DeBarros is the only colored kid on the Police Athletic League's first football team in 1956. He's the son of Emmanuel Anthony DeBarros, born in Cape Verde in 1921, who came to America at age ten with his brother Christian after World War I, to work on the cranberry bogs. His mother, my great-aunt Flora, came here in the 1930s with her whole family. They arrived in New Bedford, and that's where many of them still live, but Manny DeBarros married Flora DosSantos in 1939, when they worked on the Stillacre bogs, and they had their first son, Albert Thomas DeBarros, in 1940. The boy suffered from *petit mal* epilepsy, which

---

4   When in 1975 the high school faculty seeks a function hall for its Christmas party, the teachers are forced to look elsewhere since the Association says, apologetically, it can bend the rules for women but not for Georgina DeBarros. It's against their by-laws.

came in from his mother's side. Their second son, Anthony John DeBarros, born in 1944, did not.

Sparky Manx says Little Anthony was never destined to be a bogscooper like his parents. He remains the most talented eleven-year-old the town league's ever seen. I remember Arianna bragging about her father in grade school. She's so proud of her dad. He's smart, fast, has an amazing throwing arm, and, judging by the couple of photos I've seen of him as a child, beautiful. The beautiful boy. He could be a model, he's that good-looking. And phenomenal in youth football. Arianna says she's seen him stand on Main Street and throw a football over the roofs of the cranberry buildings, and Sparky Manx confirms this. On the field he weaves and dodges so fast no one can touch him. He's the golden boy from Hancock Street. On Sunday afternoons the bleachers alongside the Franklin Street fields sag beneath the butts of family, friends, the clubs, and the curious. People predict a glorious future for him at the high school and beyond.

There are some who cheer for the "cute little monkey from Hancock Street."

There are some who resent the "uppity little colored kid from Hancock Street."

Some just cheer for Little Tony D, Hancock Street's golden son.

For several spectacular fall weekends he's the talk of the town, the object of everyone's attention, affection even. People drop what they're doing, grocery shopping, dump runs, trips to the mall, to check him out. People who don't care about football take an interest. *The Quagmire Express* sends photographers. The two ends of town, Us and Them, blend warily into one community. Elbows are tucked and greetings muted, but when the ball goes into the end zone, community wins the day. There's no clear segregation in the bleachers. The cheers are sincere.

It doesn't last. The following summer, on a steamy July day in 1957, his big brother Albert drowns in the quarry. Because of Albert's epilepsy and history of seizures, his classmates consider him a misfit, but Albert wants to run with the cool kids, and the cool kids swim in the quarry. Little Anthony tags along. Little Anthony is there when his brother dives in and doesn't come back up. Maybe he has a seizure. Maybe he hits his head. Men in scuba gear find old cars, refrigerators, sunken junk. They never find Albert, and Little Anthony watches it all unfold. He internalizes his brother's disappearance. It scars him. He plays football into high school, but the fire has gone out. Halfway through fall of his sophomore year, Arianna is born. He quits the varsity team and doesn't graduate high school. His girlfriend runs off, leaves him with an infant daughter and no means of supporting her. He drops out and tries to enlist, but there are questions about his state of mind, his brother's epilepsy, and he ends up clerking at Brate's Liquor Emporium, working as a call fireman in his spare time, a single gold chain with a tiny winged figure around his neck. Also, in his spare time he bulks up his body, builds go-carts, flies model airplanes, works with two-way radios, and messes around with engines and circuit boards. He's brilliant with his hands.

If he hadn't been so brilliant the coaches couldn't refuse him, none of this would've happened.

Little Anthony DeBarros.

Little Tony D.

Hancock Street's golden son, handcuffed to a chair so we don't lose the quorum.

So Police Chief Crockett doesn't lose the quorum before we vote him his new cruiser to replace the old cruiser that got crushed by the ladder truck in revenge for co-opting Miss Makepeace and marring her driveway. Chief Crockett wants that new cruiser, whatever the cost in human life. And, yes, we vote to finance it out of the postage line, but until the meeting is officially dissolved, none of the business voted on can take place. Which means Tara Drummond has to bang the gavel and sing '*The Star-Spangled Banner,*' and Chief Crockett's steely blue gaze, not to mention his gun, means no one is going anywhere until the last vote is taken, gavel pounded, song sung. But Chief Dobbs storms out of the meeting, as everyone bets he will, and gets run over by the ambulance. If not for Little Anthony's arrival in cuffs, we would have lost the quorum.

(And, for the record, Chief Crockett did have gorgeous blue eyes. No one questioned Miss Makepeace's dumping of Chief Dobbs. Although they weren't a couple for long (Makepeace and Crockett, that is), and she's been gone for almost thirty years. Arizona, last I heard. She hated snow. Can you blame her? Also, she was a Republican. The good-looking ones often are.)

Not that Republican or Democrat or Green or What-Have-You matters a whole lot at Town Hall. Party politics surface during state and federal elections, but in the day-to-day governance of a quagmire, no one pays much attention to political party affiliations. It's more about what faction you belong to at bog level. There's the We-need-a-new-state-of-the-art—More-Technology! School faction and the What-was-good-enough-for-me-Damn-the-Asbestos! No-School faction, both of which feed Letters to the Editor with vehement ALL CAPS and exclamation marks!!! There's the Pro-Life Initiative and the Free Choice Collaborative that butt heads and placards outside the medical center. And there are those who think Sparky Manx paid her dues long ago, and those who still balk at the idea of a female usurping the rights of a male breadwinner to mobilize fire equipment. [5]

Back in 1976, as we celebrate two-hundred years of freedom, we are equally free to join any number of factions that divide the town. We can belong to the group that wants all-day kindergarten or side with those who think glorified babysitting is a waste of money. We can turn out cheering for the motorboat races on Cushing Pond Two every Memorial Day weekend, or we can grumble about the oil slick on the water and the litter on the green after the last Evinrude's been hauled away. We can throw our voices behind those who think a secret illegal piggery in the swamps is a health-hazard-to-be-uprooted-like-bad-truffles or join others who consider it a reasonable-venture-in-a-Right to Farm community. We support Chief Dobbs (for fear of arson), or we support Chief Crockett (for fear of arrest), or we keep our heads down and raise our hands in favor of every Town Meeting article proposed by either chief (for fear of reprisals from both).

And, you are either Male or Female. You are White or you are Colored. You're entitled or you aren't. There is no in-between or shades of gray. (This is not New Orleans, after all!)

We go into the October 4, 1976 Special Town Meeting a town divided, or more appropriately, fractured. But there's nothing unusual in that. From what I've seen, all small towns are like that. We are unexceptional.

---

5   Sparky Manx finally got appointed fire chief last year at age seventy. There have been two out-of-towners brought in since Chief Dobbs died and Biff Larson took over. It's only taken thirty-one years for people to admit that a woman is as capable of running a department as a man.

Except we have a killer about to take exception to us.

Toby Dobbs is a high school god. Like PT said, it's difficult to reconcile the boy in the photographs (and there are many. The local newspapers of the time found him irresistible) with the fat, jowly, balding, surly man who rules the fire department and keeps the town sleepless nights, wondering what (or who) will burn next. In the old black-and-white pictures, he towers over the back row of the football team, big kid, broad shoulders with or without pads, a wide smile, just the hint of cruelty in the corners. He has the blonde buzz-cut typical of the time. His eyes, by most accounts, are blue. They look a little muddy to me, but that's years after his glory days, and countless gallons of Jack Daniels.

His glory days aren't all that glorious. South Quagmire hasn't had a winning football team since the 1930s, but in the mid-50s Toby is the biggest and toughest of what they have, a bruiser who makes varsity his sophomore year and co-captains the team his junior. His co-captain and best friend is Tim Drummond, not-so-big, not-so-broad, not-so-good-looking, but a loyal lackey. They're inseparable. To a man (or boy) the jocks idolize their running back, and Tim Drummond is his biggest male fan. Together, they lead the squad to infrequent victories and dream of unlikely futures in the NFL. They are the best of a sorry lot. No pro scouts ever come to watch a Quagmire game. That, at least, is how Sparky Manx remembers it.

Needless to say, if the high school teams of that era aren't necessarily good, they are uniformly white. They're coached by fat, jowly, balding, surly men who haven't escaped the town limits and are reliving their youth through their offspring. If there's any color in town, it spends its autumns working the bogs, not chasing footballs. Color is excluded from the home-grown Athletic Association that takes root in an outbuilding behind the Highway Department garage and dispenses drinks to its paunchy members on Friday nights. No Coloreds allowed in. So, to see a photograph from 1956 of the first PAL (Police Athletic League) football team, three rows of grinning eleven-and-twelve-year-olds, miniature versions of their dads, and discover one dark kernel blatant on the white cob, is a bit jarring. The dark kernel, third from the left in the middle row, breaks the symmetry. It's the face of my second cousin-once-removed, Anthony DeBarros. It's a round face, pleasing to look at even on the reduced scale of a team photograph, with a small, sweet smile that doesn't recognize the precariousness of its position, and high cheekbones visible through pinchable adolescent chub. The helmet tucked beneath an armpit leaves a modest brush of black hair free to frame the innocence, welcome to curl over the little hockey pucks that are his ears.

But what most stands out are the eyes. With Little Anthony DeBarros, the eyes always stand out. You can say, C'mon, give me a break. It's a team photo. You can barely see the eyes. They're neither big nor small, narrow nor wide. They're dark on dark. They're unremarkable, hardly visible. You're projecting.

And you're right. I am projecting. Little Anthony has been a part of my life for as long as I remember: family, friend, local handyman, Arianna's dad, a guy I call 'Uncle' out of respect or love or, I don't know, some combination of the two. I live two houses down, grow up with him and his eyes in near constant attendance. I feel them on me often enough, questioning, protective, see how they light up when he's studying Arianna with a father's gratitude, recognize their evil gleam the moment before he shouts, "Small Package Apocalypse!" and grabs one of us in a tight squeeze, crushing our knees to chest, hands against ankles, chin to collarbone, as we're swaddled inside his arms, carried around the living room or yard shrieking and giggling. He could stuff either of us into a large shoebox, he's got us folded so securely. We're tossed onto a sofa or into the neighbor's above-ground swimming pool. When we come up for air his eyes fairly howl with glee and ours reciprocate. I never feel so happy as when compacted into Uncle Anthony's Small Package Apocalypse, knowing he's got me scared safe, big hand close, the smell of Old Spice deodorant thick in his embrace, and that his eyes are all for me and my frizzy hair and my knobby shoulders and my bony knees and my wiggly toes. His eyes are my great-aunt Flora's eyes, laughing, brooding, ready to call us home, tuck us in, sometimes narrowing with a snap to shut us out. They're dark, really dark, and the dark overshadows the whites when he's in a mood. The dark extends way back into his head, as if it seeps from holes drilled into his brain. And back there in the seepage something moves in the dark. Something in the depths speaks of purpose. Whether he's draped across a La-Z Boy watching a game on TV or bent in concentration over a circuit board for his sister's transistor radio, his eyes are restless, penetrating. I've always found them a little scary. Sometimes cold. And when I look at the team photograph from 1956 that Arianna has taped on her bedroom wall above the vanity and Chanel bottles, I see all that in those eleven-year-old eyes. Even at eleven he's intense.

Projection, yes, but not without foundation.

Still, the eyes haven't won him a coveted position on the team, but talent, talent enough that his potential as a future player at the high school overcomes any Swamp Yankee aversion to "letting the foreigners in." He can run, he can throw. He's cute. He has a winning smile. His smile is sweet enough to sap barriers. He's not too dark-skinned. Not so black he's a threat. That first season the PAL football team wins all its games against the neighboring towns. Little Anthony scores at least one touchdown in every game.

I won't be born for another two years, but I'm taking Sparky's word for this. She hasn't been wrong so far.

The little boy wonder catches the attention of everyone in town who cares about local athletics and the future of high school sports. He catches the eyes of Toby Dobbs and Tim Drummond, who are assisting the coaches in their spare hours off the gridiron, and they catch his. Maybe they see something of themselves in his eyes.

Hunger.

Intensity.

Desire.

"C'mon, boy," they say, "we'll show you how we do it in the big leagues."

Dobbs is the big, blonde, high school god in white T-shirt and single gold chain with tiny winged figure around his thick red neck. Little Anthony is small, brown, and grateful to be singled out. He goes off to hang out with the big boys, the cool guys, the white kids, although their eyes go no deeper than the shallow skim of water over a flooded winter bog. Twenty years later, he's still in Dobbs's company, dark eyes fixed with a kind of intensity we take as hero worship on a man who no longer seems worth the adulation. He's a fixture at his saggy god's fire station, first to respond when the siren sounds. If not hanging around Tubby's Phallus, he's behind the counter at Brate's, selling vices to the old deities who once-upon-a-time let him tag along when they were young and beautiful, and he was their "pet monkey." Dobbs is fire chief, Drummond's a big man in real estate, Little Anthony's still a kid (ageless) who once-upon-a-time had potential, but never took it to a happy ending. Why they're still together after all these years is anybody's guess, but nobody ventures a guess. Nobody's interested enough, except Sparky Manx, who's always been protective of him, who knows him better than he knows himself.

Hey, some people fight fires. Some play football. And some lounge shirtless outside the station on hot summer mornings, personalized coffee mug in muscled hand, single gold chain with winged figure draped across tawny brawny brown pecs, hungry for notice.

Notice from Chief Dobbs and Sparky Manx, Biff Larson, Reverend Jake and PT Wood, anyone who happens to drop in for Fire Prevention Week. He's not little anymore, but to the fine citizens of South Quagmire he'll never be anything but.

So, when he's hauled into Town Meeting in tears, having run over Tubby Dobbs with the town ambulance, the irony is not lost on people in the auditorium. The saggy old god has been killed by his acolyte, his "pet monkey."

"I didn't see him!" the pet monkey's bawling. "It was dark!"

"You were speeding," snaps Chief Crockett, who's probably not as displeased by this turn of events as he appears. His relationship with the late fire chief has proven fraught at best, as evidenced by rubber in driveways and mangled cruisers wrapped around fire hydrants, and now the second body of the night, a mountain of meat under a sheet, is being hauled through the auditorium on a stretcher. Chief Dobbs storms out of the hall, having hip-checked a cop into the wall, and a moment later we hear the squeal of brakes, the blare of sirens. People leap from their seats. Sparky Manx and the Reverend Jake sprint out the gaping door after their boss. Police swarm the exit. Chief Crockett forbids anyone to move. He goes out. Red lights pinwheel in the dark. He comes back with a strong hand on Little Anthony DeBarros's elbow. Dead meat follows, Sparky and Reverend Jake bowed under the weight. Arianna's hysterical. Her father's just run over a man. Petrified Wood's got her held tight in the sound booth doorway, trying to comfort her, without obvious success. Birnam Wood is beating his head against the console, probably in fear of having lost the quorum.

"I was late!" cries Little Anthony. "Chief Dobbs said he'd kill me forgetting to bring the ambulance in the first place." He's got both hands pressed to his forehead in despair and his biceps are popping. The short sleeves of his tight blue uniform shirt show them off in all their glory.

"You're under arrest."

Chief Crockett is searching his pockets as he forces Little Anthony onto a chair in the front row. A moment's anxiety before Wilhelmina Makepeace, executive secretary, descends from the stage where she's been hovering since the fistfight that precipitated this tragedy. Her red fingernails sparkle beneath Fresnel lights as she passes the chief a pair of handcuffs she's produced from somewhere, her purse, maybe, or her cleavage, or a concealed handcuff shoulder holster. He takes them with a nod and cuffs Little Anthony to the chair.

"We've got the quorum and we're not gonna lose it now."

"It was dark!" Tears are running down Little Anthony's face. He's not struggling. He looks heartbroken. "It was like he came out of nowhere! Like he was pushed. He was on the ground! I couldn't hit the brakes in time!" He wipes his cheeks with a veined fore-arm. A single gold chain comes with it, snagged on his wrist watch. Thirty years ago, and the image still sticks in my brain, a visual that haunts.

Arianna's sobbing, "Let me go, let me go," or something like that, if memory serves, but she isn't struggling, and Petrified Wood's holding her, throwing me frantic looks like, can I do something about his brother who's already put a dent in the sound board?

"Just sit there and shut up," says Chief Crockett to Little Anthony, and then he bends down, untangles the gold chain for him, and talks low into his ear. Maybe this takes five or ten seconds. Miss Makepeace returns to her seat onstage with the poise of a run-way model. Every old white male eye in the room follows her tush which sways to its own inner music. Arianna subsides into a whim-per. I smack Birnam on the back of the head and tell him to grow up. This has no positive effect whatsoever. Down on the floor, two tellers who count votes are busy hoisting Mrs. Doppelmeier back into her wheelchair as if she were a stuffed toy. They heave her by the armpits and fluff her like a pillow. [6]

Then the chief straightens. He glares at our temporary mod-erator, Tara Drummond, who's slumped behind the podium, cata-tonic. She's a small woman, mousy-colored, easily overlooked. Once she was a cheerleader, really cute, says Sparky, but never gifted with

---

6   She is, despite PT 's doubts, Mrs. Doppelmeier. She has been for three months. I've seen the marriage recorded in the ledger for 1976: June 29 at the Second Congregational Church. Their signatures are illegible. It's possible neither was conscious at the time.

personality. Someone's brought a box for her to stand on, and still her head barely rises above the podium.

"Let's move to the vote," growls Police Chief Crockett.

She flinches. The cops manning the exits stiffen in anticipation. No one better think of getting by them.

The room has been loud with the exclamations of the shocked and incredulous, and people shouting that they've won or lost their bets. Now it falls silent. Two deaths in the space of ten minutes constitute a windfall for funeral director, Bambi Saville. She already has her black tape measure out and is probably estimating the size of the casket. It will be a big casket. It will be a big funeral. It will be years before anyone polishes the gold ball on top of the Town Hall flagpole by means of the ladder truck again.

EMTs Sparky Manx and the Reverend Jake haul the fire chief's body out of the room on the stretcher. Bambi hurries after, giving instructions we can't hear.

Petrified Wood looks at me questioningly. Arianna's wiping her eyes on his sleeve. "Walk-in refrigerator?" he mouths. His long, lanky arms are wrapped around her in a protective embrace, and her head is buried in the crook of his elbow. I can only shrug, imagining two bodies shelved with tomorrow's mac-and-cheese. The students have a choice of sides, and Arianna needs to get out of this white boy's embrace. Her father's not the one heading for the walk-in refrigerator on a stretcher. He'll be all right. This will get sorted out. The girl needs to control her emotions, not make a scene. The last thing we need is someone else adding fuel to this public spectacle.

Down on the floor, murmurs, some of protest, some of resignation, ruffle the hall. The sound is indistinct, hushed. Selectman Nigel Brate, our town bookie and owner of Brate's Liquor Emporium, is calculating wins and losses on a candy wrapper. Chief Dobbs's temper didn't even make it through Article One. What will the payout be? No doubt it has entered a few minds that both deaths are members of TouchDown Realty. Eyes flit between its surviving members, the stunned Tara Drummond and the scowling Town Treasurer, Thomasine Épée. PT's metaphor is apt. An angry hippo is not a sight one soon forgets. No doubt Thomasine Épée is making calculations too, but of another kind. She didn't get to be Town Treasurer, or TD Realty's managing accountant, on size alone.

General Tarry, our third selectman, has just taken his seat onstage again. He says, "Move to the vote!"

We haven't introduced General Tarry yet. He's been offstage, I think, probably polishing his weapons.

General Millard Tarry is a retired staff sergeant suffering Post Traumatic Stress Syndrome (only in 1976 we still call it 'shell shock'), acquired in Korea or Vietnam, or maybe Fort Hood. He's the founder of and head of school at the South Quagmire Military Academy. His mailbox at the town end of the dirt road leading to his swamp boot camp for wayward boys is triple-locked and grenade-resistant, and postmistress Carmen Selsby, a chain smoker who recently broke nose and ribs falling down the steps of Brate's Liquor Emporium, has the only second, third, and fourth keys in existence, which she hands off to postman Bill Early, who's sick early and often, so Bill hands them off to the local juvenile delinquent, Jasper David Lovell, who stuffs everybody's junk mail into General Tarry's box, maybe as a joke, maybe because, after thirteen years in school, he's still basically unable to read. The general keeps the campaign literature from the NRA and the NEA (he's an educator) but buries the *Victoria's Secret* catalogs in hidden caches throughout the

swamp, hidden caches that his students raid and digest with enthusiasm, and the old man is overheard at The Grub Pub prophesying
the end of the world by sultry minxes packing M-16s in their apoca-
lyptic undergarments. He's a big white dude, white hair in a crewcut
tapering down to a neck the girth of a good-sized log. The camouflage jacket and pants make him look like a survivalist. Which,
basically, he is. Rumor has it, he goes commando.

This from Nigel Brate, who stumbled into him in a lavatory stall
at Town Hall and now has a horror of sitting next to him at selectmen's meetings. [7]

The general looks anxious. Two deaths in ten minutes. He may
be armed and dangerous, but not half as dangerous, it appears, as
participation in our country's purest form of democracy, and the
sooner he gets back to safety behind his barricades, the better.

Temporary Moderator Tara Drummond slowly shakes herself
from her stupor. Her mousy brown head barely clears the microphone as she mumbles, "We will move to the vote."

"Can't hear you!" shouts a voice from the audience.

She moves closer. Tears run down her cheeks. "We will move
to the vote," she repeats, barely more audible. "On Article One, all
those in favor say Aye." The sniffles are louder than the words.

There's a momentary pause. The vote? What vote? We have two
dead... Oh, Article One. The cruiser. The cruiser? What, really?
We're expected to vote on replacing the cruiser when we've just
stuffed two corpses into a walk-in refrigerator? Tim Drummond!
Tubby Dobbs! I just lost twenty bucks. This is an outrage. This is

---

7   I may have the junk mail chronology wrong here, but it was a *Victoria's Secret* catalog that
    precipitated General Tarry's death at the hands of a former student who discovered him
    burning the 1979 edition. I have to take some of the blame for that death. The kid was plan-
    ning to buy me a Christmas present from it, and he had serious anger management issues.

despicable. (This is America.) Chief Crockett's lack of propriety scandalizes the voters. But we're also aware of his gun. And the cops standing with crossed arms at every exit. We're not going anywhere until the meeting's been dissolved. We are prisoners of democracy. After the flurry of protest wears itself thin, a half-hearted Aye goes up from the floor.

"All those opposed, please say Nay," mumbles Tara Drummond.

Silence. There's no need for the tellers to take a hand count.

Maybe no one hears her. Or maybe the blue eyes and the handgun see to that.

"The Ayes have it," mumbles Tara Drummond. She slumps again. Her little hands seem to clutch the sides of the podium for support. Town Counsel Edgar Vade sidles in beside her and whispers something. He's a mousy little thing too. "Oh, oh, yes. Sorry." She pulls herself back up, an effort. "It is a vote," she adds.

Police Chief Crockett leans into the floor microphone.

"Thank you, ladies and gentlemen," he says. "We have made it through Article One despite two deaths, sorry, Mrs. Drummond, and still managed to maintain the quorum." He looks at Little Anthony accusingly. "I am confident—" He clears his throat. "—confident we will all remain in our seats, and at the end of the meeting, Mrs. Drummond will sing '*The Star-Spangled Banner*' for us as she has at every Town Meeting for the last nineteen years. Thank you, Mrs. Drummond."

He claps. Reluctantly, a few others join in. They're not happy. Sparky Manx has come back from the walk-in and handed Little Anthony a handkerchief. He's not a fan of hankies, but from Sparky he takes it and blows his nose. She puts hands on both his shoulders, leans in, and talks to him. I see him visibly relax. He trusts Sparky.

"Mrs. Drummond?" says Chief Crockett. "Shall we move onto Article Two *before* another mishap occurs?"

Mrs. Drummond doesn't seem to hear. Her head drops onto the podium, bouncing off the mike with a loud 'THUNK.' Theobald Doppelmeier, however, who until this moment appeared dead, leaps from his seat at the Town Clerk's table.

"B-4!" he shouts. "B-4!"

There's momentary confusion in the hall. Then he shouts even louder, "Got it!" and collapses onto the table, scattering what may or may not be BINGO cards. His stuffed squirrel does a back flip and lands on the floor. He retrieves it, sets it back in front of him on the table. The exertion is too much for him, and he collapses again.

Unbeknownst to anyone, his oxygen is running low.

ARTICLE 2

"To see if the Town will vote to amend the South Quagmire (Just North of East Quagmire) General By-laws, Article 3 – 5, Farm Animals, by adding a new Section 2 as follows:

Section 1: Legislative Purpose and Intent

The purpose and intent of this Bylaw is to state with emphasis the Right to Farm accorded to all citizens of the Commonwealth under Article 97 of the Constitution, and all state statutes, and regulations thereunder including but not limited to Massachusetts General Laws Chapter 40A, Section 3, Paragraph 1; Chapter 90, Section 9, Chapter 111, Section 125A, and Chapter 128 Section 1A. We the citizens of South Quagmire (Just North of East Quagmire) restate and republish these rights pursuant to the Town's authority conferred by Article 891 of the Articles of Amendment of the Massachusetts Constitution ("Home Rule Amendments").

Section 2: Definitions

The word "farm" shall include...

etc.

f) keeping and raising of poultry, swine, cattle, and other domesticated animals for food and other agricultural purposes, including bees and fur-bearing animals.

etc.

Section 3: Right to Farm Declaration

The Right to Farm is hereby recognized to exist within the Town.

etc.

or take any other action in relation thereto."

The Kernickis keep a cow in their back yard. The Cappellis have two cows and a small, horny bull that likes to hump big dogs. The Lozeaus herd sheep, a dozen or so, and the Blooms raise goats and rabbits. The Bryants and the Beymans breed horses. (Bud and Susie Beyman run a public stable and riding school.) Lots of people have chickens. Jack Keene has several and refers to them as his "girls." The Little Quagmire Grange is largely inactive now, its members fading octogenarians who sponsor the local 4-H kids and their hobby livestock, but said members harbor fond memories of pastoral days gone-by when chicks and ducks and geese scurried along the gravel roads, filling the air with birdsong. None of said creatures raise (or raised) more than a communal eyebrow, and on steamy spring days, the whiff of manure. The real stink begins with a new pig in town, piglet, actually, the latest lap love of the younger Miss Ottick, Edith, gift from an anonymous admirer (whose name, rank, and lack of underwear everyone knows) to replace the cat taken out by Fire Chief Dobbs's Colt .45 M1911 (thanks, PT!). The piglet starts a war in town that will take years and the death of General Tarry to resolve. The piglet is but the opening salvo. Our newest selectman, Nigel Brate, has announced in no uncertain terms he's throwing down the gauntlet. His lady love has been co-opted by the military. He will take his revenge. No one dumps Nigel Brate and skulks away unscathed. And Heaven help the collateral damage, curly-tailed and other-rumped.

Every town has its share of characters. Nigel Effenfield Brate is one of ours. If you can picture some old white pruney guy about as wide across as a lamp post (he looks like someone took a big straw and sucked his insides out, leaving him with more skin than innards), you've got Nigel Brate, selectman, bookie, misanthrope. He owns the liquor store on Main Street. A former Coast Guard pilot who flew sixty rescue missions and had to be rescued from, if gossip serves, eight of them, he keeps several small aircraft hangared one town over (East Quagmire) and owns a chain of liquor stores in neighboring communities where he drinks through his profits before achieving liftoff. In 1976, everyone calls liquor stores "the package store," or "the packy," as in, "I've gotta run to the packy for a case of Bud." Brate's Liquor Emporium, the packy, is a white clapboard building with no windows in front, situated on low ground between two brooks. Its full wine cellar has walls so thick we joke he has bodies bricked up in them. They can withstand spring flooding without major inconvenience, even when his postage-stamp-sized parking lot is two feet underwater. In case of World War III, the town has a fully-supplied fallout shelter where we can squeeze through nuclear winter on cheap Chablis. Six concrete steps lead to the front door with loose cast iron railings on the side that wiggle. Many a visitor to Brate's takes the steps two at a time in one direction, six at once in the other, and ends sprawled among the faded plastic flower beds and empty nip bottles.

I do not frequent Brate's Liquor Emporium. I pay Uncle Anthony to buy my cigarettes at employee's discount when he's night-clerking. The place smells dirty. The floors creak. There may be bodies decomposing below among the casks of Amontillado. I'm too young for the packy and too cheap.

Not that it matters, because Brate doesn't need me to make his fortune. He has the Ottick sisters. The Ottick sisters, Kay and Edie, are prized customers. They buy their Merlot from Nigel. The younger sibling, Edie, has her own honorary corkscrew displayed behind the counter and makes frequent use of it checking out the latest vintages with Nigel in the cellar. Gossip has it they're an item, at least when tipsy. Or were, until Chief Dobbs took out the cat.

Until the piglet, a.k.a. Porky Doodles, arrived on the scene to replace it.

Porky Doodles is a pink and cream, plumpish little thing with curly, black-tipped tail, fitting complement to pink and cream, not-quite-plumpish little Miss Edith Ottick, who's fitted him with frilly collar and tail ribbon and takes him everywhere like infant in arms. She coos, he poops, everyone rolls eyes. Everyone in town knows from whence Porky Doodles cometh. Nigel Brate knows from whence Porky Doodles cometh. The thought keeps his underpants in knots.

Aerial knots at a thousand feet.

I need you to picture, if you will, two old men in a helicopter flying low over Little Quagmire Swamp, rotors beating against a setting sun, landing skids tangling in the treetops. They are Nigel Brate, one hundred-eighteen pounds of Merlot-fueled malice, and Big Pauly Silvio, three times his weight and about equal measures of grudge, both girded in scarves and goggles, brandishing binoculars as they sweep over cedars in search of errant porkers supposedly harbored by the South Quagmire Military Academy's top-secret piggery. The as-yet-only-suspected illegal piggery General Tarry's hiding in the swamp is an affront that drives Nigel Brate to near hysteria. Word's out that someone in town is running an unlicensed farming operation, that specifically, this someone and his adolescent band of brothers are requisitioning garbage after hours from local restaurants. Day-old doughnuts and the dregs of yesterday's corn chowder disappear with a regularity that defies explanation. Kids in camo are spotted dumpster-diving in the dark. The survivalists are swiping swill. Rumors of these nocturnal raids reach the ears of town officials, and Nigel Brate and Big Pauly Silvio have spent the better part of two years playing World War I flying aces on porcine patrol. (Big Pauly has never forgiven the tires shot out from under his tow truck.) Two years and, to date, no luck. If pigs lurk in the foliage they're cagey and run for the undergrowth when they hear the sound of approaching aircraft. They've learned to recognize the martial strains of *Flight of the Valkyries.* [8]

Big Pauly is on the Board of Health and has a 'thing' about livestock code violations (the dumping of used motor oil into the swamp he's less concerned about). Also, he lost his grandmother to the Influenza Pandemic of 1918 and already this year several people have died from Swine Influenza A, or so the Center for Disease Control and World Health Organization are suggesting. President Ford himself urges vaccination. Big Pauly has a morbid phobia regarding needles, swine flu, and early death. He's a burly man reduced to panic by the arrival of Miss Edie's latest love. It would

---

8 There's every possibility it wasn't *Flight of the Valkyries.* It was a long time ago, and memory's a funny thing, but when you ask any old-timer who remembers Nigel Brate, they'll give you the same answer. When it comes to helicopters, we've all been Francis Ford Coppola'd and *Apocalypse*d, *Now.*

be comical if there wasn't a national discussion going on right now about the coming epidemic. [9]

On Brate and Silvio's most recent reconnaissance mission, a badly-aimed shot under the bow by the general's pupils damages a landing skid. The general's apologies are profuse (his boys only just beginning An Introduction to Anti-Aircraft Weapon Systems 101), and promises have been made to pay for the damages. Thus far, reparations are not forthcoming.

Instead, a pink and cream, black-tipped curly-tailed piglet's comethed, waving a red flag in front of the emaciated thunder god that is Nigel Brate. A great white whale did less to inspire one man's monomania than has Porky Doodles inflamed our Wagnerian package store titan. Not one to plan a campaign, Selectman Brate flails wildly, and his flailing hits its mark.

One dark night he raids Miss Edie's Little Lending Library, a quaint dollhouse on a curbside post beside the driveway that offers kiddie lit to the neighborhood youngsters, 'Take One, Return One," and replaces them with well-thumbed issues of *Playboy*. (He denies this, says it was the high school derelict who misdelivers mail). The following week, South Quagmire's impressionables are bewildered, their parents aghast. What's happened to *Charlotte's Web* and *Where the Wild Things Are?* In what new *Wonderland* has *Alice* outgrown her frocks? Instead of *Peter Rabbit*, *Playboy* bunnies now ride the handlebars of little bicycles with training wheels. *Goodnight, Moon* takes on whole new meanings. And while Miss May, 1967, makes a big comeback, Miss Edie's reputation suffers a blow to propriety.

---

9   Which doesn't come. President Ford is vaccinated on national television and subsequently loses the election to Jimmy Carter. Unwarranted flu hysteria may contribute to his defeat.

"How could he?" she cries and squeezes Porky Doodles until he nearly pops. "How could he be so cruel?" She's furious. She was born in this town. Her family goes back to the Mayflower. She's a maven of good taste. People solicit her opinion about which hot new beefcake romance to put on hold at the local library. She harbors literary pretensions. She's published a recipe for veal bourgignon with tarragon and tequila in *Bon Appetit*. This is so not right. It's not like they had an understanding or anything. She feeds the piglet an entire chocolate trifle and sobs in her decorative pillows. What to do?

"Don't be a fool," snipes her older sister, who is seriously pissed off by loss of trifle. "That thing has gained ten pounds in a month. It has to go. The place smells like a sty. And if we end up getting third-rate California vintages pawned off on us because of your sloppy sex life, I will cut you out of my will. Nigel's already removed your corkscrew from behind the counter!"

Edie gasps. Yes, Kay is right. Edie's corkscrew has disappeared from its place of honor behind the counter of Brate's Liquor Emporium. She goes in, spies the vacancy, and is speechless. She has to turn around and leave without uttering a word of protest. This affront to her dignity, possibly more serious than the *Playboy* offensive, provides further grounds for separation, although she's too much of a lady to confront him with her disappointment. Instead, she throws herself deeper into General Tarry's oaken arms and bemoans the inhumanity of man. Who will sell her wine at true love's discount?

(And her sister gets seriously disgruntled without her afternoon wine cooler on the veranda. Kay's been to see her lawyer. This could negatively impact Edie's inheritance.)

Edie uses her piglet to infiltrate the Grange, seek their help.

"It's simply criminal," she says at a Tuesday night gathering, "that our children are so distanced nowadays from our farming heritage, they don't have a clue where their food comes from. They think milk comes from plastic jugs. They think eggs come from refrigerated units at the supermarket. They think bacon—"

Well, scratch that. She can't think about bacon.

Porky Doodles wags his little black-tipped tail appreciatively.

The old hens at the Grange cluck their support over the Bicentennial quilt they're patching in honor of our nation's two-hundredth. It's true, these newcomers to town seem dismissive of farming. They're city types. They wouldn't know a pullet from a capon if one strolled over and laid an egg in their roasting pan. They may cheer the horses in the Memorial Day Parade and applaud the picturesque sheep added to the annual Revolutionary War re-enactment for verisimilitude, but when Susie Beyman's Black Lightning hoofs around the softball field, clopping divots, those people not born in town begin to fuss and point fingers. Their daughters could turn an ankle in one of the craters in the outfield.

It's a shame, really. We've lost Thomas Jefferson's vision of an agrarian nation of gentleman farmers, ruggedly independent and sustainable, slaves to no one's food supply but our own. If someone wants to raise pigs to supplement his diet, isn't it un-American to raise objections?

(And really, swine flu? Big Pauly Silvio's grandmother never came within a hundred miles of a pig.)

Edie orchestrates, and the old hens bustle out to talk to the Chernickis about their cow and the danger presented when city types object to good, old-fashioned, virtuous food production in the back yard. They bewail the loss of sheep grazing on the village common (South Quagmire has never had anything resembling a common), and let Jack Keene know that his "girls" are in peril, that certain neighbors have made pointed comments about the chick-enshit aroma wafting from his coop. They point to the new sign on the chain link fence that reads, "No horses or dogs allowed on the ballfield."

It's a conspiracy!

Before long, an Agricultural Commission forms in town, and its first order of business is to place a Right to Farm Article in the October 1976 Special Town Meeting. After all, Right to Farm dates to the foundation of our great country, to the Home Rule Amendments that fed Massachusetts patriots on Lexington's green and Bunker's bloody heights. Right to Farm is our national heritage. It's what separates us from the Russkys. Only a dyed-in-the-wool Soviet sympathizer would argue against the virtues of self-sustain-ability. A chicken in every pot, a long-haired goat in every garden.

Nigel Brate and Big Pauly Silvio are furious. The *Playboy* offen-sive has provoked unintended reprisals. They must defeat this article or their vendetta against the general and his floozy will be seriously, perhaps fatally, undermined. But Big Pauly Silvio is home tonight with bronchitis, and Brate, as it turns out, has nothing to fear. Two town officials drop dead, the interim moderator is incompetent, and voters are anxiously eyeing the exits.

Then, as if heaven-sent, to the microphone saunters Bud Beyman, strapping, tanned, the faint smell of hay wafting in his wake. Nigel holds his breath. This could be good. Bud's the Marlboro man in L.L. Bean flannel, a gentleman farmer who doesn't mind getting his Timberlands dirty. A little mud under the fingernails or a stray smudge of horseshit on his rolled-up cuffs never hurt anyone. He's his own mechanic, his own veterinarian, his own political theorist. He's an avid reader of the tabloid press. He knows Lee Harvey Oswald did not act alone. The government's a conspiracy ready to turn us all into soulless drones.

If you're a soulless drone who has an article on the Town Meeting warrant you care about, Bud's the last guy you want defending your article. Ever. He's articulate and passionate. He's a steam roller for Truth, a juggernaut for Justice. The more he rails against those who would curtail Our Inalienable Rights (that includes the moderator gaveling His First Amendment Rights ten minutes into rant), the more aggressive his heavy equipment gets. He'll flatten anyone to defend His...

Our...

Well, OK, His and Our Rights (but mostly His):

Our Right to Free Speech,

Our Right to Bear Arms.

Our Right to Stockpile Sand for Our Cranberry Bogs.

(Suddenly everyone in the hall remembers the nor'easter that blew silica dust all over town and wrecked Billy's backyard hockey rink.)

Our Right to Ride Horses in Public.

(Suddenly everyone recalls the manure on Tiffany's patent leather shoes in church that First Communion Sunday.)

Our Right to Raise Bees for Pollination.

(Suddenly everyone remembers the sting that triggered Joe's anaphylactic shock.)

Once he gets started, he cannot be stopped. Bud is eloquent and his vocabulary colorful. His lung capacity rivals that of Japanese pearl divers. He'll browbeat the moderator. He'll heap contempt on the opposition. His prose, like his face, turns purple. His ears threaten to combust. The article's proponents brace themselves and foresee unhappy ends. He's got their back. He's crushing it.

Opponents feel a gloat rise in their chests.

Bud Beyman's got the mike! (And just listen to the invective!)

Victory? They're screwed.

Defeat! Bring it on!

Miss Edith Ottick crosses her fingers. She believes that calves and ponies and floppy-eared puppies, lambie-kins, yellow duck-lings, Easter bunnies, and roly-poly piglets have some Hallmark hold on our hearts. She has hopes for down and fuzz and darling little bleats and peeps. Aren't we all suckers for cute and cuddly? At our most primal, don't we long for tails? But then, Bud reminds us of the Christmas when the sheep started doing it in the live Nativity on Town Hall lawn. That was nature, he tells us, not nasty, and there's no harm in letting the kids see first-hand where lamb chops come from! No need to get our panties in a twist! And the blue-bottle flies that swarmed the middle school band Fourth of July because of the horse dung strewed along the parade route??? Pesticides! Pesticides can handle that. Nothing easier! That's why we invented 'em! And it gave the Highway Department something to do the following week. They spend way too much time in the Dunkin Donuts parking lot anyway.

He gets emotional. Chokes the mike stand. Miss Edie feels hope wane. The end is nigh, and it doesn't smell pretty. It smells a little like Porky Doodles' diaper.

Suddenly, tangible as sledgehammer on railroad spike, the end comes. Bud's winding up a minor digression on falling John Deere stock prices (and declining value in portfolio) when his wife, Susie Beyman, equestrian, stands, jockey svelte and expression fearful but not yet defeated. She steps toward the aisle. Maybe she thinks she can temper his argument with a gentle, spousal hand to the shoulder. Maybe she's picturing a dump-free canter over the Town Forest's groomed trails and daring to rein this imagined amble back within the realm of possibility. Maybe she's—

But Susie is too late. Bud is on a tear. He's at the top of his game. How many hypocrites in this room right now are fertilizing their potted tomatoes with local cow manure, eh? How many? Without a glance behind he senses his wife's momentum and barks, "Susie, sit!" in a tone usually reserved for bad dogs.

The audience gasps. Necks snap. Susie sits. And that's the end of Right to Farm right there. The alleged illegal piggery in Little Quagmire Swamp remains illegal, if existential.

Up in the sound booth we four have no personal investment in Right to Farm, so the floor show ends with a lame voice vote more Nay than Aye. Bud Beyman stalks out, ears aflame. Susie waits until he's exited the hall, then stands, shrugs apologetically (careful not to make eye contact) and follows. I could go into more detail, but there's no need. Article Two will bear some relevance to our story's climax but is not otherwise noteworthy. Theobald Doppelmeier is turning bluer, but no one notices.

No one dies during Article Two. [10]

---

[10] During March Annual Town Meeting Bud went off on a rant in favor of taxpayer funding of Catholic high school transportation and after he finished (a vehement twenty minutes) there was no chance that any teenager in town would be riding a bus to Bishop O'Bannon for the next quarter century.

ARTICLE 3

"To see if the town will vote to purchase or acquire by eminent
domain the property known as Little Quagmire Swamp, as authorized by town by-law I-17, for conservation and/or water supply
protection purposes, which land is more fully described as follows: Assessors' Map 56, Lots 12, 13, 14, 17, and 129a,b,c, and r,
two thousand four hundred twelve acres referenced in Deed Book
3922, page 419, and Assessor's Map 58, Lots 3,4,5,6,7,27,37,47, five
hundred-sixty-two-and-a-half acres referenced in Deed Book 4102,
page 39—that $1,779,900 is appropriated for this acquisition, that
to meet this appropriation the Treasurer, with the approval of the
Board of Selectmen, is authorized to borrow $1,779,900 under
General Law, Chapter 44, section I-27, and that the Conservation
Commission or the Board of Selectmen be authorized to apply for
and expend any federal or state aid or private funds available for
the project, provided however that this vote shall not take effect
until the Town votes to exempt from the limitation on total taxes
imposed by the General Law, Chapter 59, Section N-31, amounts
required to pay the principal and interest on the borrowing authorized by this vote, or take any other action in relation thereto."

Three white boys in camo gear huddle at the back of the
non-voters' section in the balcony. They are students at the military
academy, teenagers. One is tall and skinny, one is short and skinny,
and one is unexceptional except for the patch over his right eye and
the secretive way he's eating something and not sharing with his

'comrades.' All three have brown hair that is shaved on the sides and flat on top. They each have numbers carved into the sides like football players sometimes do, a 41, a 43, and a 169. (Thirty-one years later, and still Birnam remembers the numbers clearly. Thank you, Birnam.) We see them around town occasionally. Number Forty-One, the tall one, drives an unregistered antique truck, a Model A from the thirties, a real junk. He makes weekly runs to the post office with mail from the school (the students are required to write home with all the news that can't be censored), and, at night, dumpster visits. The alleged illegal piggery out in the swamps is in the market for free swill, and tall, skinny Number Forty-One, Tyler McVeigh, is head forager.

Number One-Sixty-Nine, the short kid, is a runty little thing, Tommy Someone. He might be in middle school. I have no records left to check, and any medical files are confidential or lost in the transition to computerization. Number One-Sixty-Nine is being treated for Post-Traumatic Stress Syndrome (or shell shock), according to Number Forty-One, Tyler McVeigh, who tells postmistress Carmen Selsby's free-range granddaughter, Tourmaline Selsby, one hands-on evening behind the post office, that Tommy Someone was traumatized on a vision quest when a "flaming, flying dead thing" or "zombie angel of death" exploded out of the swamp and attacked him.

Scorched his clothes, singed his hair and eyebrows and lashes.

Tried to drown him.

This is exciting and fuels endless speculation. What could a "flaming, flying dead thing" be and where is it now? Is it / was it human? Supernatural? The Pleasant Street Monster, maybe? Can we see it? Do we dare?

Petrified Wood hypothesizes it's a big goose or dead swan that spontaneously combusted like in some Dickens novel, achieved lift-off, and chose Tommy as its landing site. Spontaneous combustion. Uh… is that even possible? [11] Tourmaline Selsby, who has a hyperactive imagination and libido but not much sense, is sure it's a body. She's read about human sacrifices in bogs in Europe. (So now we know she reads something besides our mail.) My boyfriend at the time guesses it's a vegetative mass reeking of methane. He knows about methane. He and his buddies have lost several pairs of underpants playing with matches.

Whatever it is (was), Number One-Sixty-Nine, Traumatized Tommy Someone, no longer speaks. Has gone mute. Dumb. Because it was a solo vision quest, only Tommy has experienced this terrifying assault on his senses. Only he's been fire-bombed by "a zombie angel of death." Whether roast goose, sacrificial human body, or decomposing muck farts, the *masse flambé* has chosen him for its crash pad. His dog tags have melted (plastic knock-offs, evidently). He's got first, second, and third-degree burns. He babbles "flaming, flying dead thing" in his sleep, but that's all he'll say, over and over and over again until his classmates writhe in their bunks and pull army surplus pillows over their ears. He's not giving up his secrets, says Number Forty-One, Tyler McVeigh, to highly receptive Tourmaline Selsby with inappropriate hand gestures behind the post office. He doesn't need to, because Tourmaline Selsby's soon inventing them for him. The postmistress's granddaughter can't wait to spread the word, no postage required. Familiarity with an armed white survivalist gives her street cred. And if anyone lights a

---

11 PT Wood is a dues-paying member of the National Wildlife Federation. Everything is water-fowl with him.

cigarette or a Colman lantern in Tommy's presence, he breaks into cold sweats. That's the word in the school corridors anyway, thanks to our freshly-pawed Tourmaline.

He looks like he's heading for a cold sweat tonight. Why is he here at all?

The assault happens on a night that Chief Dobbs is setting fire to End Zone Island (a favorite pastime), and Nigel Brate comes along in his helicopter to put out the blaze and crashes into the swamp. Nigel is carrying water in a big canvas sling from the bay to dump on the fire. These two play a circular game. Chief Dobbs sets the fire, Nigel Brate extinguishes it. The game's been repeated at least four or five times. It's impossible Brate doesn't know that Chief Dobbs sets these fires but, of course, in small towns, nothing's impossible. This night is different, and while the story changes daily, depending on to whom he tells it from behind the counter of his Liquor Emporium, Nigel Brate keeps most of the details within a mile of possibility. Chief Dobbs calls, saying those damned football kids have set fire to End Zone Island again and the whole damned swamp's ablaze. Brate rushes off to East Quagmire with Big Pauly Silvio, gets his biggest helicopter, flies to Narraganset Bay to fill a big canvas sling with water, and comes back, but he takes off so fast, he doesn't check the fuel tanks. There's a hole in the tank, slow leak, fast! Gas drains into the water. Suddenly he looks. The fuel gauge is on empty. The sky above, the fire below. Panic! He releases his load. The helicopter flips. The sky below, the fires above! Gasoline dumps onto the fire. Baboom! His helicopter ignites. It falls. It does not land on Tommy, who's finding his Zen on End Zone Island, but fuel and motor oil mix with swamp gas, methane, or some such combustible. End Zone Island goes up like too much lighter fluid on not enough charcoal. The only reason Tommy's spared from death by conflagration is that the "flaming, flying zombie angel of death" knocks him into the water (now salted) and tries to drown him.

Or so the story goes. In a small town, who knows where the legends end and the lies begin? Tommy isn't providing details. Tourmaline Selsby's making them up as she goes along. Nigel Brate embroiders the tale with each new telling, and Big Pauly Silvio, who's broken both arms in the crash but removed the casts with a hack saw three weeks early (they itched bad!), now has a party piece he'll be able to embellish for years to come.

As for the Ottick sisters, they lose their bet when Chief Dobbs storms out of the building before the end of Article Three, but Kay will make it back with interest when the town doesn't vote to buy her portion of Little Quagmire Swamp, on which she has paid minimal taxes for over thirty years, and she sells twenty one-acre lots for development. Despite the deaths of Tim Drummond and Tubby Dobbs, she'll recoup her losses. She's probably weighing the odds right now as Conservation Commission members Woodchuck and Cher Wood rise from their seats and move to the front of the hall. Woodchuck Wood takes the microphone from Chief Crockett.

We already know, thanks to PT's voluble introduction, that the Wood family has a vested interest in Little Quagmire Swamp. An assessor's map from the time lays out in detail their four parcels of property, about three-quarters of which is wetland, a portion of that cranberry bog. Their house sits on the easternmost parcel, with about fifty acres of crop field (they're heavily into sustainability) and a sizable woodlot. There's also, buried beneath the foliage, a still, a goofy-looking contraption with a big copper tub and lots of tubing. PT shows Arianna and me once how it works, but I don't pay attention. Why would anyone go through that much effort for something you can buy at the packy cheap?

PT's dad, Woodchuck Wood, is a moonshiner. From the corn and potatoes in his field he distills a family-recipe rotgut that went out with Prohibition but is prized by town elders and under-aged kids who don't have fake IDs. This he's willing to sell on the cheap.

Which presents a problem for Nigel Brate, purveyor of booze.

Nigel Brate hates Woodchuck Wood. Their mutual antipathy goes back years. Nigel's a Republican who thinks Nixon was framed, Woodchuck's an aging hippie who came late to hippie-hood because there were no hippies in his Eisenhower-era youth. Nigel was in the military; Woodchuck claims to have burned his draft card (although I'm sure if we asked Birnam about this, he'd say, "Do the math!"). Woodchuck's graying hair is tied back in a ponytail that falls almost to his waist. Nigel is bald. And although Nigel's lost his biggest helicopter to a leaky gas tank while trying to extinguish a swamp fire, he's burned out others flying aerial missions in fruitless search of the Wood family's still and the illegal piggery. Besides, his packy backs onto the swamp and there's talk in town he wants to expand his parking lot. There's no chance Nigel Brate will vote for the town to buy the swamp tonight. His squinty eyes stare malevolently down from his seat onstage as Woodchuck Wood takes the microphone, taps it loudly enough to puncture eardrums, and shouts:

"Testing! Testing! One, Two, Three!!!"

Spittle splats. People groan and cover their ears. Someone (or somefifty) holler, "Turn it down!" Woodchuck grins vacantly, moves the mike away from his mouth, and swipes at saliva, resulting in loud protests from the sound system. He's wearing a fringed leather vest over a sleeveless sweater and raises a skinny wrist to brush the hair back from his forehead. There is no hair on his forehead. It's clubbed back in the braid tonight.

His wife's beside him. She's in a floor-length floral skirt that appears to have been beaten on stones in a river for twenty years, and a baggy pink T-shirt that says, *Save The Whales!* It might actually have been worn by one before it beached itself and died. She's carrying something, a glass jar, dark, maybe green inside. Weed? I wouldn't be surprised. She's an inch or so taller than him, Aryan blonde to his gray, but he's her totem. She looks down with rapturous admiration, brushes the hair back from his forehead, the hair which isn't there. He smiles with manly condescension. Tarzan will speak. Jane will provide the show-and-tell.

Woodchuck and Cher Wood, formerly Charles and Gladys, deserve a picture frame. They are clichés, *American Gothic* on LSD: geriatric flower children, poseur wackos, wanna-be freaks, crunchy-feely organic-granola slaps at the public consciousness. (As if anyone in South Quagmire is in position to save the whales.) "Look at us, look at us!" they all but beg from their self-righteous pulpit at the front of the hall. "We will not bow to bourgeois interests. Our respect for the planet (or the cosmos, or various hallucinogenics) far surpasses your pitiful comprehension. Puny mortals, resistance is futile. Prepare for enlightenment."

We resist enlightenment. Petrified Wood winces in embarrassment and avoids our eyes. Arianna slips from his embrace. I try not to make my disdain too apparent and fail in the attempt. Parents are required by law to mortify their children. His do. Mine does (constantly. Arianna's parent meanwhile has just run over the fire chief, submitted to handcuffs, broken down in sobs, and still managed not to humiliate. Of course, he's a special case, too young to be father to a teenage daughter. Too hot in his tight-fitting, short-sleeved uniform shirt and baseball cap. Sympathy for Anthony DeBarros, that's what three of us in the booth feel, and probably others in the room too. Sympathy, and something else. Something in the flesh.)

Woodchuck and Cher Wood do not evoke our sympathy (or any positive emotion), not decked out as they are tonight. They do inspire scorn. They will speak on and on until every eye in the room glazes over. And, thanks to a cop at every exit, we're a captive audience. The itch in a hundred bums becomes audible. It's promising to be a long night. Only Birnam looks eager for the games to start.

Woodchuck opens his mouth. People fidget. Instead, from the stage, he's interrupted by our temporary moderator, Tara Drummond, who mumbles:

"We will move to— (She shuffles some papers.)—Article Three. To see if the town will vote to purchase—"

But he cuts her off with a three decibels less-than-deafening:

"I move that the Selectmen be authorized to purchase or acquire by eminent domain, as authorized by—"

But he's cut off by Tara Drummond, who's being advised by the town's lawyer:

"This is—this is a bond issue, and Edgar... er, Mr. Vade ,.. er, Town Counsel informs me it will require a two-thirds vote. Edgar, is—two-thirds? Yes, yes, two-thirds vote. Will the Conservation Commission...? Ah, Mr. and Mrs. Wood?"

Woodchuck Wood has not looked back or acknowledged Tara Drummond. He backtracks a few words and continues at an alarming pace, as if afraid he'll be cut off again. Only Theobald

Doppelmeier listens. He's still involved in his imaginary BINGO game. Fondling that small furry squirrel thing on the table in front of him and rearranging his nuts.

"…as authorized by town by-law, section I-17…"

"I-17!"

"… the property known as Little Quagmire Swamp, for conservation and/or water supply purposes, which land is more fully described as follows: Assessors' Map 56, Lots 12, 13, 14, 17, and 129a,b,c, and r, two thousand four hundred twelve acres referenced in Deed Book 3922, page 419, and Assessor's Map 58, Lots 3,4,5,6,7,27,37,47, hike, five hundred-sixty-two-and-a-half acres referenced in Deed Book 4102, page 39—that $1,779,900 is appropriated for this acquisition, that to meet this appropriation the Treasurer, with the approval of the Board of Selectmen, is authorized to borrow $1,779,900 under General Law, Chapter 44, section I-27, and that the Conservation—"

"I-27! Got it!"

"—Commission or the Board of Selectmen be authorized to apply for and expend any federal or state aid or private funds available for the project, provided however that this vote shall not take effect until the Town votes to exempt from the limitation on total taxes imposed by the General Law, Chapter 59, Section N-31, amounts required to pay the principal and interest on the—"

"N-31, N-31."

"—borrowing authorized by this vote."

"N-31. Oh, crap."

This is followed by an exhausted silence in which the audience hesitates to shrug off stupefaction, allowing Woodchuck Wood to catch his breath. After a polite interlude, his wife sings, "I second that emotion," and throws a supportive hand across his shoulders. She has long fingers.

Petrified Wood buries head in hands, but his brother is bouncing on his stool. Without a glance our way, eyes lowered, Birnam is up and sidling out the door. He commandeers a folding chair at the front of the balcony. He too has long fingers with which he grips the railing. His mother takes the microphone from her husband.

"Citizens of South Quagmire (just north of East Quagmire)," she begins, "good evening. You know me, Cher Wood, Conservation Commission."

The voters are dispirited. They know her only too well.

"When my old man Chuckie and me moved back to town fourteen years ago, we bought our first house from TouchDown Realty, Tim and Toby, God bless 'em... (She sighs, looks Heavenward, then changes her mind and glances down, shaking her head.)... just off Ridge Road. Nice little starter home, half an acre of land. Good times, good times. We grew organic vegetables in the garden. Fed the fattest little rabbits you ever saw. Free love in the cabbage patch, you hear what I'm saying?"

She's got a big smile going. No one else in the room does, although Birnam's chubby chin now rests on his baby-fat forearms on the balcony railing, and he leans over, already enthralled by the story.

"Then TouchDown Realty comes along and develops Apple Orchard Acres behind us, fifty tract houses, and diverts Little Quagmire Creek right through our basement. We have to wait till the summer of '68... you all remember the drought?... before the cellar's dry enough we can sell the place to those unsuspecting schmucks from Malden who don't speak to us anymore...

"Oh, I see you there in the third row. Hello. How's it going? You get the sump pump working? Peace, love!

"So, then we buy the parsonage on High Street, also from TD Realty, Tim and Toby, may they rest in... anyway, and figure we're good, until they develop Colonial Pines Plaza practically in our backyard and blow out our windows with the noise of jackhammers and diesel engines."

From the depths of the stage, we hear the bellow of a hippopotamus. "Get to the point!" she barks, with all the weight of hippo-critical indignation behind her. Cher Wood continues, unfazed.

"Finally, we buy sixty acres of land on Swamp Road, not from TouchDown Realty this time, thank you very much, and figure we're safely out of the way of their corporate clutches. Wrong! They're back. They've already scooped two hundred acres from Coastal Cranberries and they're raping the rivers, humping the hills. Setting fire to the swamp. They're driving out the wildlife. They killed Bambi's mother."

She glances into the audience, spots funeral director Bambi Saville, who's come back from the walk-in refrigerator, looking all excited, and says, "Sorry, Bambi."

Bambi doesn't appear to know what she's sorry about. But then, she's not alone. We're trying to envision some enormous figure with his pants down around his knees humping hills.

"I'm talking subdivision, man. I'm talking another fifty tract houses on half-acre lots on seven new streets. I'm talking fifty more backyard barbecue grills polluting the air over South Quagmire (just north of East Quagmire). I'm talking more traffic, crowded classrooms, hoodlums moving in from the city, demanding all the social services they've gotten used to in Boston… I'm talking retention basins."

A scrape of table and chair in motion. The earth shakes. The hippo stands.

"Point of order, Mister—" She catches herself. "Madam Moderator."

Tara Drummond slumps. She looks nervously toward the Town Treasurer.

"Uh—state your point of order, Mrs. Épée."

Mrs. Épée directs her point of order at the bohemian in the beluga-sized *Save The Whales* T-shirt.

"This hallucinogenic diatribe has nothing to do with the motion on the floor."

You can see the bohemian Mrs. Wood grow two inches of indignation as she snaps back, "With all due respect to Madam Moneybags here, this discussion has everything to do with the motion on the floor. This discussion has to do with TouchDown Realty. TD Realty. In the past fifteen years, at a *conservative* estimate…" She throws heavy emphasis on '*conservative*'… "these ravenous monsters of corporate greed have decimated over twelve hundred acres of farmland, destroyed valuable wildlife habitat, deflowered who knows how much virgin wilderness…"

She pauses to collect herself. You can see stick-figure Nigel Brate onstage startled by the suggestion of 'deflowered virgins.'

"…invested in at least a hundred condos, paid Wilhelmina Makepeace, health agent, to falsify perk tests, so we got diverted waterways running through people's cellars…"

She's starting to hyperventilate, and out on the balcony, Birnam looks like he might leap the railing in solidarity.

"...and split between them, at a *conservative* estimate..."

There's that *conservative* again.

"... a cool ten-and-a-half million dollars, which—"

A shout from the non-voters' section: "Divided four ways, that's two million, six-hundred-twenty-five thousand dollars apiece!"

Gasps erupt from below, gasps of envy, outrage, alarm. Heads turn, crane to see. Who's tossing out numbers from on high? God? God, no, it can't be God. God isn't hanging with the moneylenders in the temple, is He? Oh, the balcony. This is not The Rapture then. We're not being called away, the chosen few, the saved? Dammit, Agnes we couldn't be that lucky. Jeez, Lloyd, it's that freaky spawn of these freaky weirdos, hanging off the railing. What's he doing here? What are *we* doing here? Can't we all just go home to *Monday Night Football*?

Cher Wood chirps with cheerful, maternal pride, "Thank you, Birnam."

But Birnam continues calculating at a roar, and five teenagers sitting near him, a cozy little wolf pack of high school thugs who will enter our story soon, exchange glances, nudge each other. Their ersatz leader, Tourmaline Selsby, the postmistress's granddaughter, looks especially smug.

"Or, if you figure there's only two of them left, that's five million, two-hundred-fifty thousand dollars each!"

Cher Wood is beaming as she says, "Thank you, Birnam," again. The thugs (three are female. one's a big, brutish-looking lump of a male, the other's his two-bit doppelganger) mouth, "Thank you, Birnam," and break into snotty giggles. Birnam is oblivious. He waves to his mother. The voting public is shaking heads and grumbling. They check their wrist watches.

"And now," announces Cher Wood, "we have some home movies we want to show you. Miz Moderator, can we turn off the lights, please?"

The room is silent, but you can hear the quorum stifle a collective groan.

Tara Drummond doesn't move. Miss Makepeace stands, smooths the front of her black leather skirt, and goes backstage to find the lights. A portable screen gets carried in from the wings and everyone manages to relocate themselves to avoid it, except for Tara Drummond, who gets whacked on the head. She does not visibly respond.

Postmistress Carmen Selsby is knitting in the front row. She's the only person we know who can knit a sweater with one hand and sort mail with the other. She does neither well, which may explain why everyone's junk mail ends up in General Tarry's triple-locked grenade-resistant mailbox. Some people say she reads our mail, but I doubt that's true. She's never struck me as the slightest bit curious about what-goes-on around town. Also, the constant carbon monoxide fog from Winston Lights have weakened her eyes.

A third member of the Conservation Commission, she fumbles her needles as she rises to set up a Super 8 mm film projector. Her broken ribs are knitting too, evidently, but not completely healed yet from the tumble down Brate's concrete steps last month. She gives a little groan and squeezes one hand against her side. Her nose is still off-kilter. A punch-drunk middle-aged prizefighter in drag comes to mind. She turns on the projector. The reels run backward. The film flaps. The reels totter. She rethreads the projector. Her yarn tangles with the film. She struggles to free it. A splice breaks. She rewinds. Starts again. Rethreads. Five minutes of our lives are wasted.

Carmen Selsby does not manage inconspicuous well.

Miss Makepeace turns off the lights.

There follows a numbing montage depicting water, mud, trees, ducks, mushrooms, rodents, flowers, turtles, cranberries, Wood children at various ages romping in red boots through poisonous-looking vegetation (Petrified Wood is cringing in the booth; it seems he's responsible for much of the footage. Birnam is engrossed), cannabis (probably an accident, but you never know with Woodchuck and Cher Wood), and, disgustingly, two amphibians assuming unnatural positions in the muck. The film is accompanied by a stupefying narration that descends all the way to genus and species and leaves most of us narcoleptic and/or comatose.

I recall two entertaining moments not recorded in the official transcript. The first is when the screen accidentally collapses to reveal Wilhelmina Makepeace and Chief Crockett behind in a grappling embrace. Chief Crockett is caught wide-handed at the moment Cher Wood declares "only a bunch of real boobs' would miss out on this chance to attain prime real estate for open space purposes, but Miss Makepeace nonchalantly frees herself the few moments it takes to fasten her blouse and reattach the screen to its mounting.

The second comes at the end, when a view from the fire tower (no longer with us, thank you, Chief Dobbs) of the swamp ablaze (thank you, Chief Dobbs, yet again) lights up the stage, and a scream is heard from the balcony. The little survivalist kid from the military academy, Number One-Sixty-Nine, the traumatized Tommy, babbles "flaming, flying dead thing!" over and over until he is pinned down and muffled by his teenage attendants.

The show ends with a sequence of charred wasteland, ash, cinder, and smoke, that Cher Wood attributes to the members of

TouchDown Realty, living and dead, may they rot in some fabled underworld, proud purveyors of Armageddon. The whole presentation strikes me as distasteful. Certainly the hippo looks apoplectic.

The screen is removed. The lights come back on. Postmistress Carmen Selsby turns off the projector and resumes her knitting. The glass jar in Cher's hand moves front-and-center, and Woodchuck Wood takes it from her and holds it in front of his face. There's an awkward collision between the jar and the microphone.

"Finally, fellow inmates of this great lunatic asylum we call suburbia," he says, "this is it."

Everyone stares. This is it? No one has a clue what '*this*' it is, although we're hoping this '*this*' signals the grand finale, that the freaks are winding down their hallucinogenic diatribe. Reverend Jake bites his fingernails. The Rapture will never come soon enough to spare us further sermonizing.

But now, unwillingly, we are intrigued by the jar. It's a Mason jar. It's a Mason jar, and there's something inside it, something likely un-Masonic. Greenery? Probably not cabbage leaves for any fat little rabbit of voting age that may have wandered in off the street. Clearly not moonshine. Is it weed? Are they planning to get us all stoned in order to buy our votes?

"This is what we're trying to save."

He tries to unscrew the lid from the jar. Someone's poked holes in the top and they're jagged. He gives a little squeak of pain, pulls his hand away. He shakes it. Even from this distance, blood is visible on his palm. He cusses, puts his palm to his mouth, licks, sucks. Refreshed, he goes back in for the attack. The lid comes loose. He hands it to his wife, pokes his finger into the jar. Everyone watches. I hear Petrified Wood inhale. The magician is about to pull a rabbit from the hat. Instead, he rummages through the compost and lifts something small and black from the interior. He's holding it by... the tail?

"This, ladies and gentlemen," he says, and licks more blood off his palm while the small black thing dangles in front of his chin, "this is an endangered species. Isn't he a trip?"

Someone thinks he's planning to eat the thing and gives a big, "Ewww!" Is the blood his, or its? Does it matter?

Gross!

"The black-bottomed newt," he proclaims.

A shout from the balcony railing: "Save the newts!"

The wolf pack nearby almost falls out of folding chairs in hysterics. Tourmaline Selsby whacks the big lump with her purse.

"There's only a couple hundred of these left in the world, and at least three of them are procreating in vernal pools in Little Quagmire Swamp right this minute."

It takes a minute for the wolf pack to translate the word 'procreating' into intelligible gutter-speak, but once they have, the lump, sixteen-year-old Jasper David Lovell, or Juvenile Delinquent Lovell to his victims and the locals whose mail he misdelivers on a weekly basis, starts making nasty little gestures with middle finger through circling thumb and forefinger on his other hand. Tourmaline bites his finger. Jasper pulls her hair. Birnam is oblivious. He waves to his dad.

Woodchuck finishes. "And with your 'yes' vote here tonight, we can save this little feller..." His voice trails off. He's staring at the thing, a salamander (?), wriggling between his thumb and middle finger. His eyebrows rise. Evidently he hasn't studied its anatomy closely before this moment, because he corrects himself. "Uh...

little mama…" He rubs a grubby finger down its belly. "…for many years to come. Thank you." And absent-mindedly, he licks that finger too.

Jasper Lovell guffaws and makes some crack about finger-lickin' chicken.

In the front row postmistress Carmen Selsby, rises. A long, violet skein of yarn comes with her.

"Madame Moderator?"

Tara Drummond looks around, bewildered. Carmen Selsby is far into middle age and unprepossessing but for the skewed nose. She's hard to notice when she isn't mangling film in a projector. Slowly, Tara Drummond focuses. "Uh… Mrs. Selsby?"

"Yes, Madam Moderator," says Carmen Selsby, waving her needles and what may be a scarf purled from the pages of Doctor Seuss, "this project is fifty-seven percent reimbursable by the state, so we on the Conservation Commission believe the Town should exercise its option for first refusal while the land is still taxed as agricultural property. If all this grant money comes back to us, then it will cost next to nothing and further protect our water supply."

Audible mumbles and grumbles, a lone, "Hear, hear!" from the voters' section. Carmen Selsby sits with a sigh and a plump. The clack of needles resumes. A strident voice from the stage rings out. The chairman of the Finance Committee rises. She looks indignant.

"Madam Moderator!"

"Miss… uh, Rupped?" Tara Drummond stutters. "Uh… sorry… uh… is there a… a recommendation from the Finance Committee?"

Miss Rupped, Finance Committee chairperson, is a tall, white female, severely dressed in a boiled wool jacket and gray tailored skirt. Her mouth is bobbed as tightly as her hair. She has large teeth.

"Madam Moderator, it is obvious the Conservation Commission has been stacked with conservationists. How can we afford to throw our limited resources away on a breeding ground for mosquitoes, when our schools are in need of serious renovations, when our classrooms are overcrowded?"

In the balcony Birnam gasps, and the three high school girls erupt into raucous cackles.

"The state," continues Miss Rupped, "is in fiscal crisis. State revenues to cities and towns are being cut by twenty, thirty percent. I think it highly unlikely, despite the assurances of our postmistress, Mrs. Selsby, that they will be putting further funds into conservation purchases. Certainly not fifty-seven percent. We'll end up footing the entire bill for this salamander colony."

Here follows a direct copy of the transcript of the meeting as recorded by the court stenographer with the dictamask, the easiest way of fast-forwarding through the confusion that follows.

Mr. WOOD: Hey, they scoffed at the Louisiana Purchase too.

Mrs. WOOD: They called Alaska Seward's Folly.

Mr. BRATE: Go back to Russia where you belong, pinkos!

FROM THE FLOOR: Save the newts!

Mr. DOPPELMEIER: Fifty-seven? Fifty-seven what? What the hell is going on here?

FROM THE FLOOR: This is all my sister's fault.

General TARRY: Use the mike!

FROM THE FLOOR: This is all— Thank you. This is all my sister's fault.

General TARRY: State your name, Pumpkin.

Ms. E. OTTICK: Thank you, Mon Générale.

Mr. BRATE: Floozy!

Ms. E. OTTICK: Miss Edith Ottick, 292 Pine Street. This is all my sister Kay's fault. Papa left Kay Little Quagmire Swamp because she was the oldest, and now after all these years she's decided to sell it. I don't know what TouchDown Realty has offered her for the land, but you can bet it's in the millions, and, you see, Kay wasn't born in this town. She was born in Quincy and she just doesn't understand.

Ms. K. OTTICK: Give me that mike!

The MODERATOR: Miss Ottick.

Ms. K. OTTICK: Give me the mike, Edie.

Ms. E. OTTICK: Why should I?

Ms. K. OTTICK: I've lived here longer than you, you old coot. We moved here when I was four weeks old.

Ms. E. OTTICK: Yes, but you weren't born here. Only a true townie understands how important this land is for water conservation purposes, and you'll never be one. Not a true townie. Money's turned her head, but it's not our place to judge. Our place, to buy this land and feel pity for my sister who never developed a strong community bond like those of us born here.

Ms. K. OTTICK: You senile old maid, I lived in this town two years before you were even born, and I guess I have the right to sell the land if I want to. The whole place is burnt from those kids setting fire to End Zone Island. What I can't understand is why the town would waste its money on a piece of property no one wanted until TouchDown Realty made me an offer. It's

dirty. It's polluted. The water rights are clouded. Mr. Corr's
students tell me the saludi—the salty—saltiness—

FROM THE FLOOR: Salinity!

FROM THE FLOOR: The salt content.

Ms. K. OTTICK: They've been doing things out there.

FROM THE FLOOR: Water quality testing.

FROM THE FLOOR: Mr. Corr.

FROM THE FLOOR: For salinity. Mr. Corr said we should—

FROM THE FLOOR: The salinity's been rising. Someone is dumping salt in the swamp.

Mr. BRATE: Those children are not registered voters. Madam Moderator—

FROM THE FLOOR: Well, you all know it's true. Twenty-five miles from the ocean, and Rocky Mackiewicz gets bitten by a shark? That's salt water.

Mr. BRATE: It's an estuary, you morons!

The MODERATOR: Please, please, may we have—

FROM THE FLOOR: Check out the periwinkles.

FROM THE FLOOR: Krystal Tull, 14 Forest Ave. It's true. Someone's salting the swamp.

My boyfriend Rocky Mackiewicz is out there in waders testing the salinity, and he gets bitten by a shark?

UNINTELLIGIBLE VOICES

FROM THE FLOOR (Ms. TULL?): He was my boyfriend before he was yours.

Mr. BRATE: It's the tide.

FROM THE FLOOR (Ms. TULL?): Sharks don't swim uphill. And, like, who set the swamp on fire?

98

FROM THE FLOOR: The salinity's at twenty-nine parts
   per thousand.

FROM THE FLOOR (Ms. TULL?): Twenty-eight.

FROM THE FLOOR: No, thirty-two.

FROM THE FLOOR: Thirty-three.

FROM THE FLOOR: No one asked you, Turd Man.

FROM THE FLOOR: ? (Birnam. Birnam.) ?

Mr. WOOD: You're killing the newts. They don't live in tidal
   pools, you know.

FROM THE FLOOR: Save the newts!

This goes on for some time. Not from the floor but from the
balcony our pack of high school ne'er-do-wells have catapulted
themselves into the official transcript. (Their sudden emergence
into celebrity almost catapults Birnam over the railing into the seats
below.) They are The Rocks. That's what they call their little clique,
thanks to a planetary alignment of looks, brain substitute, but most
notably, names: Tourmaline Selsby, Krystal Tull, Ruby Jones-Smith,
Jasper Lovell, and Jasper's younger brother Jet. There are five of
them: four fourteen-year-olds, and their big stooge, Jasper, learner's-permit-packing mailman, who's sixteen. He's stayed back twice,
a clever educational strategy that's enhanced his career as tight end
for the Quagmire Quarrymen and somehow gotten him access to
the postal van keys. He and his Rocks are notorious at Quagmire
Regional for bad behavior. They terrorize Birnam, who's in class
with them, calling him 'Bird Brain' and 'Turd Man,' among other
niceties. They hang out behind the post office and smoke and pre-
read Nigel Brate's *Playboy* magazines (there's little reading involved).
They're in attendance tonight because they've been coerced by their

history teacher, my cousin, Miss DeBarros, to present an article, part of an extra credit project for her United States Government class at Quagmire Regional. Why Georgina trusts them to present Article Four is a mystery. She tells Arianna the object of this psychological experiment is to inspire them into good behavior by giving them a taste of civic responsibility (and maybe help Jasper graduate before he turns twenty), but this, Arianna and I agree afterward, is hopeless teacher naivete. Teachers can be so unrealistically idealistic. The Rocks are beyond salvation. There isn't a salt shaker's worth of civic responsibility between these thugs.

And tonight, we're fast approaching critical mass. With bodies piling in the walk-in refrigerator, an ambulance driver shackled to a chair for vehicular manslaughter, hippies tonguing blood and amphibians, and a temporary moderator unable to gavel anyone into order, all bets are off. The delinquents have seized the reins. Tourmaline and Krystal are bouncing up and down like the little plastic figures in Whac-A-Mole, and Tara Drummond is too far gone to apply the hammer. If not for a head jerk from Chief Crockett, leaning against the proscenium arch, that sends Officers Farrell and Willis trundling down the balcony steps, they could probably hijack the meeting. Nothing's unlikely anymore. Birnam scrambles away from the railing, where he's been shouting, "Save the newts!" and back to the safety of the control booth. He flings himself onto a stool and buries his head beneath pudgy arms, as if by hiding his eyes he might become invisible.

If you told me tonight that someday I would be married to this freak, I would have whacked you upside the head. Life is nothing, if not amazing.

A show of force from the cops, and The Rocks are cowed into a mutter of hostile subservience. Their arms cross tight in front, their eyes narrow. Their moment of fame is threatened. They get huffy and pretend they're being unfairly harassed. A few rows back the three boys from the military academy are looking plainly distressed. Their hands are inside their camo jackets. The oldest one is squirming. The littlest one has developed a tic. The nondescript one with the eyepatch crumples his snack bag and seems to be mumbling about canned beans and beef jerky. Any minute, I'm thinking, they're gonna come out shooting. The fuse is lit, the time bomb's ticking.

Meanwhile, onstage, their commander, Selectman General Tarry, has taken the microphone from Tara Drummond. He's speaking, but in a voice so low and ominous that for a minute it doesn't register. Arianna's turning up the volume. He becomes audible. Petrified looks apprehensive (I could say 'petrified' but that would be a cheap exaggeration), and soon enough, Birnam raises his head.

"Don't you prissy little butt wipes get it?" hisses the general.

Get what? we're wondering. Even the stenographer in the dict-amask has missed most of what he's said so far.

"They're coming." His hand is inside his camo jacket. I think it's on a gun. "Hundreds of them. Millions of them. From the cities, the slums, the mean streets. The millennium is upon us." He's heating up now. This is fun to watch. "They're gonna take our town, burn our homes, hijack our ladder truck. Eat the kids. Our children need to be armed and ready. I train my boys out there. We know how to survive, don't we, Forty-One?"

The tall boy, Number Forty-One, Tyler McVeigh, stands in the balcony. Slow motion. His hand is in his camo jacket. He appears to be nodding in a vague, hypnotic stupor.

"We have our secret shelters," the general announces. His eyes widen and his crewcut stands on end. "We have our battle plans."

The other two are standing now. Trauma Tommy is shaking. His mangled dog tags dance in sympathy across his narrow chest. The nondescript one with the eyepatch is mumbling something about devil dogs.

"Be prepared. Save the swamp. When they come to get us, it'll be our town's last refuge."

He's pulling out all the stops. I swear I hear bomber jets overhead. "We will fight them in the bogs. We will fight them on the landing strips. We will never surrender."

The tension in the hall has become palpable, as if a fuse has been lit and we await the explosion. Chief Crockett puts his hand on his gun. Officers Farrell and Willis are gripping their pistols. Tara Drummond begins to bang her head against the podium microphone in General Tarry's hand.

But before the place erupts in gunfire, before the bomber jets drop their payloads, Cher Wood takes the floor microphone in hand and, oblivious to the high anxiety around her, turns to the hippo onstage. She's got a hand on her floral hippy hip. Her face is pinched.

"Could she—our Town Treasurer—explain to us why shopping plazas are more important than black-bottomed newts?"

Cher Wood has marched in Washington, resisted arrest protesting the war in Vietnam. Petty civil servants are no threat to her righteous indignation. She's challenging Mrs. Épée, Town Treasurer, TouchDown Realty, to engage.

The hippo rises. Pushes back her chair in disgust. You can see the audience stiffen in its seats. She crosses to the podium. Everyone onstage backs away a few inches. With one big, fleshy arm, she shoves aside both Tara Drummond and General Tarry, seizes the mike from his surprised grasp, and engages.

"I don't think it possible to explain my position clearly enough to people—" she begins, and at the sound of her condescension, the hall relaxes. We're back in familiar territory, lambs before the wrath of our town's chief beast. There are certainties at Town Meeting. We'd feel deprived without them. Tubby Dobbs will storm out early. Tara Drummond has to sing the national anthem. At some point in the evening Edie Ottick will go off on a tangent about being born in town. Nigel Brate will have a meltdown over General Tarry's alleged illegal piggery. And, as sure as rising real estate assessments, Thomasine Épée will voice her disgust at a volume that shatters hearing aids before storming away to the bathroom. Thomasine Épée's epic scorn and weak bladder are as predictable as death and taxes.

General Tarry retreats to his seat at the selectmen's table. His arsenal is no match for her displeasure. Taking cue from their fearless leader, the three boys in the balcony slump into their folding chairs, guns clicked back to safety. Chief Crockett catches Tara Drummond just before she falls face first into the wings.

"—people only barely higher on the evolutionary ladder than this—this black-butted slime mold, but for the hundredth time, I will try to explain in terms that even the lowest primeval slug can grasp."

Thomasine Épée strangles the mike en route to center stage. We are enraptured by the sheer eloquence of her disgust.

"Little Quagmire is just that. A quagmire. A cesspit. A breeding ground for icky, slimy, revolting pests that lower our property values and, very possibly, our life expectancy. Sharks. Sharks!! TouchDown Realty is doing—I am doing—this town an enormous favor by proposing to turn this wasteland, this leaching field for leeches, into a viable commercial property—at some deserved financial gain, admittedly."

At the front of the stage three steps descend to the hall floor. She approaches them warily, her little feet in their ruby red shoes pawing the air for traction. Beneath her thunderous calves, the tiny ankles look like they might snap. She starts down. We hold our breaths, waiting for the fall which would surely make the evening's entertainment complete, but does not come.

"I assure you, citizens of South Quagmire, there is nothing in Little Quagmire Swamp worth saving. Nothing. Nothing! So—"

She's at Woodchuck Wood's side. He's a rat beside a boa constrictor. If she opens her mouth just a bit wider she can swallow the little man whole.

"So, let us take this revolting specimen from the primordial sludge..."

For a moment I think she's referring to Woodchuck Wood.

Gingerly, she plucks the salamander from him by the tail. Woodchuck Wood is powerless to resist. She raises it above her head, "—and kiss its little black ass good-bye—," opens thumb and forefinger. It drops to the floor, a sickening fall. Even the voters who despise Woodchuck Wood and his hippy-freaky ways gasp. It lands with a wet plop at her feet. Those of us not in position to see it strike the floor imagine the splat. She lifts one thunderous calf, one tiny ankle, one little ruby red shoe, and steps squarely on the creature. Then she grinds it into the floor with her heel.

There are shrieks. The whole front row pulls back in alarm. A guy vomits on his warrant.

Over them, she snarls, "—and get on with the vote!"

She turns on her ruby red heels and stomps back up the three steps and returns to her seat.

Woodchuck Wood is screaming in horror. "No! No! Ahhh! Monster!"

Arianna and I are aghast. Petrified Wood fairly tackles Birnam, who has lunged for the door with a roar that must be heard but for the pandemonium below. Above the shouts I can hear their mother calling, "Bambi! Bambi!" and Mrs. Saville hollering back, "I don't do amphibians! Nothing with gills!"

Uncle Anthony is on his feet, gold chain in flight around his corded neck. He's shouting something, maybe, "Murderer! Murderer!" I half expect him to rip the cuffs from the arm rest. Sparky Manx and the Reverend Jake have moved in and are on the floor beside Woodchuck Wood. Woodchuck Wood is sobbing. Sparky runs out and comes back with a dustpan and spatula. Reverend Jake is performing last rites, or whatever Baptists do when a victim, possibly soulless, has been squished. The school custodian is summoned to mop up blood and barf.

Eventually, the banging of the gavel breaks through the din. Sparky leaves with the corpse. I'm thinking, Please, not the walk-in refrigerator! Cher Wood and Reverend Jake lead an inconsolable Woodchuck out of the hall to find a brown paper bag. The Wood family seems to have this thing about breathing.

Tara Drummond says, "We will move to the vote."

She looks like she might throw up herself. Town Counsel, Edgar Vade, is at her side again, patting her forehead with a handkerchief, whispering.

"What? I'm sorry. Two-thirds?" She looks out at her audience, although one doubts she sees anything past the hankie. In a dull monotone, the Town Counsel's ventriloquist dummy, she parrots, "Article Two requires a two-thirds vote to pass. I will search the house for a unanimous vote." There's a momentary pause while she chokes back a dry heave. "All in favor, please say aye."

There are some ayes, most notably from General Tarry onstage, but they are unconvincing.

"Those opposed?"

The nays are stronger, but still unconvincing. Town Counsel whispers in her ear.

Tara Drummond sighs. "The tellers will take a hand count."

And they do. The two main proponents of the article, Woodchuck and Cher Wood, are not there to lead the resistance. Postmistress Carmen Selsby is tangled in her knitting. General Tarry looks stunned into submission by the hippo. Has the swamp been lost to her oratory? Hands are raised. The tellers count. They come to the front, to the microphone, and call out numbers. "Ayes, five. Sixteen. Thirty-seven."

"And those opposed."

The process is repeated.

"Twenty. Seventeen. Six." [12]

---

12 Thirty years later, and still Birnam remembers the numbers. They're burned into his psyche.

Tara Drummond is beyond calculating, but Edgar Vade tallies the numbers, and whispers in her ear. "The ayes fifty-eight, the nays forty-three. A two-thirds vote has not been reached. The article is defeated."

Afterward, there is some confusion as Carmen Selsby wrestles free of her Gordian skein and insists that the article does not, in fact, require a two-thirds vote. She reads a letter from the state division of conservation and recreation that says, "The autonomy of conservation commissions being maintained, a majority vote is necessary for any land purchased for conservation purposes," which leads Town Counsel to rebut with, "The autonomy of conservation commissions was revoked by passage of Massachusetts General Law c N-39 in 1960," which ends in shouting, and Theobald Doppelmeier bleating, "N-39! N-39! Got it!"

Carmen Selsby staggers out of the auditorium, hand on ribs, a long, Seussian tail of violet yarn trailing behind her.

At the last, Katherine Ottick and Nigel Brate convince Town Counsel to side with TouchDown Realty (money will pass hands), and, just when we think we're done, Woodchuck Wood staggers back into the room, paper bag over his head, on his wife's supportive arm and lifts the bag enough to holler, "I move to reconsider Article Three."

A cautionary wave from Chief Crockett's pistol, and Woodchuck Wood pulls the bag down over his face and collapses into a chair with a mumbled, "I withdraw the motion."

Birnam is actually crying.

We move on.

ARTICLE 4

———

"To see if the town will vote to transfer from Article 7, line B-5, Memorial Day Observances, 1974, the sum of $750 to purchase a plaque to dedicate the new municipal swimming pool to the memory of Albert Thomas DeBarros, or take any other action in relation thereto."

Georgina DeBarros got tenure the first day of classes in September. This is her fourth year teaching at the local high school. She's one of the more popular teachers at Quagmire Regional, and the fact that she's dating fellow faculty member, Mr. Corr (who is white), only makes her more attractive in the eyes of her students. Bill Corr is sitting beside her in the voters' section tonight. He is everyone's favorite biology teacher. His science labs are held almost entirely out-of-doors, and while few of us believe that his student, Rocky Mackiewicz, was actually bitten by a shark last year while testing salinity in Little Quagmire Swamp (Rocky's the kind of way-too-cool knucklehead who might have had a chunk taken out of his hip boot waders in any number of creative ways), we all wish that we could have Mr. Corr every year, every class. He's fun, funny, and even educational.

And he definitely has his sights on Miss DeBarros. Their secret romance is the talk of the student body. Since the student body is mostly white, few of the kids are in a position to know that she's also dating the black Wampanoag minister at the Baptist Church, Reverend Jake White (ironic), who delivered tonight's opening prayer and has spent the last hour ferrying bodies to the walk-in refrigerator. He may or may not know that Bill Corr is a contender. They've both spent a lot of the evening throwing glances Georgina's way.

Georgina is the youngest daughter of an attractive family. The DeBarroses are all good-looking. Her parents, Emmanuel Anthony DeBarros, and my Aunt Flora, are Cape Verdeans, born on the islands and brought here as children. There was no chance they wouldn't have attractive children. Aunt Flora passed away several years ago from congenital heart failure, but my Uncle Manny is still alive, a member of the school committee and handsome at fifty-five, graying at the temples and distinguished. I plan to join him on the board next year, my first run for elected office, although this, it turns out, will not happen until after college. [13]

If the old photographs are any proof, their oldest son, Albert Thomas, was handsome like his dad. He died before I was born, quarry diving, age sixteen. He shouldn't have been anywhere near the quarry. None of us should. Tonight's Article Four is about him, a reminder that water can be hazardous, whether you're an epileptic non-swimmer like Albert, or just a way-too-cool knucklehead like Rocky Mackiewicz, who met a similar end in August. Rocky's body was recovered, alleged shark bite and all. Albert's has never been found.

Then there's my Uncle Anthony, still handcuffed to the chair. He's got himself back under control after the outburst with the

---

13   Emmanuel DeBarros is the only person of color serving in an elected town position in South
     Quagmire in 1976, which probably means the Cape Verdean population bullet voted.

newt. Even at thirty-two, Uncle Anthony (cousin, really, but due to the difference in our ages I think of him as Uncle) is still movie star gorgeous. High cheekbones, strong chin, the beautiful black eyes, and a full head of hair that glistens without the aid of tonics or fluorocarbons. Right now it's under a Red Sox cap, tilted sideways, the height of bro cool. Normally he'd never wear a hat indoors (Aunt Flora would have killed him!), but in all the excitement of Chief Dobbs's untimely end beneath the tires of the town ambulance, the hat's been overlooked. His unshackled hand hasn't gotten around to observing the niceties. He's been crying. I don't ever recall seeing Uncle Anthony cry. He's too macho to cry, too jacked. His skin-tight uniform shirt showcases everything. He's a member at the racquetball club (which, unlike the Athletic Association, lets anyone in) where he lifts weights to the edge of obsession, and he spends the warm months shirtless so we can ogle his physique. He wants the world to know he can take care of himself. He's the Master of His Universe. Nothing can touch him. No one can hurt him.

Even red-eyed and under restraint, he looks good. If he wasn't such a law-abiding citizen, he would rip the handcuffs from the chair right now with a mere flex of his wrist.

And his daughter, Arianna, my best friend, takes after him. She's the prettiest girl in the high school, also the nicest. If not for skin color, she'd be the most popular kid at Quagmire Regional. She's a beautiful person inside and out. The few people who remember her mother say she looks just like her. I don't remember her mother, and no pictures remain. She left when Arianna was less than a year old. The family doesn't talk about her.

Personally, I think Arianna looks like her father, the same cheekbones, the same deep, dark eyes. They are beautiful people.

And Georgina, Uncle Anthony's baby sister, shares their DNA. She's six years younger than her brother. There's a lot of good genes running through the DeBarros clan.

Georgina and Bill Corr are seated in the second row. I can only see the backs of their heads, so I can't tell if they are anxious or excited, apprehensive or proud, as their problem children preen their way from the balcony to the floor. The Rocks jostle and elbow and giggle their way to the front of the hall, to the microphone at the foot of the stage. They toss Officers Farrell and Willis looks that dare them to disapprove.

"Time to rock and roll," squeals Krystal Tull, petite, blonde, snidely adorable. She's only a sophomore, and already making my skin crawl. She wears a mini-mini skirt over purple leggings and way too much eye shadow. A pink-and-white purse with kitty ears hangs from one bare shoulder. Naturally, she's a cheerleader, status she wields as a weapon. No one breaks into the clique without her say-so. Tourmaline Selsby and Ruby Jones-Smith sashay behind her, equally under-dressed, over-kohled, and kitty-purse accessorized. These are three girls who deserve each other and the mindless boys who worship them (including the late Rocky Mackiewicz). Sixteen-year-old lump Jasper Lovell drools at their rear, big, broad, a wide, dim smile that looks more like a leer. His little brother Jet makes a stealth entrance from the locker rooms where he's been smoking. Jasper gives him a punch, then produces a belch. People on the aisle pull in and away as their learner's permit-packing substitute mail-man passes. Jasper has a reputation for knocking down mailboxes with the postal van and they are taking no chances. It goes without saying that all five Rocks are white.

The clock by the flag reads 9:15 PM. Petrified Wood is cradling his brother and mumbling about an English paper he has yet to write. I must say, this meeting is way more interesting than March Annual Town Meeting, which went on for three nights and was boring beyond belief. Public executions are entertaining. And now, if we're lucky, I'll get to see The Rocks crash and burn. At least, that's my hope. I hold these low-lifes in the same contempt our Town Treasurer holds the rest of us. Sorry, Georgina, I should be rooting for your derelicts, but I'm not.

Georgina (Miss DeBarros) teaches five classes: two U.S. History classes for juniors, two freshman Western Civilizations, and a seminar in United States Government which is required for underclassmen. The Rocks are underclassmen, or rather, beneath class. They're mean-spirited, self-absorbed, and insular. They'd as soon step on you as recognize your humanity. So it's a testament to Miss DeBarros's popularity that these thugs have agreed to present an article honoring her late brother Albert. Even before they start to speak, I'm thinking this whole experiment is doomed. No sane adult, even doddering old white men with one foot in the grave (or in tonight's case, the walk-in refrigerator), is going to take these delinquents seriously. But The Rocks do seem to hold Georgina in some esteem (She doesn't assign too much homework. I remember I appreciated that about her), and she's hopeful they will rise to the occasion. We can only admire her misplaced optimism. The future of her brother's memorial plaque rests in the hands of five swaggering morons and a misplaced intention of raising grades through coercion.

While they careen toward the microphone, Tara Drummond, temporary moderator, mumbles, "We will move to Article Four. This is a special article prepared by the United States Government class at the high school with the help of their teacher, Miss Georgina DeBarros, and we ask the Town Meeting if they will allow her students, all non-registered voters, to speak before this meeting. Is there any objection?"

The hall is silent but for the grating giggles of The Rocks, another burp from Jasper.

"Hearing none, all those in favor of letting these future voters of South Quagmire speak to this assembly, please signify by saying, Aye. Those opposed? The floor is yours."

The microphone is Krystal Tull's and she starts:

"I move that the town vote to transfer from Article 7—"

But before she can finish, Tourmaline Selsby has pulled the mike from her hands and begun again.

"I move that the town vote to transfer from Article 7, Line B-5, Memorial Day Observances, 1974, the sum of seven-hundred-and-fifty dollars to purchase a plaque to dedicate the new municipal swimming pool to the memory of Rocky Mackiewicz."

Tourmaline sighs through a vacant smile. The name, Rocky Mackiewicz, seems to have triggered some erotic memory. Not to be outdone, Krystal (offended) and Ruby (half-a-mind elsewhere) sigh in unison. Theobald Doppelmeier is busily searching his BINGO cards, imaginary or otherwise, for a B-5.

Maybe Tara Drummond is coming out of her stupor at last, because she says, "I'm...uh... sorry, but the motion, as I read it, is "to the memory of Albert Thomas DeBarros."

Her eyes are on the podium. She doesn't look at the girls.

Krystal grabs the mike. She flips back her bobbed blonde hair as a political statement.

"Well, we just decided—"

But Tourmaline snatches it back. Then she flips her shoulder-length brown hair to greater effect and gets Krystal in the face.

"We just decided—unanimously—to change the name to Rocky Mackiewicz."

A muffled shout is heard from the sound booth:

"I didn't decide that! It wasn't unanimous! I didn't vote for Rocky—!"

And a confused mutter works its way across the hall. Who? What?

Georgina stands. Bill Corr touches her hand as she does.

"Miz Moderator," she says. "Tourmaline, this is not what we—"

But Edgar Vade, Town Counsel, has sidled in beside Tara Drummond again and taken the microphone from the podium.

"There can be no discussion of this motion as presented until the motion is seconded."

Jasper Lovell responds in a belch, "I second!"

"Please state your name and address."

"Jasper David Lovell, 146 Congress Street." He turns around and beams at his audience. He's big enough that no one questions his age. He has beautiful teeth. Damn!

Georgina starts from her seat, edging past the person next to her. Bill Corr takes her hand and physically holds her back, as Town Counsel says, "Now someone has to amend the article."

"Tourmaline Selsby, 1492 Main Street. So how do we do that?"

TOWN COUNSEL: You write your amendment on a piece of
    paper and hand it to the moderator.
Ms. SELSBY: I can do that. I need paper.

She bats her eyelids. In the balcony survivalist Number Forty-One, Tyler McVeigh, rummages through his camo pockets, but he's too far away to be helpful. Young Jet Lovell, thug Rock, pulls paper from his jeans' pocket. Rolling paper for tobacco, I'm guessing. He hands it to her with coy adoration.

Ms. SELSBY: I need a pen.

FROM THE FLOOR: Don't give it to her! This is demagoguery! No taxation without representation!

Ms. SELSBY: Miss DeBarros, can I borrow a pen?

Ms. DEBARROS: Georgina DeBarros, 44 Hancock Street. Ms. Moderator, please, may I speak to this amendment?

Mr. LOVELL: Like, Ms. DeBarros, we all—all of us—we talked about it—you know— and like it was you said Town Meeting is anarchy in its purest form—

Ms. DEBARROS: Democracy.

Mr. LOVELL: Democracy, right. So, we took a vote. Don't get mad. This Albert DeBarros, your brother, I mean, he died like, yikes, twenty years ago. No one even knows who he is now. That was, like, before Pink Floyd, man. Before *Dark Side of the Moon*.

Mr. DOPPELMEIER: I-20. I-20.

Ms. SELSBY: Before *Stairway to Heaven*.

Mr. DOPPELMEIER: I-20. Got it!

Ms. SELSBY: Interrupt me again, you old fart, I will take your squirrel and break his nuts!

Mr. DOPPELMEIER: Not the nuts, not the nuts!

Ms. SELSBY: He was an awesome swimmer.

Ms. TULL: Rocky. Rocky was.

Ms. SELSBY: Rocky. He was an awesome swimmer.

Ms. TULL: Who drowned.

Ms. SELSBY: Who drowned.

Ms. TULL: He made all-state with his breaststroke.

Ms. SELSBY: Breaststroke.

Ms. TULL: He was my boyfriend before he was yours.

Mr. LOVELL: And then he drowned in the quarry. Driving drunk.

Ms. TULL: Diving.

Mr. LOVELL: Diving.

Ms. TULL: Dunk.

Mr. LOVELL: Dunk.

Ms. SELSBY: He got dunked and he drowned.

Ms. TULL: He had an awesome breaststroke.

Mr. LOVELL: Now they electrified the fence, none of us can dive there anymore without you get neutered. (Expletive.) Your nuts roasting on an open fire.

Mrs. EPEE: Madam Moderator, these painful prepubescent reminiscences cannot alter the fact that there is no money for a memorial to Albert DeBarros, or anyone else.

Ms. DEBARROS: But the Memorial Day Observance line—

Mrs. EPEE: Has a balance of twelve dollars and thirty-five cents.

Ms. DEBARROS: I was told—

Mrs. EPEE: You were misinformed.

Ms. DEBARROS: Free Cash then.

Mrs. EPEE: Not a penny.

Ms. DEBARROS: The Reserve Fund.

Mrs. EPEE: Allocated.

Ms. DEBARROS: Allocated?

Mrs. EPEE: Allocated.

Ms. DEBARROS: What about the back taxes the town just got from the Fortin property?

Mrs. EPEE: Uncertified. Unavailable.

Ms. DEBARROS: Could we raise and appropriate? It would cost so little, and mean so much—

Mrs. EPEE: This is not an annual Town Meeting. One cannot raise and appropriate at a special. Any ignoramus knows that.

Ms. DEBARROS: What about the Albert Thomas DeBarros Burial Account?

There's a moment, just before she mentions the burial account, when Georgina pulls herself up straight and you get the feeling she's about to spring a trap. Although not indicated in the transcript, I seem to remember a dramatic pause, followed by:

Ms. RUPPED: What in Heaven's name is the Albert Thomas—?

Mrs. EPEE: I know nothing about any Albert Thomas DeBarros—

By now, Georgina has pulled free of Bill Corr, excused her way past the other people in the row, and gained the microphone. You can see she's upset, but The Rocks are too excited by their new-found celebrity to feel chagrinned. Tourmaline Selsby even readjusts the mike stand to accommodate her teacher. Georgina has to steel herself. She didn't expect to be standing in front of the voters herself. Arianna and I knew this was going to end badly.

"The Albert Thomas DeBarros Burial Account." She looks toward Uncle Anthony, but his back is to us and if he's showing any expression, we can't see it. She speaks directly to the voters in a voice just this side of audible. "My grandfather, Christian DeBarros—when they couldn't find Albert's body—he put five hundred dollars in a special town account for the eventuality that it might someday be recovered. That was almost twenty years ago. After all this time and interest, it must have accumulated at least enough—"

Behind, the hippo is so angry her wattles are shaking. She pushes back her chair and rises yet again, making a big show of her vexation.

"I know nothing of such an account," she hisses. "It was certainly before my time." She swells like a balloon. Everyone on stage deflates in self-protection. "Madam Moderator—" Tara Drummond cowers behind the podium. "I am deeply, deeply offended by these machinations on Town Meeting floor. Miss DeBarros has obviously abused her position as an educator to hoodwink these—these lemmings—into rushing headlong in here with an article whose sole intent—sole intent, citizens of South Quagmire (just north of East Quagmire)—is to coerce us into using the Town's already strained resources to finance her nostalgia trip—yes, nostalgia trip! Albert DeBarros! Rocky Half-a-Wit! There's a quarry full of these lemmings who took the plunge. How many other plaques—to what end? This is not democracy in action. It's a ticket down Memory Lane at the taxpayers' expense—a flagrant abuse of common sense by a teacher with too much time on her hands. Maybe if she corrected more homework, she could realign her priorities, instead of imposing her stale family genealogy on our pockets, our purses—!"

Georgina stands speechless before this assault on our senses. Magnificent in its fury, almost Shakespearean, no speech at Town Meeting has since reached these heights of vituperation. Thomasine Épée's massive bosom heaves. She has to catch her breath. She's made protest futile. This is our Town Treasurer's greatest performance (or so it will be remembered in years to come, accompanied by the shaking of heads). Her audience anticipates the finale, spellbound.

And it comes, exactly as we've anticipated. She spins on Tara Drummond, invisible behind the podium, and snorts, "Tara, I am going to the bathroom, and don't try to follow me."

She exits stage right, practically foaming at the mouth.

There should be thunderous applause, or maybe we're waiting for an encore. The Rocks are wondering what on Earth's a lemming. Georgina has to make a decision and make it fast. It will be impossible to top the Town Treasurer's showpiece. Should our civics teacher surrender to the inevitable or play for sympathy? She turns to Tourmaline, accusatory, gets no response. She looks out over the hall. She decides to go for it.

"Our brother, Albert Thomas DeBarros, died in a quarry accident twenty years ago," she begins, but she can't get any farther before Krystal Tull pipes up, "Rocky Mackiewicz drowned in August."

"Not even a month ago," adds Tourmaline.

"Two months ago, and two days!" comes a shout from the altitude.

"But Albert—"

"Rocky Mackiewicz was a god!" cries Krystal Tull. She pulls a Bic lighter from her kitty purse and holds it, lit, aloft. Immediately, Tourmaline and Ruby are scrambling for theirs, and Jasper and Jet produce two more from hip pockets. All are lit and thrust high in honor of the Half-a-Wit with the awesome breast stroke. There are muffled screams from the balcony, the words "flaming, flying dead thing" stifled, and then a respectful pause as the voters of South Quagmire question their sanity.

Why are they still here?

Has the world gone mad?

Who in his/her right mind will ever attend Town Meeting in South Quagmire (just north of East Quagmire) again?

Georgina can't go on. I can see tears all the way back here. If she was in fact setting a trap, the trap has failed to grab. Chief Crockett shouts, "Put those things away!" and The Rocks, with little snorts of indignation, extinguish their skimpy funeral pyres. Uncle Anthony stands. He's calm, perfectly, alarmingly controlled. The single gold chain with winged figure has settled back into the deep cleft between his chest muscles. He takes a step toward his sister and the chair follows. He stops.

"Let it go," he says. "It was a nice thought. Albert doesn't need a plaque."

"He was your brother too."

"Let him rest in peace. In the quarry. He doesn't care. No one does."

"But there might be money in his burial account."

"Maybe—and remember, sis, that's all it was for. Burial."

"Rocky was cremated," says Tourmaline. "It was so sad."

Whether she refers to fire or water is impossible to tell.

Jasper Lovell moves close to his teacher, offering moral support by way of an awkward arm around her shoulder, which she shrugs off indignantly.

"Now they've chain-linked the quarry and got us a new pool," he says, unsure what to do with the arm, "no more drownings,"

Georgina wipes at her eyes. "No, no one will drown in the quarry anymore." She looks at her brother. He whispers to her. I'm missing something but I've no idea what.

Edgar Vade, Town Counsel, leans in to the podium.

"Is there any further discussion on Article Four?"

No one says anything. No one but Georgina seems invested in this article. I for one never gave it the slightest chance of success, and I'm not even sure of her motivation.

But then, surprisingly, Tara Drummond, temporary moderator, leans in and nudges Town Counsel aside. She takes the microphone in both hands. They're shaking.

"I'm... I..." she begins, a stammer, "it's highly commend... commendable that Miss DeBarros has given her — gone this extra mile to give her pupils — her students — a very educational and worthwhile experience with — democracy in action, and I just — I applaud her efforts — I know we all do — and I do remember Albert DeBarros, and I do think he deserves to be remembered in this way." She looks like she might be crying too. Her gray cheeks are damp. "That's all I wanted to say."

The explosion announces itself via our feet and our butts, a vibration transmitted through floor and chairs, except that none of us know it's an explosion, not yet. There's a muffled bang from somewhere outside the hall, a boom, really. I can feel the floor shake through the soles of my sneakers. Heads snap in the apparent direction of the noise. Birnam squeaks in alarm. Several people stand. A moment of silence shorter than that observed for either of our recently departed follows, then confused chatter. "Did you feel what I felt?" General Tarry ejects from his seat onstage and, in unison, the three boys in the balcony leap to their feet and are scrambling for the stairs. The cops at the exits shift nervously in their boots.

Someone gasps, "Earthquake," loud enough to make it into the official transcript. This is a world before terrorists. We had an earthquake in May, a small one, around nine at night. It felt a little like this, a sudden thump, as if a big truck passing by had dropped its tailgate.

"Stop!" booms a voice through the sound system, and Chief Crockett has the mike. "Don't anybody move!"

The cops stiffen. Even the three boys freeze where they've collided in the doorway.

Chief Crockett glances up at the acoustic tiles on the ceiling. Maybe he's expecting a shower of dust or something, but, no, nothing. The shimmy has stopped almost as soon as it began, and there's no sound beyond the murmur of protest.

"Farrell, Willis," he says, and two officers run off to a jerk of his head. Sparky Manx says something, and he nods. She and Reverend Jake go out another door. "Until we know, don't anybody move."

People respond quickly to a show of authority in crisis, although none of us are clear yet we've achieved crisis. We're intrigued and confused, but the protests end almost as quickly as they begin. Several people crowd the stage. Miss Ottick gives the police chief her thoughts through a pointed finger, but the microphone doesn't pick up those thoughts. It seems he's turned it off. Uncle Anthony is looking around for Arianna. He doesn't know she's in the sound booth. The chair executes a few dance moves as he scours the hall. Then Arianna's out to the balcony railing, waving. He sees her. He looks relieved, maybe questioning. Petrified Wood's beside her. He's waving too. Uncle Anthony sees them together and nods behind thick, dark eyebrows. An expression passes between them, but I'm at a loss to guess what it means. He's OK. She's OK. We're all OK.

Safe.

We wait in modest suspense for the meaning of the boom to be revealed. Two of the exits are now unmanned, but the intimidation factor lingers. No one is leaving until the replacement police cruiser is a done deal, and the cruiser is not a done deal until the meeting is dissolved.

Officer Farrell comes in through the back of the stage. He's a big man, middle-aged, balding, snug-bellied into his uniform. He's been a cop for thirty years, a known commodity, comfortable in his authority, and everybody's comfortable with him. But he looks uncomfortable now. He motions Chief Crockett aside and they confer. Chief Crockett remains expressionless throughout the conversation which lasts less than a minute. Then Officer Farrell goes out and Chief Crockett takes center stage and turns the microphone on.

"It's a plumbing problem," he says. "For the time being the ladies' room is out of commission. So let's see if we can finish business and adjourn the meeting before anyone has to use the facilities. There's water everywhere. Mrs. Drummond?"

I suddenly have an irrational urge to pee. I doubt I'm alone.

General Tarry stands, all big bull neck and camouflage.

"I move to adjourn the meeting."

Maybe he's desperate to get out of here alive, maybe he's shaken by the shake. Maybe he's being political. If the meeting is adjourned without finishing its business (never mind Tara Drummond singing '*The Star-Spangled Banner*'), nothing voted on thus far can take effect. That includes the town's failure to buy the swamp, a swamp that General Tarry takes a proprietary interest in thanks to his military school. New home construction will have a deleterious effect on target practice.

Chief Crockett reminds him, "There's a motion on the floor."

Town Counsel pipes, "A motion to adjourn takes precedence over a motion on the floor."

Chief Crockett pulls out his gun and points it at Town Counsel. Edgar Vade stares down the barrel of the pistol and rules, "A man with a gun takes precedence over a motion to adjourn."

General Tarry pulls an assault rifle from behind his back and points it at Chief Crockett. People sink into their seats. In the balcony doorway, Numbers Forty-One, Forty-Three, and One-Sixty-Nine pull out guns in solidarity. We knew they were packing heat, and now no cops man the balcony to inspire concealment.

Three selectmen (persons) make up a trio behind the table onstage. General Tarry is standing, armed and blustery. Katherine Ottick is seated next to him. Nigel Brate is at the end. Nigel Brate jumps up. He's incensed. Maybe he sees that, unless the meeting reaches a satisfactory conclusion, it will have to be reconvened another night, and there's always the possibility that the conservationists will stack the meeting and demand reconsideration of Article Three, and there goes his expanded parking lot. Whatever his motivation, he decides to take on General Tarry, a match stick going up against a Lincoln log. They may be close to the same height, but the general makes five of the package store bookie. The bookie is not intimidated, however. A match stick has one thing going for it the Lincoln log does not. A match stick is incendiary.

"Put that gun away, you asshole," growls the match stick, "or I'll see your whole operation's taken down along with that illegal piggery!"

General Tarry goes wide-eyed, takes a step backward. "What illegal piggery?" The assault rifle pivots to Brate.

Brate is lit. He could lose his expanded parking lot to these machinations. "The illegal piggery you and your juvenile delinquents are using to stuff yourself with pork chops out there!" he flames.

In the balcony Nondescript Someone Number Forty-Three practically hurls himself at the railing, screaming, "Pork chops? Who's got pork chops? Where's the pork chops?" He lifts his eye-patch to see who's holding out on him. Someone needs to feed this kid a sandwich.

"Shut it, Forty-Three!" snarls General Tarry from the stage.

Brate advances. The general takes another step back. He's dumb-founded. He's used to boys dropping into submissive pose before his bulk, to townies giving him a wide, respectful berth. Nigel Brate, fellow selectman, is threatening to ignite, and without the use of paramilitary devices. Now the general recalls himself, ultimate warrior. He has the gun. The package store bookie will burn himself out. To Brate he retorts, "There's no piggery. No code violations. We got no pigs out there!"

Brate doesn't back down. He shouts, "Running from restaurant to restaurant every night, hauling garbage and slops outa the dumpsters?"

"Raccoons! Wild dogs!"

"Your boys are chowin' down on bacon and pulled pork sandwiches!" Spittle sprays from Brate's lips on the 'pulled pork sandwiches.'

From the balcony, we hear, "Pulled pork sandwiches? Where? Where?"

"You don't talk about my boys! You leave my boys outa this! Don't you mess with my boys!"

"Swine flu! Swine flu!" Brate accuses. "You're settin' us up! We know where that pig came from! You stole my woman with that pig! You're tryin' to kill us all!"

'Swine flu?'

'My woman?'

Them's fighting words. General Tarry doesn't take aim and fire. He's nuts but he's not crazy. Instead, one-handed, he flips the table on Nigel Brate and Kay Ottick. There's a crash. Brate squeals and goes down. Ottick yelps. The audience watches, spellbound, drop-jawed. This is better than any action movie. Brate's under the table, Ottick has been knocked onto her boney butt. The table relishes its moment in the limelight and thrashes around like a live thing. It releases Ottick, buries Brate. Ottick comes up, all sparks and steam. Her wrinkles wrinkle, her creases crease. She's going to blow. Men! She despises them all, their little boy tempers, their baby-brat tantrums! They're not of the slightest use to anyone. Let them blast each other into oblivion. Better yet, let her have the honors. Too angry for discretion, she goes for the gun. The general flinches, retreats behind the Finance Committee. The Finance Committee, all five of them, duck their heads under the table. Then all other eyes are on Sparky Manx, who's run in from behind stage, oblivious to the OK Corral re-enactment. She skids between Chief Crockett and General Tarry, doesn't see the guns, doesn't see Ottick pawing at the Lincoln log for his assault rifle, doesn't see the FinCom members burrowing their way to safety. Or, being Sparky Manx, she sees it all, but has more important business at hand. Sparky is urgently speaking at the chief. Everything stops. The guns do not go off. Bullets do not fly.

Brate struggles to extricate himself from under the table.

Now Chief Crockett is looking toward Uncle Anthony in the front row while Sparky makes inaudible demands. The chief is shaking his head. Sparky persists. We can't hear a thing, but she's using her hands as exclamation points. Chief Crockett squirms to deflect punctuation marks and dodge incoming periods. Sparky persists. The chief shakes his head. He holsters his gun and comes down the three steps, rummaging in his pockets. By the time he's reached Uncle Anthony, it's clear he's lost something. Clear also to Wilhelmina Makepeace, who stands, smooths the front of her black leather skirt. She crosses the stage with the air of a runway model and comes down the steps to him. She hands him the key. Chief Crockett thanks her and unlocks the handcuffs. He hands her back the key and sticks his face into Uncle Anthony's ear and gives him instructions. Uncle Anthony shakes out his wrist and rubs it as he listens. Then he nods and thrusts hands into pockets.

He glances up to the balcony, to us. We've retreated into the sound booth. Whether he can see us behind the glass I don't know. He gives an odd little tilt of the head, squints, then turns away and bounds up the steps and exits backstage with Sparky Manx. All eyes in the hall watch the second skin of his blue uniform shirt, the tight jeans, and raked baseball cap disappear through the curtains.

Most of them will never see Little Tony D alive again.

Chief Crockett motions Miss Makepeace to precede him back onto the stage. She awards him a glorious smile that says to everyone, "In Crockett we trust," and goes up the three steps. He follows, not at the bound, but a study in calm. Her black leather bottom sways before him as they ascend. Then, ever the gentleman, he waits until she's smoothed the back of her skirt and resumed her place, before taking the microphone again, and, as if nothing untoward has happened, he says ever-so-calmly, "Let's move to the vote. Mrs. Drummond?"

But Tara Drummond, although physically present, is far, far away. She's lost in space, or maybe the walk-in refrigerator. She does not respond. Selectwoman Miss Ottick, meanwhile, having regained her spindly legs, glares at General Tarry, who hides his rifle behind his back. She decides that oblivion must wait, gives a big, theatrical sniff of displeasure, leaves her colleague Brate fighting his way from under the table, and marches to center stage. "Give me that," she snaps at Chief Crockett, and he surrenders his gun to her.

"Not that, you nincompoop!" she growls. She practically flings the gun back in his face and grabs the mike. She carries it to the podium and elbows our temporary moderator back to consciousness.

"Tara," she snaps. "Tara!"

"Huh? Oh, oh... I'm... sorry. What?"

"We will move to the vote. Say it."

"Oh. We will move to the vote." To Selectwoman Ottick she mumbles, "What vote?"

Georgina starts to protest, then stops. She looks after Uncle Anthony, gone, and gives up.

"On the amendment. All those in favor—"

"Say aye."

The transcript records no ayes. The Rocks don't realize they're in favor of the amendment.

"Those opposed?"

Georgina says nay. A few others, Bill Corr, maybe one or two more, voice their objection. That's it. The Rocks are milling around her, confused, as Miss Ottick announces, "On the motion as printed in the warrant, those in favor?"

No funding mechanism has been determined, but nobody notices or cares. Georgina says aye. Bill Corr too. Maybe one or two more.

"Those opposed?"

A general, unconvincing nay from the crowd.

"The nays have it. It is a vote. Article Five."

Bill Corr has Georgina by the arm and is leading her out of the auditorium. She's holding back the tears. She doesn't want to go, but he's insisting. Quietly. He's feeling protective of her. If Reverend Jake were in the room right now, there might be a scene. Sadly, he isn't, but then, how much more excitement can one ask of a Special Town Meeting? Everyone watches them go, the white guy shepherding the black girl away. Tara Drummond watches them go. When Tara doesn't return to this world, Miss Ottick snatches the warrant from her and reads:

"Article Five: I move that the Town vote to amend Article 1, Section 6 of the Town By-Laws to read as follows: "Section 6: No article involving sums of monies shall be acted upon at any Town Meeting unless there are present at least seventy-five registered voters of the Town."

Nigel Brate hollers, "That article was proposed by the moderator. He's dead."

General Tarry, guns and politics abandoned, shouts, "Move to pass over Article Five!"

Nigel Brate: "I second."

Miss Ottick: "Is there any discussion?" She doesn't give the room a chance to open its mouth before she continues, "Hearing none, we will move to the vote. All those in favor—" and she gives Tara Drummond a serious poke in the ribs.

Tara squeaks, "Say aye."

An unenthusiastic aye resonates, and before we know what's happening, Petrified Wood whispers, "Come on," and is out the door of the booth. At the rear of the balcony stairs lead to an exterior fire escape and, while the three survivalists glower at the balcony railing, waiting for any kind of sign from their general (or for pulled pork sandwiches), and The Rocks are wondering if they should scamper back to their seats or ditch this scene for a cigarette, Petrified starts down the stairs. Arianna and I are nonplussed, but we follow him, and Birnam is so close on my heels he gives me a flat tire. The tape recorder is left behind for posterity.

After this, we are too preoccupied to care how the meeting ends, but here, according to the official transcript, are the final moments of the October 4, 1976, Special Town Meeting:

Ms. K. OTTICK: Article Six: I move that the Town vote to accept the recommendation of the Fire Chief—that the Town assume the financial responsibility for the ambulance service.

Mr. BRATE: That article was proposed by the fire chief. He's dead.

General TARRY: Move to pass over Article Six.

Mr. BRATE: Second.

Ms. K. OTTICK: All those in favor?

FROM THE FLOOR: Aye.

Ms. K. OTTICK: The ayes have it unanimously. Article Seven. I move that the Town vote to transfer from available funds in the treasury a sum of money to cover the increase in cost of Group Insurance for the premium for the months of May and June 1976.

Mr. BRATE: That article was proposed by the Town Treasurer. She's in the bathroom.

General TARRY: Move to pass over.

Mr. BRATE: Second.

Ms. K. OTTICK: Any discussion? Hearing none, all those in favor.

FROM THE FLOOR: Aye.

FROM THE FLOOR: Wait, wait!

Ms. K. OTTICK: Unanimous.

Article Eight. I move that the Town vote to transfer from available funds the sum of $55,000.00 to revalue all property in the Town of South Quagmire (just north of East Quagmire) under the decision handed down by the Supreme Judicial Court in its Sudbury case for equalization of value at a full and fair market—

General TARRY: Move to pass over.

Mr. BRATE: Second.

Ms. K. OTTICK: All those in favor? It is unanimous.

Article Nine. I move that the Town vote to transfer funds from Capital Improvement, line O-71, for the purchase of a BINGO console and board to facilitate local revenue... enhancement. Oh, I'm sorry. Mr. Doppelmeier. That's you. Mr. Doppelmeier? Teddy?

Chief CROCKETT: Mr. Doppelmeier?

Ms. E. OTTICK: He's not breathing.

Chief CROCKETT: Mr. Doppelmeier?

Ms. K. OTTICK: Theobald? Teddy?

Mr. BRATE: Mrs. Doppelmeier's wheelchair's on top of his oxygen tube.

Chief CROCKETT: The wheelchair. It's cut off his oxygen supply.

Mr. BRATE: I think he's dead.

FROM THE FLOOR: I challenge the quorum.

Chief CROCKETT: I can feel a pulse.

General TARRY: Move to pass over.

Mr. BRATE: Second.

Ms. K. OTTICK: Those in favor? It is a vote.

FROM THE FLOOR: I challenge the quorum.

Ms. K. OTTICK: Move to dissolve.

Mr. BRATE: Second.

FROM THE FLOOR: Wait, wait!

MS K. OTTICK: Those in favor?

FROM THE FLOOR: Aye.

Ms. K. OTTICK: It is a vote. Meeting dissolved.

The meeting dissolves at 9:37 PM. It ends, having fulfilled every-one's expectations and so much more. Tubby Dobbs has stormed out early. Edie Ottick has announced she was born in town. Thomasine Épée's vented spleen and bladder, and Nigel Brate's had a meltdown over General Tarry's illegal piggery. Only one requisite has been overlooked in our haste to depart. Tara Drummond has not sung the national anthem. We don't know it then, but Tara Drummond will never again sing the national anthem at Town Meeting. The good citizens of South Quagmire (just north of East Quagmire) have heard the last of Tara Drummond.

As for the actual business of Town Meeting, it might be argued that the good citizens of South Quagmire (just north of East Quagmire) have been less-than-conscientious about fulfilling their civic responsibilities. How will the increase in the cost of Group Insurance for the premium for the months of May and June, 1976, be covered? No one cares. Should the Town assume financial responsi-bility for the ambulance service? That's been kicked down the road. And what of the decision handed down by the Supreme Judicial Court in its Sudbury case for equalization of value at a full and fair market value? A lone voice shouts, "Wait, wait!" and is ignored by our Board of Selectman, three selfless individuals elected to office when no one else bothers to contest the seats. Are two deaths (not counting the newt) and a plumbing crisis reason enough to cut the good citizens of South Quagmire slack? Or did we just want to get home for *Monday Night Football*? So ends Town Meeting, the purest form of anarchy.

Er, democracy.

But now, the unexpected. There is one last entry in the official meeting transcript. Police Lieutenant Brian Watson, a big, gruff, friendly officer who's been blocking one of the exits all evening, is suddenly standing center stage. He has a big roll of yellow 'POLICE CAUTION' tape in one hand. He takes the microphone from Miss K. Ottick.

Police Lt. WATSON: Ladies and gentlemen, I need you to clear the hall immediately. Do not touch anything. Do not take anything you did not bring in with you. Please go quickly and quietly. Thank you.

The silence is deafening. Purses are clutched. Warrants are dropped. Eyes go wide as Lieutenant Watson begins cordoning off the stage. All at once, people who moments before were desperate to leave are now desperate to stay and see what's happening. A crime scene???!!! He repeats his instructions and, reluctantly, they go, but they aren't happy about it. By that time we've made it down the fire escape, run around the building, and snuck in through the rear boys' locker room door. We are unprepared for what awaits us.

ARTICLE 5

OUTSIDE THE FEMALE FACULTY'S BATHROOM,
and any other action in relation thereto.

The locker room is dark and smells of disinfectant and cigarette smoke, and I bang my shin on a bench, but the first thing that
hits our senses when we come out into the brightly lit corridor is
the overwhelming smell of bleach. Serious bleach. Or is it? The odor
stings my nose. There's also noise, voices loud and incoherent at first,
but I can make out Sparky Manx shouting orders down the hallway
to our left, which is, as I recall, the direction of the female faculty's
bathroom. Petrified Wood leads. We follow him, uncertain, but any
hesitation has been overcome by curiosity. We have to know what's
happened. Whatever it was, it was no earthquake. Earthquakes
don't smell like bleach and, what, ammonia(?), and I've had enough
high school chemistry to know those two chemicals don't mix. The
auditorium is behind us. No one's coming out the doors yet. So we
continue on, come to the corner near the school cafeteria (where I
am thinking about two bodies and tomorrow's lunch), and take the
turn. Petrified Wood slams on his brakes and we execute a series of
rear-end collisions. Birnam flat tires me again.

"Would you stop that?" I snarl, but then I am silenced. The door
to the women's bathroom is lying on the opposite side of the corridor

against a bank of lockers. There's water everywhere. There's blood in the water. There are fragments of white porcelain and a ball of violet yarn in the blood in the water. There's a body in the porcelain and yarn and blood in the water.

The body is that of our Town Treasurer, the hippo, Thomasine Épée. She's on her back. Sparky Manx is bent over her, not straddling because there's too much to straddle, administering CPR. Sparky has white latex gloves and a small white mask she puts to her nose to breathe in, then removes to exhale. Officer Willis is feeling for a pulse. He too wears gloves and has his collar over his nose. Inside the bathroom we can hear someone retching.

Officer Willis looks up and sees us.

"You kids get out of here!" he says through his collar. "Now!" when we freeze in disbelief.

Before we can exchange questioning glances ('What do we do?'), the cafeteria doors swing open to our left, and Uncle Anthony is kicking the door stoppers to hold them in place. He sees us and his black eyes open wide.

"What are you—?" he begins, doesn't bother to finish.

Sparky Manx bolts upright. The mask is in her left hand.

"Ambulance?" she barks.

"Loading dock," Uncle Anthony answers.

"No lights."

"No lights," he says.

Sparky looks at Officer Willis. "Is she alive?"

"Yes," he coughs. "Hard to feel her pulse through all the…" And he lets the thought of blubber go unspoken. "Yes."

Sparky looks right past us to Uncle Anthony.

"Gurney's outside the walk-in," she says. "And get a backboard."

Officer Willis grunts, "Get a forklift," which would be funny except at this moment it isn't.

Uncle Anthony nods and disappears. Sparky puts the mask in place for another inhale, then locks lips with the hippo, resumes mouth-to-mouth. We decide to follow Uncle Anthony. He's already ahead of us, through the kitchen, and onto the loading dock before we catch up. Breathing is easier out here. He's pulling a backboard out of the ambulance. Petrified Wood grabs the ambulance door handle, opens the door wider, holds it.

"Can we help?" he asks. He looks so earnest it would be hard to refuse, but Uncle Anthony is moving fast.

"What are you kids doing here?" He jumps onto the loading dock with the backboard under a thickly muscled arm

"We came to help," says Petrified Wood, the perfect lackey. He tries to take the end of the board, but Uncle Anthony is already across the cement platform and into the kitchen. We step aside as he pushes past.

"Go home. You can't be here."

His lackey chases him in and we're right behind. "But what's going on?"

"Not now." He turns to find Arianna, then changes his mind and looks at me. His black eyes narrow. "Take Arianna home. Get out of here." If he notices Birnam he doesn't register. I can hear Birnam starting to hyperventilate behind me. "Go!"

I take Arianna by the elbow. "C'mon," I say. But she doesn't move, and then suddenly Uncle Anthony's saying to his lackey, "If you're coming, come. Get the gurney by the walk-in."

Petrified Wood beams at his hero's recognition and darts off through the counters. Birnam goes after him, panting. Arianna looks at me. Those beautiful brown eyes of hers are all concern and question. I have no answers. Petrified comes back through the counters, pushing the gurney. He's a lousy driver. Things bang and crash as he comes through. He almost takes out Arianna and me. Birnam's behind him, counting, "Eighty-three, eighty-two, eighty-one..."

Then they're past and into the cafeteria, where they manage not to hit any tables, and they're into the corridor. Arianna has made up her mind to stay, and I'm not going anywhere if she isn't, so we pursue. By the time we're back in the hallway, there are more people, but the smell is keeping them at bay.

Chief Crockett is telling Sparky, "I've called in reinforcements. We've got Andrews directing traffic. Where's Farrell?"

"Throwing up in the bathroom. You might not want to go in there."

"Carmen Selsby?"

"Parts of her."

"Plumbing?"

"I dunno. Where's that gurney? Oh."

Petrified Wood wheels it up, and Sparky doesn't protest. She and Uncle Anthony are cautiously rolling Mrs. Épée sideways, trying to slide the backboard underneath her. Uncle Anthony glances up.

"Chief, can you help?"

"What're these kids—?"

"Now!" Uncle Anthony's intensity is frightening. "There's a chance we can save her."

Chief Crockett gives him, then us, a dirty, blue-eyed look, then drops to his knees in the water and blood and broken porcelain and takes an end of the backboard, trying not to breathe, while Uncle Anthony and Sparky roll her, and the lackey drops onto his knees and grabs the other end of the backboard. Between the four of them they manage to maneuver it into position and her onto it. Sparky hollers, "Jake, get out here!" and Reverend Jake comes out of the bathroom, mask askew, drenched in blood. We can hear the sound of Officer Farrell vomiting, only there's no longer a toilet to vomit in. More by instinct than conscious thought, I grab a side of the gurney, trying to hold my breath, and Arianna and Birnam grab ends and we steady it while six of them lift the victim with a mighty, collective groan. Then she's on it, and Uncle Anthony shouts, "Move!" and we scatter while he and Reverend Jake wheel it back through the cafeteria, the kitchen, onto the loading dock, and into the ambulance.

Officer Willis secures the corridor at the turn, and stops the Ottick sisters and Nigel Brate, also Bambi Saville, funeral director, who's come galumphing along to see if she has more customers.

"They're all TouchDown Realty," says Selectwoman Katherine Ottick.

Officer Willis coughs, "Not Carmen Selsby."

Edie Ottick coughs. "There go your plans for the swamp, dear. I told you."

"Be quiet, Edie," snaps her sister Kay.

Chief Crockett says, "Clear the corridor."

Kay: "Tara Drummond? Has anything happened...? Is she—?"

"Makepeace is driving her home. Saville, don't go in there without a mask. Deal with the two in the walk-in, and leave the one..."

"Pieces of one," adds Officer Willis. His eyes are watering.

A loud groan from inside the bathroom, and then another gag and gush is heard.

Bambi Saville pushes her way past Officer Willis and hurries into the lavatory. She doesn't come out. Brate and the Otticks are held back by Officer Willis and the smell. Brate's got his face in his sleeve, the Otticks hold hankies to their noses. Mr. Carroll, our school superintendent, appears with the school janitor who's pushing a wet mop and bucket. Mr. Carroll's a distinguished-looking old man with a big white moustache and horn-rimmed glasses. He lives in the neighboring town of West Bridgewater. [14]

"Call school tomorrow," says Chief Crockett. "Call school for the week. All the food in the walk-in… dump it, and there's… no, don't go there. Not yet."

The janitor, Joe Mastico, has made a move toward the bathroom and is stopped. Police Lieutenant Watson lumbers up.

"I've cleared the hall, Chief," he says. "Got the place taped off."

"Get back there. It's a possible crime scene. No one goes in."

"Crime scene? You think?"

Chief Crockett sees us.

"You!" he hollers.

"We're going," I say, and pull Arianna with me toward the front door. Petrified Wood's gone. It doesn't take a genius to guess he's gone off with his hero, but the genius, it turns out, would be wrong. I'm stuck with Birnam, who has reached the mid-thirties but is still gasping for air. "You," I growl, "c'mon."

Birnam stares at me like I'm speaking in tongues. I grab him by the arm and haul him off. He tries to fight me, but for all his size, there's not much strength.

This is not the beginning of a true romance. Not even close.

I don't make it home until after midnight.

---

14 In 1976 he's only 48, but I'm 18, and 48 is old! So, here I am today, 49. How does old happen so fast?

ARTICLE 6

TOWN HALL, TUESDAY

I already know there'll be no school, so I tell my mother not to answer the telephone in the morning, as it will be some message on the emergency call tree announcing cancellations, but my mother never listens to me and answers the phone anyway. It isn't the school. It's Town Hall calling. Could I please come over immediately as there's no school?

So much for sleeping in. I get dressed, skip breakfast and cigarette (which always leaves me in a bad mood), and drive off in my 1962 Ford Fairlane. It's a boat with an ash tray. When I sail past the middle school I see several police cruisers (our old, battered Chevy Caprice, a couple from East Quagmire, others I can't read) plus the fire truck, the ladder truck, and the ambulance. Also, Channel 4 news has a van there. Hmmm. The place looks like a crime scene.

Funny thing about that.

At Town Hall the flag is flying half-mast. I'm greeted by both Miss Otticks in the Town Clerk's office, a pair of spindly spinsters with a wrinkle for every complaint they've ever registered at Town Hall these past sixty plus years. Selectwoman Katherine Ottick, the spindlier, gives me an appraising look and asks my name. When I tell her, she wants to know if I was at Town Meeting last night. What am I, invisible? Didn't I get called down to the floor last night and then told personally by Selectwoman Ottick that I was too young to fill in as Town Clerk?

But she launches into a long-winded explanation about how the present Town Clerk, Mrs. Tara Drummond, will be incapacitated for some time, and how the Town is asking Miss Edith Ottick to fill in as temporary Town Clerk, but she will need help getting started, and I won't have school for the rest of the week, so of course I should be honored to continue my unpaid internship and help run things.

The Town is asking?

Isn't hiring your own sister nepotism?

Selectwoman Ottick assures me that Miss Edith Ottick is not her nephew, that there's no conflict-of-interest in an emergency, and that I'm the only one who knows where Mrs. Drummond keeps the burial permits and death certificates. The Town's going to need several burial permits any minute now.

I suggest the burial permits might be filed under 'B'. I want to add that any semi-intelligent person could figure that out, but my mother has drummed it into my head to respect my elders, even when they don't respect me.

Selectwoman Ottick doesn't appreciate my tone.

Neither does Miss Edith Ottick, the younger, who is, may she add, a townie. Am I?

Should I dig my birth certificate from the files and show it to her? I won't lower myself. Of course, I'm a townie. I was born here—well, Saint Anne's in Fall River, actually, then brought home to Hancock Street as soon as my mother could leave the hospital. But for these two persnickety old crones, skin color trumps documentation. I might as well bark at a fire hydrant. Or do whatever else one does with a fire hydrant.

So I unearth the burial permits and wait.

The Otticks go off into the bowels of Town Hall to swill coffee and gossip, and I'm left to man the fort. This is not how I intended to spend my unanticipated school vacation. I need a smoke, but I'm out of cigarettes and I'm trapped here.

I'm behind the counter, sorting mail, when Arianna comes in. She's been dropped off by Georgina who's doing something for her father. She starts crying again. Our Town Treasurer died last night in the ambulance en route to the hospital, and her father's in jail. Chief Crockett took him directly from the hospital after they delivered the body.

Although startled by the news I feign nonchalance. It's only a matter of form, I tell her. Uncle Anthony did, by his own admission, run over Fire Chief Tubby Dobbs with the ambulance. That's vehicular manslaughter, but it was an accident and he was on duty. No one's gonna blame him. They might even cheer. Arson will take a big hit with Tubby Dobbs gone. The cops are doing their duty, that's all.

I'm telling Arianna to quit the histrionics, that it will all work out, when Petrified Wood gangles in, all tall and lanky. He's in tight jeans high at the ankle and a sweater two sizes too small with wolves on it. The wolves are loping across his not-insubstantial chest, howling at a white, vinyl moon.

"I saw your Ford Fairlane outside," he says to me. Then he gives Arianna a big, dopey, heartsick look like he understands what she's going through. No boy with wolves hugging his chest will ever understand what Arianna's going through, but then, she's never going to understand what he and his *Call of the Wild*-pack are going through either, so their confusion is mutual.

They exist in different worlds.

Until last night, I never had much to do with Petrified Wood. I saw him play opposite her in *South Pacific* last year but didn't pay attention. He wasn't all that much shirtless. Just very white. I doubt I'd know who he was if not for his having reneged on inviting Arianna to the Sophomore Swing. (Now there were histrionics!) He doesn't even drive yet. But it seems boys pay attention to vehicles, and he knows mine.

"Where'd you go last night?" I demand. "Off ambulance chasing with...?" But I'm not sure what to call Uncle Anthony in his presence, so I grunt instead. "I had to drive your stupid brother home. You live halfway across town. You know how much gas costs?"

He looks stricken, deer in the headlights.

"No, I left my bike... I mean, I told..." He looks at Arianna. "...your dad... I said I'd... he had an errand he... asked... me if...."

"What errand?"

"His... wallet." Hesitation gives away the lie. "He left it in the chair when they handcuffed... It fell out... somehow. I said I'd go back in for it."

"You went back into the auditorium?"

"Yeah."

"It's a crime scene."

"I know. Lieutenant Watson almost caught me." He looks to Arianna. "Where's your father? I went to the station and he isn't there."

Arianna doesn't answer him, so I do. "He's in jail."

"What?" He looks genuinely shocked.

I don't bother to explain the obvious. "Where's his wallet?"

He can't look me in the eyes. "I couldn't find it."

"Convenient." And pretty lame.

"Someone will turn up with it."

"Right."

Arianna's saying nothing, so it's up to me to grill him. But now that I've got him and his knitted wolves pinned against the counter, I can't think of anything else to say. This is all a lot bigger than I'm ready to handle.

He says, "Why's he in jail?"

He looks at Arianna, but she says nothing. She's uncomfortable with him in the room.

I throw out, "He killed Chief Dobbs, in case you've forgotten."

"But that was an accident."

"Right. But he killed Chief Dobbs." Then it comes to me, and I can't resist adding, "Not to mention, he's black."

He looks genuinely confused. "Who's black?" When I fail to answer, he says, "Little Anthony's not black." And glances to Arianna for corroboration, which doesn't come.

"He's not white."

"He's... What's that got to do with anything?"

"Nothing at all, white boy," I tell him. "Or maybe everything."

"You're not black," he says.

What's this got to do with me? What's he trying to say? Instead of arguing with him, I go to the file cabinets near the window and pull open the second drawer down. This is not the same as lowering myself for the Ottick sisters. It takes less than a minute to find my birth certificate.

Karen Angelina Pina.

April 7, 1958.

8:42 AM.

Saint Anne's Hospital, Fall River, Massachusetts

Mother: Rosario Maria Gomes

Father: Thomas Joseph Pina

Color: Black.

He's stunned.

"But you're not… You're… from Cape Verde…" He pronounces the final 'e' as a separate syllable. "Portuguese." Again, a look of entreaty to Arianna, but, no, nothing. She does not commit.

"Or whatever they write," I tell him. "I'm not white, white boy, never have been. And it'd probably be better you stop calling him 'Little.' Or maybe that's just a thing white boys…"

I leave it hanging. I've got him and his wolves cringing tight where I want them. Wolves! What the hell does a white boy in Massachusetts know about wolves? And isn't that sweater itchy against his baby powder white skin? Then I see the bulge in his jeans' hip pocket.

"I need a smoke."

I know Arianna doesn't smoke. This kid, I don't know much about, but that bulge looks promising. "Got a cigarette, white boy?"

White Boy shakes his head.

"I don't smoke."

And then, just like that, his face changes expression as if startled. He's remembered something. Or felt it in his jeans' hip pocket.

"What?"

He says, "Nothing."

I persist. "What?"

"No. Nothing. I…"

I lower my brows, give him the accusatory stare. I can see him wince, struggle, then surrender before superior force. He reaches into his tight jeans' pocket, fumbles around. He pulls out a crushed pack of Marlboros. He hands me the pack.

"Afraid I'll squeal to Mommy?"

He just shrugs and looks guilty as hell.

"Don't worry," I assure him. "Your secret's safe."

The pack is squishy in my hand. It's definitely short a few cigarettes. I tap it against my palm, shake one loose, pull it out. I check out his tight jeans' pockets for another bulge.

"Got a light? I left mine…"

He shakes his head, and this time the pockets don't look promising. Arianna's clearly confused. She doesn't know he smokes, it seems. I go to Tara Drummond's desk. There's a lighter in her top middle drawer. She smokes Virginia Slims. I find it and light up, hand him back the pack. I don't thank him.

Funny. For a second I sense there's something different about the cigarette, but I'm not sure what it is. I inhale, and just like that, it all feels good. My hostility for White Boy drops several degrees. He goes back to studying my birth certificate like he's discovered the Declaration of Independence or something.

"Your parents were born in Cape Verde." There's that 'e' again." He reads over the paper which is bound in a small, thick book of records, four years' worth, 1955 - 1958. "Wait. What? This says your mother's white, your father's black. Aren't they both Cape Verdean?"

I cut him off. "The Army decided. My father went along with it."

'*...that all men are created equal, that they are endowed by their Creator with certain, inalienable rights...*'

He says, "Chief Dobbs calls him 'Little.' So does Biff Larsen."

"White boys." I exhale smoke in face, taking pleasure in his discomfort.

He looks like he's been impaled.

Another puff and I drive the stake home through the wolf pack with, "How about Sparky Manx? She call him 'Little'? Reverend Jake?"

The three of us descend into an uncomfortable silence which I fill by re-filing my birth certificate. I looked it up the second day I worked at Town Hall. There's an education to be had in archaeological digs. "The old order changeth," but not fast enough.

I'm thoroughly enjoying my first drag in the last twelve hours when Miss Makepeace comes along the hallway. "That will age your skin prematurely," she says with a smile. I could hold that against her but I don't. She's always pleasant to me. She's an attractive woman. Not beautiful. Nothing about her stands out as perfection, but she's perfectly put-together. Her smile is lip-sticked to sincerity, her eyes lined and shaded and welcoming, and her hair's so perfectly coiffed and lacquered the ozone layer's having a meltdown. She wears an autumnal pantsuit ensemble and a neck scarf of silk foliage.

And cowboy boots.

Cowboy boots? Somehow or other, on her they work.

"Miss Pina," she says, "I heard you were volunteering... or should I say, drafted. Miss Ottick is nothing if not persuasive." She passes a knowing smile. I take a deliberate drag on the cigarette to let her know I'm too old to take advice from anyone. "Are you here for the week? Welcome to The Snake Pit. I'll give you some paperwork to fill out and we'll see you get paid. Substitute line in Wage-and-Personnel. Modest, but you deserve something for your service."

Next she turns to White Boy and beams. "Mr. Wood," she says, "what a pleasant surprise on a Tuesday morning. And after such a difficult evening. I imagine your parents are disappointed with last night's vote."

Dead bodies everywhere, and she's asking after his parents. Her composure is as assured as her ensemble.

White Boy says, "Yes," but is unable to continue in the presence of such charm. You can watch the temperature rise in his cheeks. She has that effect on males, even males whose preferences are, as yet, indeterminate. For now, he thrusts both hands in his jeans' pockets and fiddles nervously. The Marlboros, maybe?

"Are you ready for coffee?" she asks. "I have your mug place of honor in my office. And this," she says, turning to Arianna, "must be Anthony DeBarros's daughter. You look so much like your father. Your eyes…" She extends a perfectly manicured hand. "Wilhelmina Makepeace. Please call me Willy."

Arianna mumbles, "Pleased to meet you," and White Boy adds, "Arianna," by way of introduction, in case Miss Makepeace doesn't already know, although I get the feeling that Miss Makepeace knows a lot more than she lets on. She invites me to her office for coffee but I'm hesitant to leave my post, which she finds commendable. Besides, I want to finish my smoke in peace. "Milk, two sugars? Got it," she says, then, "would Mr. Wood come and help with the delivery?"

Clearly, this Aryan Youth would go through fire to grant her any request. He can barely get another, "Yes," out his throat, and may have to start counting down from one hundred himself if she gets any closer.

"Miss DeBarros," she asks, "do you drink coffee? Come along. I have tea, if you'd prefer, peppermint, English breakfast?" I notice she's careful not to dwell on Uncle Anthony's incarceration, at least not in a public space. She ushers them away, then turns back to me. "A word of warning. You might steer clear of the Rec Director and the Board of Health agent. They're feuding again. This time it's s'mores." The small smile and arch of the brows includes me among the few and kindred sane.

She goes. I'm left behind to hold the fort, but the fort is not attacked. Several people come in, secretaries, commission members, glee and expectation plastered all over their pasty faces, but at sight of me in the Town Clerk's office, they pass on, pretending I don't exist, and disappear into other corners and crannies of The Snake Pit where they can recount last night's events with improvements. The cigarette is gone too soon.

Arianna and Petrified Wood come back with coffee. Sure enough, Miss Makepeace has fixed mine just the way I like it. We drink, say little. Then they announce they're going to the police station to see Uncle Anthony, but before they can go, the police come to us.

Chief Crockett, specifically.

"I heard I'd find you here," he says, and his blue eyes examine us so thoroughly I think maybe he intends to buy us. Makepeace has obviously let him know our whereabouts.

"You were in the corridor last night when the accident happened," he says. "I didn't get your names."

He pulls out a notepad, points. We give him our names. He doesn't make a face when he hears Petrified's, so I assume he's heard it before. "You're the kid hangs out at the fire station," he says. "Friends with Anthony DeBarros?"

"Yessir," says Petrified Wood, looking like he's committed about ten thousand crimes since last night.

"Where'd you go after I saw you?"

There's a stunned silence. We're being questioned by a police officer. We're being grilled. It's like in the movies. We're material witnesses. Or are we suspects?

I say, "Home," when it becomes clear my companions are lost for words.

"All of you?"

"Yes. I drove. I have a car."

He looks me over, seems to change his mind, and turns back to PT.

Again: "You're friends with Anthony DeBarros."

"Yessir."

"You didn't by accident happen to pick up anything when you were leaving, did you?"

Petrified Wood finds his voice, barely. "Nosir." He maintains eye contact. Thankfully, he does not look down at his tight jeans' pocket. Good stage presence.

"Why," I ask, valor overcoming discretion. "Is something missing, sir?"

I hit the *sir* hard.

"He can't find his wallet. Afraid somebody stole it." Beat. "You smoke?"

Petrified Wood shakes his head slowly. He looks scared stiff.

"Nosir," he says. Two beats. "We never saw his wallet."

"Thanks," says Chief Crockett. "Just checking. It'll turn up."

He gives us one last look, then heads off for Makepeace's office. The three of us feel like we've had the wind knocked out of us. We exchange guilty glances, say nothing. Petrified and Arianna go off to the police station.

About an hour later Petrified Wood comes back alone. He looks miserable.

"What're you doing here?" I ask. "Where's Arianna?"

"She's with her dad," he says. "So's Miss DeBarros, and their father, and a bunch of women. There wasn't…" He wipes at his face. "Crowded."

"Too many Blacks?" I offer.

"Mostly Cape Verde, I guess. And Sparky Manx and Lieutenant Watson. They said Officer Farrell's in the hospital from breathing that stuff. Inhalation. Everyone else is at the school looking for evidence."

"So you didn't stage a breakout."

"I left."

"And came back here?"

"I didn't know where else to go."

"Answer to a prayer. Give me another cigarette."

Immediately he looks guilty as hell.

"I can't."

I can see the bulge in his tight jeans' pocket. It strikes me they're not tight as fashion statement but because he's grown out of them. Don't his parents buy him new clothes?

"You can, White Boy. I'll pay you back."

"They're not mine."

"Right." I hold out my hand.

"They're Mr. Drummond's."

That stops me short. I give him the look.

"Mr. Drummond's." A question, stated, and I realize White Boy doesn't smell like a smoker.

He stares at me.

"Well," I reason, "he's not gonna need 'em. Gimme." I flex my fingers.

Reluctantly he reaches into his pocket and takes out the pack. He hands it to me. I shake the pack, take out another cigarette, get the lighter.

"Thanks, White Boy."

"Don't call me that."

"OK."

"My name's PT."

"Petey?"

"Initials. P.T."

He waits for me to say something snarky, but I restrain myself. He has just given me a dead man's Marlboros. I should be grateful. "Compromise," I decide. "I'll call you PT if you quit saying 'Cape Verde' like it's two syllables. It isn't. Just say 'Cape Verd'."

"OK," he says. A big tear wells in his right eye.

I take a few puffs and this time I do not exhale in his face. He cries anyway. I am not about to comfort him. I wait, and eventually he stops and blows his nose in his wolf-sweater sleeve. The blonde hair on his wrist is very fine. It comes to me that he does love a DeBarros. I don't think it comes to me to wonder which one.

The cigarette burns down way too soon. I take the pack to cadge another. This time though I notice something. The top of the pack is crushy from cigarettes gone, but the bottom of the pack is solid, firm, like there's something in it, something, my fingers detect, with hard corners. I shake out another cigarette and when I examine it, I see it's shorter than it should be. Not a lot, but, yeah, it's been tampered with. The filter's intact, but the end has been... amputated(?). I try to tear open the pack, but it resists, and I'm not keen on using my teeth, not in front of wolves, so I take scissors from the desk and cut.

"What're you doing?" he asks.

I say nothing and snip apart the pack, cellophane and paper. Three cigarettes fall out, which I catch and lay on the desk. From the bottom of the pack I pull out a small, thin piece of metal, not more than an inch thick.

"What is that?" he asks. He moves close to see. He smells like shampoo. Baby shampoo, maybe? I haven't smelled baby shampoo in years.

There's fine wired circuitry inlaid on the surface of the metal.

He looks at me, questioning. I look at him.

"Where'd you get these?"

"They were... you remember how Chief Dobbs, he threw the pack of cigarettes away when he did CPR on Mr. Drummond? They were in Mr. Drummond's shirt pocket."

I do remember that.

"Pacemaker."

Did I say that out loud?

We study the thing closely. He takes it from me and turns it over, holds it close to his eyes. This is not right. This is dangerous. Even the woolen wolves are holding their breaths.

"Why do you have them?"

"I... when I went back for the wallet, I just... they were lying on the floor in front of the stage."

"So you just happened to pick them up... because you're sixteen and your parents won't buy for you."

"I don't smoke."

I believe him about not smoking, but something's fishy, and what is that thing in his hand?

"Someone cut the cigarettes so this would fit inside the pack."

His expression is pure bewilderment. "Why would anyone do that?"

"How do I know? Heart attack. This... He sent you back for these, didn't he?"

He ignores my question, takes the metal thing over by the window where the light is better. I follow, but at a slight distance. Suddenly he looks up, startled, from it to me. "His pacemaker!"

OK, so either I did say it out loud, or we've both come up with the same idea independently. This thing was in close proximity to Mr. Drummond's pacemaker. He turns it over a couple more times. An idea is taking shape in our heads, an unpleasant idea.

"What is this thing?" we ask each other, almost in unison.

He looks at me. I look at him. The wolves look at the white, vinyl moon. None of us say a word. I take the thing and the pack and the cigarettes... all at once I don't want to smoke any more Marlboros... and find a manila envelope to stick them in and crumple the whole bunch up in a messy ball and bury it in the trash basket by the desk, which I will empty in the dumpster outside as soon as he leaves.

"You're destroying evidence," he says. He's watching me beneath lowered brows.

"Yes," I say.

There's a long pause, and then all at once the brows lift.

"Right," he says.

We're in agreement. But he reaches into the trash can and fishes the envelope out.

"What're you doing?"

"Too risky," he says. "I'll get rid of them."

He's got the mutilated pack and the metal thing in his hand when Sparky Manx walks in. She sees him clutching the Marlboros, minus the Marlboros, and glowers.

"You smoke?" she asks. Her voice is hoarse, raspy, probably from inhaling those chemical fumes. "Since when?"

"I... I... just... coupla years."

He's not even close to believable, and Sparky's no fool.

"Woody, tell the truth," she says, and her disappointment shows. "Where'd you get them?"

Before his stammer incriminates him further, I confess. "I bought them for him."

"Really?"

"I'm eighteen. Legal."

She eyes me funny. She's not convinced. Clearly, we're neither to be trusted. She holds her hand out, waggles her fingers.

"Spare one?" she asks. "It's been a hard twenty-four hours."

But before I can lie further, PT Wood blurts, "I just smoked the last one," and he crumples the pack and throws it back into the trash basket. The metal thing he palms. Luckily, I'm blocking the desk so the three modified cigarettes are out of view behind me.

Sparky coughs. "Make sure that's your last Marlboro, Woody." And she looks at him funny on the word *Marlboro*. "Quit now. Seen MakeLoveNotWar?"

"I think she's in her office." I've heard this joke before. PT Wood too, evidently, if the weak grin is any evidence.

She goes with an accusatory backward glance at us. PT Wood looks even whiter than I thought possible for a white boy. The color, what little he's got, has drained out of him. I'm not sure I trust him, but, as he stands there, all wide-chested wolf moon sweater lanky tight jeans tear-streaked Aryan Youth, I realize, we are in this together.

And we have to protect Arianna.

We have that much in common at least.

When I come back from lunch an hour later, someone's emptied the trash.

ARTICLE 7

———

'DEATH BY DEMOCRACY'

Town Hall is closed on Wednesday in respect for the deceased, who number several, but not, it turns out, Thomasine Épée. She is not quite dead or, rather, she was dead for a minute before the emergency staff resuscitated her at Quagmire Medical. She's on a ventilator, lungs damaged by chemical fumes, but the ventilator does not prevent her venting spleen, and the spleen she vents spews its venom on Anthony DeBarros.

"It was that maniac, that butt-licking monkey Tim and Toby let follow them around with his face so far up Toby's ass it's a wonder he didn't suffocate. Little Tony DeBarros! He was no TD, no matter how they nicknamed him. And we bore no responsibility for the death of his half-baked brother, that loser. He drowned himself. It had nothing to do with us!"

So she is later quoted by our town accountant, Mrs. Sandy O'Reilly, a lovely woman of unmathematical bent to whom a spreadsheet might as well be cuneiform and the means of calculating a fifteen percent tip honors calculus. Mrs. O'Reilly and the chairwoman of the Finance Committee, she of the boiled wool jacket and big teeth, go to the hospital bearing flowers and get an earful which they then pass on free-of-charge to diners at The Grub Pub Wednesday night. I'm listening over the meat loaf and instant mashed potatoes and it makes me sick to my stomach. Many eyes, some sympathetic, keep pretending not to look at me. Our customers know Anthony DeBarros is my uncle. Or at least they know I'm Cape Verdean, which means I must be related to Anthony DeBarros by default. I have to go home early with cramps.

Her accusation doesn't make that evening's Channel 4 news, which dwells on the death of the fire chief by ambulance and misses completely the business in the bathroom, but it is mentioned obliquely in *The Quagmire Express*, first page article, 'Death by Democracy,' just not so obliquely that everyone doesn't get the gist of it. Accompanying photographs of the moderator being administered CPR, of Uncle Anthony handcuffed to the chair, and the still-wriggling black-bottomed newt in the hands of Charles Wood, Conservation Commission, before the blurred amphibian meets its untimely end beneath the heel of a ruby red shoe make visually clear the thrust of the accusation.

"Little Tony DeBarros is a mass murderer!" Thomasine Épée, newt killer, snarls from her urgent care bed, voice singed and rancid. "He ran over Chief Dobbs with the ambulance. We were all there. And he tried to blow me up in the bathroom! I was just lucky Carmen Selsby was in there instead of me, knitting and reading our mail. That woman takes forever!"

Her accusations may not be responsible for keeping Uncle Anthony behind bars. Certainly, the town isn't taking Thomasine Épée's conclusions seriously. A heart attack, faulty plumbing? True, he ran over the fire chief, but he confessed. He didn't hit-and-run. Everyone likes Little Anthony. And everyone's used to Thomasine Épée's vituperation. It's just the kind of thing she *would* say. Her ruby red shoe and the bloody salamander impart a visual eloquence with which no rant can compete. But Tuesday comes and goes, then Wednesday comes, and Anthony DeBarros, the former Little Tony D, is still in jail. He's agitated. "Let me out!" he shouts and shakes the bars. "Why are you keeping me here? I want out! Get me a lawyer!"

Chief Crockett sends in Sparky Manx to calm him down, which she manages with some effort. Sparky and Reverend Jake plead his cause and get sympathetic responses but nothing else. Uncle Manny comes and argues with Chief Crockett, but Chief Crockett claims he's helpless to assist until Anthony DeBarros goes before a judge, and that won't be before Thursday at the earliest. Arianna and Georgina visit, but Uncle Anthony sends them home distraught. He doesn't want them to see him like this. The aunties arrive in bulk from Fall River and showcase their righteous indignation. Chief Crockett doesn't budge. He says his hands are tied.

There's a rumor circulating Town Hall that something's gone missing from the crime scene. I hear the building inspector telling the Appeals Board secretary that the police and the County Bureau of Criminal Investigation have done a thorough search of the school and auditorium, and something's not there that they need. Is it a pack of Marlboros? I need to talk to this Petrified character, but he's not where I need him either.

Wednesday evening Uncle Anthony refuses to touch his supper.

Wednesday evening I get a telephone call from, of all people, Petrified Wood. Petrified Wood has never called me in his life. I'm taken aback. How the hell did wolf moon sweater white boy get my phone number? [15]

"This is an outrage!" he howls. "They can't do this to him! They're denying his civil rights. I'm going over there and do something about it."

"Do what?" I snark. "They're not going to listen to a kid."

"I'm going to stage a sit-in, like my parents did for Vietnam. I'm going to sit there in the station and not move, and they'll have to let him go."

"They don't have to do anything, moron," I say. "You still have the thing?"

A nervous pause, then a hushed, "Yeah."

"I think the cops— I think they know the cigarettes are missing."

"Don't say anything else. The phones may be bugged."

"What? Get a grip."

"Gotta go."

"Go where?"

"To the station."

"You keep showing up there, people will get suspicious."

"He's not gonna make it till Thursday." He hangs up.

White boys are so emotional. But they're also sure of their position in the hierarchy and expect to be heard. So I am taken aback, chagrinned even, when my mother tells me later that night that there's a white kid staging a sit-in outside Uncle Anthony's cell and the cops aren't making him leave. He's sitting on the floor, big as life, his back to the bars of Uncle Anthony's cell, and Uncle Anthony's

---

15   From a telephone book or directory, of course, which people used back in the day of land-line telephones and dinosaurs.

sitting on the floor on the opposite side, their elbows interlocked through the bars. The prisoner's refusing to eat the tuna sub the cops brought him for supper.

I'm more chagrinned when, next morning at 9 AM, Petrified Wood shows up at Town Hall, re-opened, and announces he's spent the night there, has been sent home by Uncle Anthony to shower because he smells (he doesn't, not really. If anything, the scent of Old Spice deodorant lingers), and then is going back to continue his sit-in. He's wearing a single gold chain with a tiny winged figure on it. He can't look me in the face. I offer to sit-in with him. He says OK, that would be nice.

And while he's off showering at home, Uncle Anthony is left alone in the police station and hangs himself.

ARTICLE 8

FIVE BURIAL PERMITS AND RAMBO

Miss Makepeace calls me into her office and closes the door. She breaks the news to me, gently, I guess, although I have no recollection of the scene. I must have blocked it from memory. She sends me home.

The old police cruiser is sitting two doors down in front of the DeBarros house, so I spend the rest of the morning with Ma, who's already heard. News travels fast in a small town. We have nothing to say to each other. We're too heartsick for platitudes. My father died when I was an infant and his parents soon after. Since then I've had no close encounters with death except Aunt Flora's, and that was eight years ago. The several deaths at Town Meeting touched me but lightly.

Now Uncle Anthony's suicide hits me harder than I thought possible and I have no one but Ma with whom to share the pain. I go over to Arianna's in the afternoon, but the doors are locked, the shades drawn. No one responds to my knocking.

I'm alone with my grief and nicotine, unaware that Uncle Anthony's body is still at the police station. No one has come to claim the body.

Bambi Saville is out straight. She's won three out of four funerals, two burials and a cremation: Moderator Tim Drummond, Fire Chief Toby Dobbs, and Postmistress Carmen Selsby, with dibs on Theobald Doppelmeier who's in limbo somewhere. Carmen Selsby's being cremated. None of us know if she's in pieces or not, but Sparky Manx says three bodies are lined up on a conveyor belt at Bambi's Salon and Funeral Parlor, with select bits of our postmistress in a picnic cooler. The rumor mill is relishing the gore factor.

Before the news of Uncle Anthony's death reaches me, before PT Wood comes to Town Hall bearing the smell of Uncle Anthony and a gold chain, Bambi Saville bustles into Town Hall.

"Who are you?" she asks. "I need two burial permits."

I have them ready. She goes away and comes back an hour later.

"Who are you?" she asks. "I need another burial permit."

I hand one over. She goes away again.

Miss Makepeace brings me to her office. I go home. I work my Wednesday evening shift at The Grub Pub, hoping to get my mind off things, only to hear the town accountant's retelling of Thomasine Épée's accusations. My head is not in a good place.

Nor my guts.

Out of respect for Mrs. Drummond, I go to Mr. Drummond's wake on Thursday afternoon, although there's only one death I care about, and it isn't Tim Drummond's. I've already filled out our Town Moderator's burial permit. *Cause of death* reads, 'Pending.' Town Hall is closed. The line is long. Evidently he was a man of some consequence, or else TouchDown Realty has long arms. Even our state senator, Ed Norquist, is there. I'm in and out, just long enough to tell Mrs. Drummond how sorry I am, although I'm not sorry at all. I didn't know him. An awkward moment, as she offers her condolences for Uncle Anthony and bursts into tears. I'm embarrassed. Everyone's looking at us. I can't help thinking about the little metal thing in the cigarette pack which was not there by accident, and the emptied waste basket, which may or may not mean anything. I leave quickly and ponder the word, 'Pending,' as I drive home.

The Woods come in just as I'm leaving the parking lot, the whole family. They only stay a minute or so, the bare minimum. The youngest member of the commune, six-year-old Woodstock, goes home with a bouquet he's culled from the funeral arrangements. Friday morning the talk at Town Hall is all about this hippy sacrilege. [16]

Friday's assembly line wake is Carmen Selsby's. *Cause of death*, 'traumatic damage to body parts from plumbing misfortune, including dismemberment of fingers on the right hand and chemical burns to face, torso, and nether regions.'

The closed casket, fortunately, doesn't distract from the main event, the epic grief of her only granddaughter, Tourmaline Selsby, Rock star. My mother and I go together, not intending to stay, but Carmen Selsby comes from a big family, several brothers and sisters and their grown children, an ancient mother, uncles and aunts and cousins, elderly but not infirm, her only son, Archie, who lives with her, and, last but not least, the Academy Award production that is *Tourmaline in Mourning*. Visitors and well-wishers are discouraged from extending their condolences by the obscene overacting she offers up to her adoring public. The ranks of the bereaved are

16 A week later, Krystal Tull will tell Birnam Wood that his brother Woodcock is a grave robber, and a week after that, Tourmaline Selsby tells him his brother Plywood pisses in the baptismal font. That's how names and news get mangled in a small town, or at least in a small town that has Rocks.

reduced to extras passing Kleenex in support of her pity party piece. It's one helluva show, performance art on the scale of Greek tragedy. No one knows whether to strait-jacket her into some familial, avuncular embrace or don raincoats before entering the splash zone.

Tourmaline Selsby, Queen of Grief. She's all in black, of course, black mini-skirt short enough to reveal black panties, black high-heeled boots, a low-cut black chemise (black bra straps visible but not much cleavage as Tourmaline isn't blessed in that department), a black shawl worn hip level, and a little black hat with a black veil that lends such dramatic flair her groupies, Krystal Tull and Ruby Smith-Jones, have purchased identical items and are squeezed in beside her, sharing the pain behind flirty films of black lace. They're intent on playing her ladies-in-anguish.

There's clearly been telephone coordination involved.

Not to be outdone, male Rocks Jasper Lovell and brother Jet are lurking just off-screen, uncertain of their princely status, but decked for the occasion in scuffed black sneakers and cuffed black jeans. Jasper sports a Black Sabbath T-shirt, sleeves cut-off at the shoulders, with a leering skull on front. Jet has opted for Metalhead and a ghoulish Grim Reaper, appropriate to the occasion. They think they're making a statement. Carmen Selsby's kin eye the hoodlums askance but the heavy metal punks in the corner can't compete with Tourmaline's operatic bereavement.

My mother and I've been in the same spot for at least half an hour when an unexpected visitor in camouflage, bandoleer of bullets over one shoulder and across his chest and dog tags, appears in the doorway. It's one of the survivalist kids from the military academy, the one who's supposedly had a few nocturnal layings-on-of-hands between dumpster runs. Traffic is at a standstill thanks to Tourmaline's histrionics. It'll be hours before we get to shake hands and offer condolences to even the most distant relation. My mother and I are going nowhere fast when Rambo cuts the line and starts breathing down our necks. *Rambo* the movie won't come out for several years, but the country's only recently emerged from Vietnam, and we get the image clear enough. People behind decide not to press the issue.

There's nothing much for Ma and me to do but stand there and hope he doesn't go full metal jacket on us. That's what we do. We wait. A minute passes. Five. Twenty. A lifetime. The line barely moves.

Then there's a tap on my shoulder. I pretend I don't feel it but, when repeated, I'm forced to acknowledge. I turn around.

"Hey," says this tall white boy with dark hair shaved on the sides, cut flat on top. The number 41 is carved over his right ear.

"Hey," I say. This is awkward. My nose is practically in his bullets.

"Number Forty-One, Tyler McVeigh," he says. "Didn't I see you at Town Meeting?"

My mother's giving me a discreet elbow that says, 'Don't engage.'

I pretend I'm invisible, but now that I could be grateful for a little invisibility, I'm evidently not. He taps my shoulder again.

'That Tourmaline Selsby, she's somethin' else, i'n't she?'

He's watching her with bemused detachment and gives me one raised eyebrow.

"How long you been standin' in this line? Gawd, I could use a smoke. You smoke?"

I hesitate, but then, for some reason I can't explain, I engage with a nod. He grins.

"Got a cigarette I can...?"

My mother gives me a not-so-discreet elbow when I say, "Actually, I could use a smoke too. But we'd better take it outside."

I've surprised myself, but after half an hour in one spot, watching Tourmaline playact, any distraction, however weird and unexpected, is better than none. And I am intrigued. I've never been hit on by a tall, white survivalist before. And there's no question in my mind he's hitting on me.

My mother gives me a look of disapproval when I say, "I'll be right back," but there's not a lot she can say in earshot of all these people, and she long ago gave up trying to talk me out of smoking, since she's a chain smoker herself.

"I'll hold your spot," she says, and pinches my arm hard.

"Thanks."

I smile winningly. There'll be a bruise later.

Number Forty-One, Tyler McVeigh, lets me go first. The funeral guy is unnerved to see a black girl stepping out with full metal jacket boy, but he holds the door for us and nods politely.

The line extends well onto the sidewalk, so we have to cross the parking lot and stand by the border of arbor vitae. I take the pack out of my purse and offer him the first one. He thanks me and waits to light his until he's lit mine.

"I really appreciate this," he says. "I was desperate."

He looks sincere. He takes a drag, holds it for what seems like forever, then slowly exhales. I recall second-hand accounts of Tourmaline Selsby's grope-fest behind the post office with this kid, and I'm tempted to disregard them.

I'm not that naïve.

When the smoke clears, he says, "Nice to go civvy."

"What?"

"Civilian. Nice to be out of uniform."

I stare at his camouflage outfit and bandoleer and dog tags and try to imagine what a uniform must look like if this is casual. He sees me staring.

"The bullets aren't real," he says. "I left the real ones home. We're not allowed to go armed off campus." He takes a long drag, blows his smoke into the foliage. "So, you're from town."

I don't say anything, but he doesn't seem concerned. I turn away and pretend to study the cars in the parking lot. The cigarette tastes good. I wonder what it was they were packing at Town Meeting then. Toy guns?

"Dumb question. Yeah, you are since you were at Town Meetin'. Pretty crazy, huh? I saw you guys behind the glass. What were you doin' back there? Didn't look like a lotta fun. Didn't seem like anyone wanted to be there. Why'd you even go? What, four people dead? Five? And none of it involving weapons. Seems like a dumb way to run a town. How the general kept his cool, I dunno. Buncha sheep yammerin' about nothin'. Can you imagine the general callin' us all together, sayin', Hey, we need a new car. Shall we vote on it? Yeah, like that'd ever accomplish anything. But ya gotta say, it's suspicious. Three of 'em part of that real estate company wants to develop the swamp? That can't be coincidence, can it?"

"Dunno. Maybe." OK, this one's a talker, that's obvious. White boys love to talk. They think they're entitled to be heard. Nice smile though. Still has all his teeth.

"And when the fat one killed the newt? Man, that was some sick shit. We heard she almost died, but didn't."

"She didn't. I work in the Town Clerk's office and do the burial permits, so I'd know."

"Too bad. That is one mean lady. I bet she was killin' 'em off so she could get all the money, like the dopey kid said, the one you were with who talks to himself with numbers. And after all that, we never got to hear the other one, the lady who ended up with the gavel, sing the national anthem. That's why we came. The general says Town Meeting's a waste, but she's worth the price of admission. Number Forty-Three and me, we love music, and we thought maybe music would do somethin' good for One-Sixty-Nine. He's the little guy, Tommy, was with us. Hasn't spoken a word since he got whacked by that 'flamin', flyin' dead thing' in the swamp, except in his sleep when he's goin' nuts. It's sad."

I take a couple of light puffs and then, not with any particular motive, ask, "So what was that 'flamin', flyin' dead thing' exactly?"

He shakes his head. "No clue. Shoulda gone lookin' for it at the time, but I had to carry Tommy outa there, the place was on fire, even the water, and then the general had us on lockdown for, like, two weeks. And after that I forgot about it. Why? You got any ideas?"

"Not really."

His face lights up.

"We could go look for it."

"Why would we do that?"

"I dunno. One more dead thing in a whole bunch of dead things all of a sudden? Can't be a coincidence, can it?"

Well, yeah, it could be. I guess I haven't given it any thought.

"I hate swamps."

"It'd be an adventure." He looks eager for me to join him. He really is hitting on me. "Live a little."

"No, thanks."

"Free Saturday?"

And he's persistent.

"No. I work Saturdays. And I got stuff to do for my uncle's funeral." Mostly I'm thinking that Arianna's gonna need company. She's finally opened the door to me, but she's not handling this well, and why should she?

"Your uncle? Jeez, I'm sorry. He the guy hung himself in jail? The black guy handcuffed to the chair?"

The black guy. No surprise there. I should've known. I take a long drag before answering.

"That's him."

"That's tough. Looked like a good guy."

"Right."

"Wicked strong. Bodybuilder?"

I take another drag. I'm annoyed.

"When's his funeral?"

"Tuesday."

"How about Sunday then?"

"I got mass."

"Mass?"

"Church, y'know? Sunday morning."

"Oh, mass, right. Catholic stuff. Yeah, we got mornin' service too."

"Really?"

"Yeah. The general, he wants to keep us on the straight."

"The general's religious? OK, I didn't know that."

"Oh, he isn't. Not anymore. But he was an army chaplain till he lost God and became a general. And he thinks it's better to play safe, in case we got souls, or at least keep us from gettin' criminal records. We all got issues. I got a wicked temper. Almost killed my brother. He stole my bike. I got mad, beat him so bad... That's how come I'm at the academy." He grins. "Hey, Sunday afternoon. Go for a ride? No funny stuff, promise. Just a ride. Check it out."

And right then, the Wood family pulls in. They climb out of the car like clowns in a circus. PT Wood sees me, sees us, says something to his parents, and comes over. Suddenly I'm the most popular girl in town, a white boy magnet. His family goes in without him, since the line has finally moved indoors, and about fifteen minutes later my mother comes out, steaming because I never go back inside. Tourmaline's been removed by her minions and the process has sped up.

"I'm leaving," Ma says. "You coming?"

"Of course," I say with my most winning smile, and bid my companions good-bye.

"Sunday afternoon, right here," says Number Four, Tyler McVeigh, action hero. "One o'clock?" When I hesitate, he shrugs his broadest grin. "Live!"

"I'll be there," says PT Wood.

Was he invited and I missed it?

Ma and I drive home and prepare dinner. I think about Number Forty-One, Tyler McVeigh, unconfirmed racist. I think about his litany of misadventures, shared between puffs of second-hand smoke and wandering eyes, how he was committed to the academy for almost beating his brother to death over a stolen bicycle (he was eight, and it was only borrowed). How he had to claw, bite, and pummel his way to King of the Barracks. Almost got expelled for mistaking a teacher for a clay pigeon. Gave up cussing for Lent and hasn't uttered a swear word since, "No shit!" He loves the discipline. He worships General Tarry, thinks of his warden as "The Man." He's certified to teach marksmanship. He's tired of pork. He'll graduate this May and go to college on ROTC (won't happen), then join the Army (won't happen), and after a distinguished career in the service return to South Quagmire and teach at the school (won't happen).

Meanwhile, six-year-old Woodstock Wood makes off with an entire vase of white lilies that reads, 'Beloved Aunt.' Birnam is too busy counting the people in line and calculating estimated total body weight to notice, and PT Wood is mortified, but his parents think their youngest son's interest in horticulture is sweet.

I don't go to Fire Chief Dobbs's funeral on Saturday because I work until three, and anyway, I didn't know him. Also, I can't keep drawing on my false sympathy account, as it's already overdrawn. People come by Town Clerk's office and assume I must be heartbroken for Mrs. Drummond, when really, I'm just pissed that Miss Edie is off with her lap pig somewhere and I'm doing all the work. Chief Dobbs didn't have family. He was married once but his wife ran off with a Boston lawyer and lives high and happy in a western suburb with a maid to do the laundry, so there isn't anyone I need to use crocodile tears on. But I hear the shindig's packed anyway. Everyone enjoys a good *Cause of death*, 'blunt force trauma by vehicle, fracture of skull, cervical spine, ribs, humerus, left hip, femur.'

An altercation ensues over "We all know where that pig came from" and "Who replaced the *Stuart Little*s with *Playboy* centerfolds?" It escalates to illegal piggeries and anti-aircraft weapons. Miss Edie wails, "Can't we all just get along?" but General Brate is enjoying the give-and-take too much and sends Nigel Brate home with a black eye.

Reverend Jake delivers the benediction.

Because he's a call fireman and clearly feels admiration for our departed hero.

And should be honored to participate before a white congregation.

By the time Uncle Anthony hangs himself, Bambi Saville is all apologies. There is simply no more room in the meat locker. She's landed Theobald Doppelmeier after some bureaucratic back room dealing that involves forging Mrs. Doppelmeier's signature on various documents, as the woman is no longer lucid, and they've never given anyone power-of-attorney. Bodies line Bambi's conveyor belt, a regular queue of carrion, and Carmen Selsby presents unique difficulties. The black tape measure has gone limp with exhaustion. Bambi is terribly sorry but she must decline. So, the aunties make arrangements with an undertaker in Fall River to handle the details of Uncle Anthony's service. The undertaker is Portuguese (from the Azores, not Cape Verde, as it happens) and associated with the Cathedral of Saint Mary of the Assumption. The DeBarros family is Catholic, but Uncle Anthony hasn't attended mass since Aunt Flora died, and that was eight years ago, so when Reverend Jake petitions Georgina to honor him with her brother's last rites, she agrees.

Reverend Jake and Uncle Anthony were friends at the fire station, and he and Georgina are something else. At least the eulogy will be more personal than the one at Tubby Dobbs', which supposedly had something to do with asphalt.

Thursday morning the undertaker from Fall River shows up at Town Hall.

"I need a burial permit, please," he says.

"Decedent's name?" I ask.

"Anthony DeBarros."

"My uncle."

"I'm so sorry. My sincere condolences. Your aunts spoke highly of him. He sure took good care of himself. Sorry. Very sorry." He thanks me and hurries out with it.

Ten minutes later, Bambi Saville bustles in.

"Who are you? I need a burial permit. Theobald Doppelmeier."

She goes without thanking me.

I feel invisible again.

It strikes me that quite soon I'm going to have to record my uncle's death for the Town records, so I dig up his birth certificate.

Here's the first surprise: Uncle Anthony is white. His father, my Uncle Manny, is also listed as white. My Aunt Flora is Portuguese. Who knew Portuguese was a color? And she was darker than either of my parents.

I look up my parents' marriage certificate. They are both black, both born, according to the certificate, in Cape Verde, although I know for certain my mother was born in New Bedford, and she's listed as white on my birth certificate

I look up Aunt Flora and Uncle Manny's marriage certificate. They are both white.

I look up Arianna's birth certificate.

She's white.

She and I are the same color. I'm no darker than she is.

Now I'm really on a tear.

I look up my cousin, Joe Cabral. He's black, his mother's white (Flores), his father's Portuguese.

My cousin Jimmy Gomes is black, but his brother Sam, five years younger, is white. Their parents have changed from black to white in that five-year span.

Who decides these things? Our parents? Ourselves? Do others make the determination for us? None of it makes sense. We are at the mercy of whoever the person in the hospital or the morgue or the Town Clerk's office happens to be that day. We are what the attending doctor or medical examiner or Bambi Saville decides we are.

Or what we want ourselves to be. Can we pick and choose what DNA, African or European, takes precedence? And does that change over time with pride or longing or advantage?

Why can't we all just be brown?

We *are* all brown, to one degree or another.

It's crazy. And after I've dug out a dozen Cabrals and Silvas, Teixeiras and Diases and Deases and Diazes (first cousins, different spelling… so I have to add immigration officers to my list of incompetent nincompoops), I'm crazy too. I go through a pack of cigarettes in an afternoon, obsessively convulsing about race.

And me.

Miss Edith Ottick doesn't show up the whole day. Her piglet is indisposed and enjoying a spa treatment at the local veterinarian's. I close the office on my own and go home and rage against The Machine, or is it The Man, to Ma. Ma sighs and lets me have her cigarettes, no strings attached. That's what good mothers do for their children.

ARTICLE 9

LITTLE QUAGMIRE SWAMP

I will not wax poetic about nature. Thirty years later I am still no fan of swamps. I never liked foreplay in a tippy canoe, and heavy petting on moss and pine needles is not my idea of romance. I won't even get into the leeches! But on that Sunday afternoon in 1976 I'm in the minority, because PT Wood and Number Four, Tyler McVeigh, are in their element. From the moment we leave the funeral home parking lot in the military academy's Model A Ford pickup, they're jabbering like long-lost friends about duck blinds and super-secret wood trails and World War II anti-aircraft guns and where the swans lay their eggs.

Wolf moon sweater white boy is so excited he's practically hyperventilating. And, yes, he's wearing the sweater again, the machine-knit wolves stretched and straining against the not-insubstantial chest that swells their happy hunting ground. Someone needs to set this boy straight about his wardrobe choices. If his mother dresses him, it's time she stopped.

I'm hanging on for dear life. I can't believe this thing counts as a vehicle. It has no roof. It has no doors. Someone forgot to put glass in the windshield. Without seat belts to hold us in place we're bouncing around, butts two feet in the air above the rumble seats. A smoke screen of dry leaves and exhaust follows as we abandon the tarred streets of civilization and careen onto a dirt road that serves as the academy's main entrance and portal to Little Quagmire Swamp. We are on a wild goose chase minus the goose (which may or may not have spontaneously combusted).

We skirt the academy. Nothing to see but trees and, high atop one, three boys in a corrugated metal tree fort, staring down at us through blackened eyes. Tyler tells us no outsiders are allowed on campus. Especially not girls. He neglects to reference skin color. For a little while we're in shade. The road has ruts and my butt feels every one. On a narrow bit with water on one side Tyler brakes and PT and I pitch forward.

"Stay," he says, as if we might bolt. He jumps out of the truck. In front of us two young boys in camo are throwing rocks at the biggest snapping turtle I've ever seen. It squats in the middle of the road like some armored prehistoric beast, an ugly head on a long, snaky neck. Its mouth is living up to its name. The boys are keeping a safe distance. The rocks bounce off its shell.

Tyler strides toward them. "Two-Twelve," he says, "Gun," and one boy unslings the rifle on his back and hands it over. Tyler takes it, pulls something, clicks something, barely aims, and fires. A loud crack, a small splat of blood between the turtle's eyes, and the huge head drops into the dirt.

"Clear the road," Tyler says. Both boys grab it gingerly by the tail and drag it to the verge. Tyler hands back the rifle, returns and jumps into the driver's seat. "Turtle soup," he says as we drive off. The boys stare after us. 'Who's the black girl Forty-One's bangin'?' the stares want to know. 'And the big sissy with the wolves?'

The big sissy looks stricken, eyes wide and pained. I don't know him well enough to understand his love of creatures great and small and ugly and evil-tempered, but the casualness with which Number Forty-One, Tyler McVeigh, kills is disconcerting. Wolf Boy is shaken. I am shaken. Every joint in my body tightens with unease only to get shaken loose moments later by violent jolt and bump. Gears grind. Tires churn. Tyler howls. And then, after a mile of jostle and cling, we take a corner on two wheels and the whole world opens wide. Suddenly, life gapes, one vast, wide-screen possibility into which we roar. The turtle is forgotten, its death ancient history. PT Wood throws his arms skyward, front seat on the roller-coaster. "Bog 19!" He grabs the metal top of the windshield frame. "I love it I love it I love it!" He loses hold and is thrown backward.

It's October, and the cranberry harvest is underway on (reputedly) the biggest undivided cranberry bog in the world. The dirt road runs straight east-west, almost to the horizon, a vast expanse of flat that ends far off in a small rise of trees in East Quagmire that hardly separates water from sky. Some bogs are kept dry and bog pickers go out with machines and scoop the berries off the vines. My grandparents used their hands and wooden scoops, but nowadays the work is mechanized. These bogs are flooded. In the distance I see men at work on a wet harvest, the floating boom in use to corral bright berries across the surface of this shallow sea. The machinery's already gone through and plucked the fruit. Now it bobs on the surface, a million crimson baubles crowding the workers in their waders and hip boots. The men pull in one shiny, undulating carpet of red that's sucked up into a truck on the far bog road. My cousin Joe Cabral might be among them, towing the ropes for Miss Ottick, who owns these bogs. He might be driving the truck. But the sun is bright off the water and they're too far away to make out faces. They turn at the sound of the Model A, one continuous belch and bellow towing a dust storm in its wake. It hasn't rained in over a week and the road is especially dry. Tyler's flying along at a bone-rattling thirty miles an hour, which on a narrow rise of gravel with water on both sides is death-defyingly fast enough for me. Then PT Wood, who's on the front passenger seat, a milk crate turned upside-down, hollers over the roar, "Can't you make this junk go any faster?"

Evidently his period of mourning for Uncle Anthony is over. The turtle too. That didn't take long.

Tyler grins. "You got it, Woodrow!" He guns it, pedal to the floor, and we hit G-force or, at least, thirty-five. As there's no speedometer, no dashboard to speak of, I can't be sure. The hurricane's eye passes over us. I'm choking on dust. I'll never get this washed out of my hair. No wonder people in the old days clad themselves in scarves and goggles before setting out for a jaunt in the horseless carriage.

The road goes on for what feels like forever. The sun beats down. Beyond our personal cloud of sand and fury the sky is bright, the water's bright, the afternoon is bright and Indian summer warm. I'm blind and barely breathing. Then suddenly Tyler brakes and banks a hard right turn I don't see coming. We graze a jumble of miscellaneous boulders that someone's placed to prevent access, and someone else has since helpfully removed. "Hang on!" he shouts.

I have nothing to hang on to. 'Woodrow' clings to Tyler's jacket sleeve with a "Whoa!!"

The trees close in. We're on an even narrower road... no, track... no, overgrown path, that shrinks into cedars. The dust storm withers behind. Now root and rock and leaf and needle hold sway, and we have to duck as low-hanging branches come at us from both sides.

The trees press in close, the branches slap and graze.

All at once, there are no trees, only water ahead, then water underneath, spraying up through the floorboards, and a bump and jolt that almost tips us over, and a scream from me, and then we're on solid ground again, but not any solid ground I've ever encountered. The red and green and gold and blue are gone. Blackened trees stab charred earth. Tyler slams on the brakes and geysers of ash erupt front and rear and side. PT Wood almost flies through the windshield that isn't there.

"End Zone Island!" announces Number Forty-One, Tyler McVeigh. "All ashore that's goin' ashore!"

I cough and sputter. My legs feel weak. The ground's all dried mud baked with charcoal and cracked from a week with no rain. End Zone Island? I have been here before, but last time here didn't look like this. Last time here was green and gold. Last time the trees on End Zone Island had branches and the branches had leaves and the ground was carpeted with pine needles. Last time I was in the throes of teenage love. (That didn't last long.) For the first time I confront the magnitude of Fire Chief Tubby Dobbs's villainy, the arsonist and his toys. This is no campfire gone bad, no careless teenage indiscretion. He's incinerated the place, Smokey the Bear's worst nightmare, a landscape so inhospitable that no one will fuss if he fills it in or paves it over. He's removed all signs of life and cleared the way for TouchDown Realty's development scheme. Football victory parties on End Zone Island have come to a sorry end. No one will ever make out here on a carpet of pine needles again.

"Oh, wow," says PT Wood. He looks around, appalled. "I didn't know. I never come out this far."

We get out of the truck. Tyler points across a charred half-acre to a dinky indentation in this dinky island. "Indian Cove," he says. I should ask Reverend Jake what he knows about Indian Cove. There's something about the Wampanoags and a refuge during King Philip's War, a last stand, when white skins and red skins went on a killing spree and took each other out in the hundreds or thousands. This place could be littered with centuries' old corpses, not just one "flaming, flying dead thing angel apocalypse," goose *flambé*, or whatever it was supposed to be.

Tyler plants his black, high-laced military boots in the soot and looks around with a conqueror's wild surmise. For a minute I think he's going to plant a flag. Instead, we walk.

"So we all get assigned this vision quest," he explains without further introduction. "We each of us get sent out to a spot where we have to sit for twenty-four hours, livin' on nothin' but food and water, and just wait and think until we have some kind of hallucination or somethin'. Somethin' the general says is what separates men from boys. I'm over World's End, no gun, nothin' protectin' me from my thoughts, which aren't all that much, when all of a sudden I really think I'm havin' a vision when… it's just a little before dark… I can see the sky gettin' bright over here, and here is where Tommy is. He's got assigned Indian Cove. I can see Indian Cove's on fire. What do I do, follow orders and stay where the general says, or go rescue Tommy? The general will kill me if I disobey orders, but the swamp's on fire, and Tommy's one of my grunts. I'm between a rock and a hard stone. I got to rescue my grunt. I don't know then, but Chief Dobbs is out here torchin' the place with his flame thrower. He doesn't know Tommy's here, and Tommy doesn't know he's here, just the trees are on fire. So Tommy wades out in the water to get away from the flames. And then... then there's this loud sound, and I can hear that music playin', the music Nigel Brate plays when he's flyin' his copters out here lookin' for our piggery. He's blastin' it over loudspeakers and comin' in low with a big canvas sling under the 'copter that's carryin' water. Salt water, I guess, though I don't believe that crap about great white sharks. I can see him over the trees and I can see the fire, but I'm like a mile away. So I start runnin'! To hell with the vision thing! I know Tommy's here and no one's closer to him than me, so it's gotta be me. And I'm out on the bog road and I got a clear view when the 'copter comes in low to dump water on the fire, but it turns out it's been leakin' gas into the water he's carryin', and when the 'copter flips, the whole place explodes. Goes up like, Kaboom! Like the burnin' of Atlantica!

"I come runnin' the road we just came on, and I'm screamin', "One-Sixty-Nine! One-Sixty-Nine!" and there's flames all out there, but they don't get me, they just burn on the water and the island. And I have to go around through the water, like tryin' not to get incinerated myself, and when I finally find Tommy, he's standin' out... right out here, somewhere right around here, soaked, bawlin' his eyes out, his hair burned right off his head, and cryin' somethin' awful about how this "flamin', flyin' dead thing" came out of the water and tried to kill him. "Zombie angel of death," he says.

"I carry him outa here. Brate's 'copter's on the other side of the island. It's just lyin' there on its side in the mud. Dunno how Brate made it outa there alive, but he did. Chief Dobbs too and the fat guy with the tow truck, I guess, but I never saw any of 'em."

"Whoa," gasps PT Wood admiringly when Tyler's done with his tale. "That's crazy!"

"So I'm thinkin' that 'zombie angel of death' 's gotta be right around here someplace."

PT Wood and his wolf pack take a deep, expansive breath. "I think you're right," they agree.

"You game?"

PT Wood grins. "Game on," he says. The wolves give a silent yelp of assent. "Think there's sharks?"

"No way," says Number Forty-One, Tyler McVeigh. "C'mon, let's find that son-of-a-bitchin'-flamin'-flyin'-dead-thing and see if it's really who we think it is."

Who do we think it is? I'm at a loss, but he's off again at a quick march, not stopping to take questions. He leads us across the wasteland. There's a narrow rise of land that cuts across the water, and beyond it, a small copse of swamp maples, strangely untouched by fire and huddled on a little hillock. There's a little wooden dock there too, a makeshift landing kids patched together long ago, also unburnt. I remember it from when we canoed here, my boyfriend at the time and me. I remember sitting on it while my boyfriend fished and caught nothing but mosquito bites.

Tyler pauses at the top of a small embankment above the dock and waits for us to catch up. He lifts his bandoleer, its full metal jackets gleaming in dappled sunlight filtered through floating ash and soot and blackened trees and swamp maple foliage, and hangs it respectfully from a low, bare limb. I expect him to pull out a gun next, but that doesn't happen, and I remember he borrowed a rifle to kill the turtle. He's not allowed to carry a gun in town.

The most unexpected thing happens instead. Tyler removes his camouflage jacket. He takes his jacket carefully by the shoulders and folds it back and in half lengthwise. Then he holds it with one hand while with the other he folds the two sleeves neatly in behind. Next, he drapes it over a forearm and folds it in half again. With the kind of reverence reserved for the vestal garments of priests, he lays it carefully on a bed of pine needles. He takes off his long-sleeved camouflage shirt and repeats the process exactly. Then he pulls a green T-shirt over his head and does it again, each layer piled carefully atop the previous. I have never seen anyone disrobe with such care and deliberation. I have never seen anyone so thin. Or so white. Below the neck he's practically radiant. Clearly, whatever this boy does over summer vacation, no beach is involved. His face has a little color, but that's the extent of it. When I first called PT 'White Boy,' I had no idea a boy could be so white. This is white meat like I never imagined. And there's not much meat.

Without layers of clothing to pad him, Tyler is the literal bean pole, a bean pole with no pigment. He's all skin and bone and sinew and tendon, and there's muscle too, but muscle starved on a diet of calisthenics. Are all General Tarry's boys this skinny and ill-fed? I recall the kid in the balcony, Nondescript Someone Number Forty-Three with the eyepatch, obsessing over devil dogs and pulled pork sandwiches, and I check out Tyler McVeigh, the number 4 shaved into the side of his head, and don't think I've ever seen anyone with less meat on him. The ribs are outlined against his pale lack-of-flesh. His collar bones stick out like matching soup spoons under the stingiest skim of cream cheese. He's a stick with dog tags. Uncle Anthony used to boast he only had seven percent body fat. Tyler McVeigh has zero.

He looks at the two of us. "You comin'?" he asks.

"You couldn't pay me enough," I snap back, and glance PT Wood's way for corroboration.

"Woodrow?"

And now the unexpected repeats itself. 'Woodrow' pulls the wolf moon sweater over his head, takes it carefully by the shoulders, and folds it back and in half lengthwise. Then he folds the two sleeves neatly behind. With the kind of reverence reserved for the vestal garments of priests, he lays it on the pine needles beside Tyler's. Half-a-wolf gazes at the white vinyl moon. He's wearing nothing underneath the sweater except the gold chain with the tiny winged figure which he removes and lays in a tight coil inside the moon. PT Wood looks Tyler's way for approval and Tyler gives it, a motionless nod. I cannot believe this is how Petrified Wood disrobes normally, but Number Four, Tyler McVeigh, has some kind of strength or force or personal presence that expects protocol to be followed. PT Wood follows protocol.

I am standing here in a remote corner of a swamp with two tall white boys, both naked to the waist and looking down on me as if they half-expect I will do the same. Clearly that isn't going to happen, and they must know it, but they're white boys, and what do I know?

Tyler is an inch or two taller than PT Wood, and both have half-a-foot on me, but PT Wood has more meat on his bones, less muscle and no hard lines, not so far removed from Birnam's baby fat. He's also got some color left over from the lounge chairs outside the fire station last summer. He sees me studying him and looks embarrassed. Tyler seems not to be aware he has a body to be embarrassed about. I pretend I've seen it all before and am unimpressed.

But am I? Really?

"Leave your boots on, Woodrow," Tyler says to PT Wood. "There's no tellin' what's on the bottom."

"Is it deep?" 'Woodrow' asks. He's studying Tyler's naked torso too. I'm thinking he's as startled as I am by the unveiling of a body so devoid of mass.

Tyler seems unfazed, standing here with nothing covering ligament and rope and sinewed knot but dog tags and air. For a moment I'm afraid the pants are coming off next, but if the boots are staying on, I guess I'm safe.

"You see all these tree trunks stickin' outa the water?" he says. "That tells you this was woods one time, before they built the dikes and ditches to irrigate the bogs and flooded this part. It's not deep, but it's uneven. And there's leeches."

"OK," says PT Wood. He doesn't seem put off by the idea of leeches. I want to shout that I will not be a party to leech removal after the fact, but I hold my tongue. Already my company is fading into unimportance. I'm becoming invisible to them.

Tyler wades into the water. PT Wood gives me a last glance of, whatever, and goes behind him, the lemming. They are two tall lemmings, one with cropped brown hair, one bushy blonde, no other bodily hair apparent. Their boots vanish in the mud, and in another moment their knees are underwater. PT grabs a tree trunk for support in passing, but Tyler moves smoothly and thinly into the not-so-shallows, hands tucked neatly into his camo pockets. Tyler's shoulder blades flare out like wings. PT's are buried beneath rolling shoulders and his hands are everywhere at once, seeking balance.

"Careful, submerged log," warns Tyler, and he steps cautiously over it. PT does the same, trips, and falls into Tyler's steadying arms. They cling to each other for a moment and burst out laughing. I wait for them to turn around, invite me in on the joke, but already I'm forgotten.

Invisible.

Somewhere ahead are the remains of a 'flamin', flyin' zombie angel of death.' Maybe? And why should I care if two white boys, code-named Number Forty-One and Woodrow, search for a needle in the muck? Thigh deep in disgusting swamp water, they glow against dark pool and rotting vegetation, shrink into sunlight. I find a big rock up the embankment that looks fairly free of soot, brush it off anyway, and settle down to wait. Do I get a code name too? I watch them recede in parallel, staggered lines as back and forth they go, bending unsteadily, tentative stoop and fumble become smaller and smaller. If there were more people to help, Tyler would have this comb-and-seek functioning like a well-drilled military exercise. Instead, two frosted sugar babies stumble about, sometimes into each other, and laugh brightly, if faintly, in the distance. I sit on my rock and stew. Time passes. I catch myself singing *White Boys* from *Hair* under my breath, which somehow segues into *'Aquarius'* until a bunch of ducks squawk in protest and rise and flap away in a rumble of feathers. After that there's nothing much to do except brush away flies.

I am not a fan of nature.

Especially not swamps.

ARTICLE 10

"LAND OF THE FREE…"

They come back empty-handed, not even a leech, but it doesn't appear to bother them. They're giggling and punching shoulders, or mainly Tyler's punching PT's shoulder and his punches sting, but PT has flesh enough to absorb the impact and he beams in gratitude. The blows land with the ring of newfound friendship. I sit on a rock for two hours, accomplishing nothing, until they emerge from the mire, slosh in their boots, sun at their backs. PT's incandescent. His blonde thatch crowns him like a halo. Tyler's scant flesh glows. "Nothing. Nada. Niente," the holy boys proclaim, and conceal their radiance in camouflage and wolves. We head back. PT bicycles off home, a wave and a luminous grin. Number Forty-One, Tyler McVeigh, fiddles with his dog tags. "Can I see you again?"

I'm in a bad mood. Again? Has he seen me at all? "I have school," I growl.

"Me too," he says, not the least put off. "But next weekend."

"What about Tourmaline Selsby?" I probably should ask, What about PT Wood?

"Who?"

"You know who."

He scrunches his face. "What's she got to do with anything?"

"You tell me."

"She's a kid." He looks offended.

"How old are you?"

"Seventeen and five months. I graduate May, same as you. Tourmaline's only when I do the mail run, nothing more. She's, what, fourteen?" He registers my scowl. "She been talking? I never touched her, I swear."

"I gotta go."

"I know you work Saturday, but you free Saturday night? I got leave. Maybe we can see a movie. I haven't seen a movie since *Texas Chainsaw Massacre* and that was ages ago."

I should put a stop to this silliness right here and now, but he smiles nice and I am weak.

"We'll see," I say. It's the best I can come up with.

"OK then. See you at the funeral."

I want to protest but he's already roaring off into the sunset in a cloud of dead leaves and exhaust. Of course, it isn't even close to sunset, but somehow, from my rear-view mirror thirty years later, Number Forty-One, Tyler McVeigh, mixes up with movies, sunset endings, *Rambo,* I dunno. In 1976 most likely it's *M*A*S*H* on TV: helicopters, red sky, and a newly-acquired, meatless action toy. I lean against my Ford Fairlane and think I may invite him to dinner next Saturday night if he does, in fact, show up for Uncle Anthony's funeral.

Ma can cook.

I've neglected to mention there is school on Thursday and Friday. We do not have a week-long vacation after all. The middle school walk-in refrigerator gets cleaned out, and while the first-floor female teachers' bathroom is closed indefinitely, there's one on the second floor still operational. I hear from a young cousin that the cafeteria pizza features ground human remains masquerading as hamburger. Rumors of last Monday night's events have filtered down to the pre-pubescents. However, I skip school both days and man the Town Clerk's office, less an honor than an obligation. Miss Edith Ottick is barely present (for a lifelong townie, she's not much in evidence in town), and I deal with burial permits and daily correspondence. My guidance counselor marks it as part of my internship and commends me on my civic responsibility.

Basically, I just want to skip school. I'm not ready to go back yet.

I'm not ready to go back, ever, but Monday, the day after swamp and rock, I go to class for a half-day, then in the afternoon and evening I attend Uncle Anthony's wake, *Cause of death,* 'Suicide by hanging, belt.' I have no real memory of the wake. Certainly, our whole extended family is there, and enough friends and townies to make a respectable showing, but nothing and no one stands out. By this point, one wake bleeds into the next. I've been waked out. It's the funeral on Tuesday morning at ten o'clock that I recall, and that only sparsely. The family takes up most of the seating in the black Baptist Church, or rather, the Christian Calvary Baptist Church, which is mostly black, not to be confused with the First Baptist Church, which is entirely white, or with Crusaders on horseback charging up San Juan Hill, which is likely Cavalry, on East Hockomock between the lakes. We are Catholic, and the liturgy is unfamiliar. There's a nervous silence at the end of the Lord's Prayer when Reverend Jake and his black congregants, several of whom stand in the vestibule to make room for the mourners, continue speaking after we've stumbled over the Amen, a strange echo of words we haven't said. A few of us pick up the cue and echo the echo. Most don't.

The assemblage is not entirely colored. Sparky Manx is there, of course, and Acting Fire Chief Biff Larsen who's wasted no time making himself heir apparent to Chief Dobbs's position. Nigel Brate's sporting a black eye. MakeLoveNotWar is there with Chief Crockett, also a big group from the racquetball club and the high school. Bill Corr is there. Town Hall is largely absent. So too the Athletic Association. In the far back row, Petrified Wood and Tyler McVeigh sit together in a shaft of sunlight. Tyler gives me an angel eye when I turn around. PT Wood looks haunted. The glint of gold shimmers off his tie.

There's no recording of Reverend Jake's eulogy, no notes or transcript for me to quote. I remember it being disjointed. He talks about friendship, love of friends, love of family. He asks who would exchange intensity of living for longevity? He says we should stand up for one another. Does he use the words "protect one another," or is that memory rewriting history? I don't know then what I surmise later. I'm groping in the dark. We all are, or most of us are. I'm sitting beside Georgina. She's being brave. It seems to me that Reverend Jake is talking specifically to her and that every time she reaches the verge of tears he changes the subject again. There's something about respecting our heritage, remembering our past but not letting it burden us. I think about End Zone Island and Indian Cove and Wampanoags making a last stand among the cedars, or something like that. I sit on a rock and watch two white boys splashing each other among the pillars and posts of charred tree trunks. There's also sun and autumn maple etched in stained glass, although the Black Baptist Church doesn't have any stained glass.

Does Reverend Jake have ancestors who made a last stand and died on End Zone Island? Are their bodies in the peat? I should look up his birth certificate. It might be interesting. Unfortunately, he wasn't born here. Plymouth, maybe, or Lakeville. (Miss Edith Ottick would sniff her disapproval.) As I said, the words from the pulpit don't seem to flow. I think Reverend Jake is too close to his subject to be eloquent. He cries at one point. I do remember that. Or maybe it's just me. My head's not in a good place and I can't seem to hold onto a thought. Any thought.

I do remember thinking that his regular parishioners are proud of their pastor. Clearly they love and respect him. After the service they serve a collation in the church basement [17] and we all go down and eat cucumber sandwiches and drink a lot of coffee, while they praise his eulogy to the heavens. Doesn't Reverend Jake give the most beautiful eulogies? He's such a caring man. Miss Makepeace circulates and lives up to her name while Chief Crockett politics and gets everyone nervous. People think he's casing the joint for suspects. He comments on PT's gold chain. PT pales. Tyler tries to smooth maneuver me aside but I'm busy with the aunties, and he has to leave, get back to class, whatever class is at his weirdo school. How to survive on fifty calories a day? I invite him to dinner Saturday night, tell him I'll cook. What does he like? He likes everything not ham-pork-bacon. He looks happy, hungry, grateful as he goes.

---

17 Collation being a fancy word we Catholics have never heard. In this case, it means food.

PT Wood drifts in the background, alone and hangdog miserable. Or maybe the suit jacket and tie make him appear so. I think I'm missing the wolf moon sweater. I have issues.

By noon, people are leaving. The extended family climbs into cars, Jeeps, pickups, and we all go back to Aunt Flora's house. Arianna rides with her grandfather.

PT follows, unseen, on his bicycle.

Aunt Flora's been dead eight years but the house remains Aunt Flora's house. She and Uncle Manny bought this place a year after marriage, and she used Uncle Manny's income and forbearance to make over this bungalow, once a summer cottage on the lake, now winterized for year-round, in her own image. The knotty pine cabinets in the kitchen are of her choosing. She's picked out the Formica countertops and the copper-bottomed pots and pans. The absence of all things cranberry speaks her bog Creole. The over-stuffed sofa in the living room is hers, and the comfy arm chairs and antimacassars, end tables and lamps with fringed shades, the framed Currier-and-Ives prints of horse-drawn sleighs on the wall, the banjo clock on the mantel above the wood stove, all these things say, 'Aunt Flora, with love.' She loved them, she left them. The four people who've remained since her passing have done little to re-make this house in their own image. Uncle Manny is comfortable with his late wife's furnishings. He has no desire to re-paper walls or change the curtains. Georgina's too busy being young and attractive to bother replacing furniture or the threadbare Oriental rug under the dining room table. True, Arianna's bedroom has transformed with her from rainbow-tailed ponies to teenage boy bands, but none of the Bay City Rollers posters or ruffled pillows migrate beyond her walls, and Uncle Anthony's confined himself to his underworld for years, refusing to meddle with the artifacts of his mother's life above ground.

In other words, Aunt Flora's house is comfortable in its familiarity, and I always feel good in Aunt Flora's house, whatever storms rock the outside world. Today, I feel comfortable and not.

The house is packed tight with close friends and family, family from the street, family from every day, and family we see only at weddings and funerals. The living room is crowded with uncles. Four of them are stuffed on the sofa, commiserating in their Budweisers. Others are perched on the arms of settees. Uncle Manny has place of honor in his frayed wingchair by the window. Reverend Jake is admiring the banjo clock. He says reverse glass painting is new to him.

The kitchen is full of aunties, eight of them: four big and bosomy, two stringy and critical. Aunt Rose is fashionable in an ensemble she's sewed herself for the occasion, and she has flawless skin. Ancient Aunt Elvira is tiny and garbed in the widows' weeds she's made her signature piece for thirty years, give or take a century. Several nieces cater to the aunties, their mothers, who expect nothing less. Georgina's at the stove, taking directions, suggestions, hints from everyone at once. Two women I don't know flank her, working on a big pot of *canja*, the chicken-tomato stew every funeral's required to serve on pain of death. I can smell the garlic and bay leaves from the hallway. The two stringy aunts voice their disapproval of the garlic powder which in no way can be said to adequately substitute for fresh garlic. Shortcuts! That's the trouble with people today. Everyone's moving too fast and taking shortcuts. It isn't healthy.

Arianna is carrying plates of chips and salsa to the dining room table. A female cousin I haven't seen since Aunt Flora's funeral assists but mostly manages to get in the way.

I don't want to get in the way. I free myself from Ma's insistence on hugging every aunt and being hugged, or groped, by every uncle, and hang out near the front door where I can see who's coming in, going out, and I obsess on everyone's skin color. Darker than me? Lighter than me? White? Black? Portuguese? Do their birth certificates, marriage certificates pretend to any kind of reality? What is race and why does it matter?

Uncle Manny is white. Is his brother Christian white? His sister Camila? Why is Arianna white and not me? And aren't I too proud to pass myself off as something I'm not, and have no desire to be? Do we have any choice in the matter of identity?

Arbitrary!

Race is so arbitrary. I foolishly believed the world ran on some kind of logic, that life was rational. The world has betrayed me. Life has slapped me upside-the-head. One night of Town Meeting and suddenly nothing is clear anymore. Nothing is secure.

Then PT Wood comes in, and an unwelcome, fleeting thought tells me maybe some things can be counted on.

White boys!

...milk, wolves, vinyl moons, baby shampoo...

We share hard evidence. We harbor suspicions. We are complicit, except we 're not sure complicit in what. It strikes me that Petrified Wood has no friends. He travels alone or hangs with grownups. He's a kid adrift in the universe, looking for a lifeline to a passing space ship. Uncle Anthony was that lifeline and Uncle Anthony's ship is gone. I'm in no mood to throw him a line.

"What are you doing here?" I ask, heartlessly, then adjust his tie, which has tangled in the gold chain. The gold chain makes me uneasy. I touch it with reluctance. I see Uncle Anthony's eyes as I do.

"I'm here for Arianna," he says. "And if I go home my mother will make me finish off the day at school."

"I don't know it's such a good idea you being here."

"Isn't Sparky here?"

As if that excuses his presence.

And, yes, Sparky is here. She's mingling with the aunties in the kitchen like she's family. But then, isn't she like family to half the people in South Quagmire? Even the aunties from Fall River who don't know squat about this town know that Sparky Manx was close to Uncle Anthony, surrogate mother practically, though there's not more than eight years between them. Sparky belongs to everyone, everywhere, or maybe it's the reverse. Everyone belongs to Sparky.

There are people to whom race doesn't matter, and Sparky is those people.

Anyway, PT Wood is staring at me with that hangdog, haunted expression, begging to be taken in. Any plea in a storm.

"Well, go find Sparky then," I snap, "but leave Arianna alone. She's got enough to deal with and you're not hanging around with me."

Sparky finds us instead.

"What are you two doing, hanging out in doorways?" She looks sternly at PT. "Not planning to sneak off and smoke, are you, Woody?"

"No, no," he stutters. He almost bolts but I've still got him by the tie which I drop, embarrassed. I get the strong vibe Sparky came to find us, find him. She definitely looks at him funny, as if she's sizing him up. Then she gives a little shrug and a sniff.

"Well, make yourself useful," she says to me, but somehow she's including PT in the deal. "Go downstairs and find your uncle's boombox and bring it up here. We need music."

I'm not clear the uncles and aunties are into *Herb Alpert and the Tijuana Brass*, Uncle Anthony's favorite music, but maybe he has other cassettes downstairs I can rifle, or there may be an easy listening channel on the radio, so I grunt my agreement, and head for the basement door which is in the hallway by the stairs.

PT Wood follows.

"Where are you going?" I ask.

"I've never seen where he lives."

He loosens his tie. His face does look a little pink, like maybe I tried subconsciously to strangle him.

'Where he lives.' Present tense. Life hangs in the present tense. Living is now. It strikes me that, well, yes, eight years later Aunt Flora lives on in this house. Her house, still her house, present tense, as if she's just stepped out to the store and will return any minute. Will Uncle Anthony be waiting in the basement, his basement, living on years after he's gone? Gone for a shift at Brate's packy, or making an ambulance run, be back shortly? We excuse our way through relatives who check out PT Wood in passing as if he's some strange animal in a zoo, maybe because he's taller than anyone else in the house, except possibly Reverend Jake. They make way for me and the giraffe (the giraffe keeps mumbling, "'Scuse me, 'scuse me") and we descend to the basement, Uncle Anthony's domain. I can almost hear the low grunting sounds of bench-press as I descend carefully in the dark.

The light switch at the bottom of the stairs illuminates an underworld immaculate to the borders of sanity. Combination bedroom / weight room / work space / man cave, the basement is an environmental amplification of his obsessive-compulsive bid for perfection. Uncle Anthony regards this space as an extension of his body and keeps it pristine. Whatever his physique represents, his living quarters represent that and more. They're crowded to bursting, but the bursting is organized past the edge of geometric. Everything is plumb, square, laid out in neat, corrugated lines and tight corners. His bed is at right angles to the wall, weight bench perpendicular to the bed, weights stacked symmetrically in ascending pyramids of diminishing kilograms. A wooden wardrobe fits snugly under the stairs. A shiny upright vacuum cleaner stands sentinel beside it, exactly where it belongs. The long wall that fronts the house is a continuous work counter of Formica polished to luster, with shelving and cabinets above and below, television and Betamax tape player housed neatly in a well-proportioned, homemade console dead center, the throw rug made by Aunt Rose (for a wedding that never happened) equidistant between screen and La-Z Boy facing. Above his tool bench every tool hangs vertical or horizontal in clearly defined, muscular precision on linear racks, hooks, sockets, and straps. Nothing is out of place. Everything is as he left it.

He's here. I feel him. Uncle Anthony has not yet passed into past tense.

PT Wood comes down the last couple of steps, stops, says nothing, but is clearly overwhelmed. I watch his face for a reaction, am pleased that he's, what, surprised, impressed? Unless you've spent time down here with my uncle and Arianna, you can't imagine so much could be crammed into limited space with such intensity of purpose. It doesn't jibe with the dude lounging bare-chested out-side the fire station, soaking sun and coffee, warming friends with the radiance of his smile, the depth of soul in those black eyes, the magnetism of his personality and pectorals. Although nothing PT could reasonably expect of his hero, this room is a true manifesta-tion of Uncle Anthony, his inner sanctum turned outward, the holy revealed in hardware, a bitter struggle prying order out of chaos, abs from flab, life on the verge of something terrible. The white boy's trying to take it all in, too surprised to speak. He stands beside Aunt Rose's throw rug and studies the greenery she's stitched into the fab-ric, foliage from Sao Vincente, our family's origin island. I go over to the cubby beside my uncle's bed and remove the boombox from its nest. People used to carry these big, black plastic-housings of knobs and dials and antennae around on their shoulders when they wanted to keep the world at bay with their music. I bring it over to the counter and, so doing, feel a profound sadness, or maybe anger, rising inside me for, or maybe against, Uncle Anthony. I have no personal interest in his combination radio/ tape recorder, but in his space with his thing, I feel his absence suddenly and sharply. I want to crouch, squeeze knees to chest, tuck myself into Small Package Apocalypse, feel safe again.

I want to go prenatal.

I resist.

Black eyes watch me from the shadows.

'Where's he keep his tapes?' I ask myself and remember the drawer beneath the cubby. I think that's where I'll find Herb Alpert lurking, better yet, something a little less sombrero. But the corner's dark, and while I'm on my knees, fending off his gaze, trying to read the bindings on the plastic cases, PT finishes the rug and goes to the counter. He spends a minute eyeing soldering irons and spools of copper wire. Then he pops open the cassette recorder. He takes out a tape. My back is to him. I hear him grunt.

"Huh."

There's nothing in the drawer that's hitting me as appropriate for upstairs. We may have to opt for the radio. I get up, come back his way. The eyes follow.

"Nothing," I say. "The aunties aren't *Beatles* fans. What's that?"

He's staring at the cassette. He looks at me.

"Tara Drummond," he reads off the label. *'The Star-Spangled Banner.'*

My eyes narrow and pop at the same time. I swear I feel Uncle Anthony's do the same.

"What?"

"This is what he had in the recorder."

I don't say anything, but my mind is moving, and he sees my concern.

"No," he says, "it doesn't mean anything. Not necessarily. My mother has one of these. Half the town does. They were selling them a couple years ago to raise money for tennis courts. It was some fund-raising thing."

He hands me the cassette. I take it, not because I want to, but because I must. The label is hand printed: *Tara Drummond sings 'The Star-Spangled Banner,' 1974.*

"I don't like this."

"What's not to like?" he asks. "She has a beautiful singing voice. Mom plays it, then the Jimi Hendrix version. I think her version's nicer. Haven't heard her do it live, but when she hits that high note, it's, like, effortless. She nails it, and then she jumps, like, four notes above what she has to, and nails that too. Pure pitch. She should sing it before the Super Bowl."

Even as he babbles, I can tell he's uneasy. He's talking one thing, thinking something else. This is not right. Why would the last thing Uncle Anthony listened to on his boombox be Tara Drummond singing the national anthem? The police were down here Thursday, checking the place out. Georgina says Lieutenant Watson and some guy from the BCI spent a good hour poking around, didn't find anything. His stuff looks untouched. It doesn't seem they disturbed anything. Couldn't bring themselves to sully perfection. Did they check his boombox? See this tape? I'm thinking not.

There's not much tape in the cassette. It looks like this may be a one-track knock-off. I put the cassette back in the recorder, close the little plastic door, press Play. I heard her sing at the March Town Meeting. It was fine. She didn't blow me out of the water or any-thing. She did go high, I guess. I wasn't feeling patriotic that night.

A few seconds of white noise, then she begins. 'O, say can you see by the dawn's early light...'

She starts soft and sweet. Doesn't belt it out. She caresses the words. Different.

PT Wood and I exchange glances. Neither of us hums along. We're listening to a woman who last week lost a husband, whose position I've been filling since.

'Whose broad stripes and bright stars through the perilous fight...'

She does have a nice voice, actually. She's easy listening. I'm not a big fan of the song, but she's doing all right, not over-selling it like lots of the professionals do. Not like a former cheerleader would do.

Kind of pretty and self-effacing. Uncertain, maybe? Like the question itself? Can we see? Can we? Do we even want to?

She starts climbing o'er the ramparts.

'And the rockets' red glare...'

Still not belting. Still not calling attention to herself. She's offering up America gently, without striving, without the strident jingoism. The way the hippo, Thomasine Épée, went at her at Town Meeting, mocking her, mocking us as willing participants feeding into her greed for glory, I would have guessed Tara Drummond was a show-boater, which doesn't go with the woman I intern for at Town Hall, mousy and gray and definitely not an attention-seeker. Thomasine Épée is a foul creature. She almost got what she deserved. What does Tara Drummond deserve?

And here it comes. The question hanging ever in the air:

'O, say does that star-spangled banner yet wave...'

The dip before the soar. A poem, and not a battle cry.

'O'er the land of the free..."

And she does this thing, which PT will explain to me later, because I'm not particularly musical, don't pay much attention to these things. She hits a high F, then jumps, no, floats above it to a B flat. I don't know what I'm talking about here, although PT shows me on a piano at school. The thing is, he's right. She does it effortlessly.

And as she hits the note, we hear a strange ping or, maybe, buzz somewhere on the shelves, almost like the little ringing sound a typewriter makes when it comes to the end of a line.

Just a buzz.

Or a hum.

And she finishes the song, no fuss, no flourish, doesn't hold the 'brave' too long.

Another few seconds of silence and the tape stops.

PT Wood looks at me.

"Did you hear that?"

"Yeah."

"What was it, do you know?"

"No clue."

But we are both noticeably shaken. Tim Drummond dropped dead with a pack of Marlboros in his pocket. Tubby Dawes stormed out of the meeting and got run over by the ambulance. Thomasine Épée went to the bathroom and had a near miss with an exploding toilet (Carmen Selsby was not so lucky). Tara Drummond did *not* sing the national anthem.

"Play it again," he says.

I rewind the tape and we play it again. At 'free', we hear the hum again. I hit Stop. The humming doesn't stop abruptly but fades. We look around, at each other. I hit Rewind for a couple of seconds, hit Play. Again, the 'free', and again the hum. This time we're ready for it though. To the right of the television screen on a shelf stands a U-shaped metal bar humming with the B flat, continuing the note after the note has stopped on the cassette. PT Wood lifts it carefully from its perch. The note fades out. He studies it.

"Tuning fork," he says. "B flat." He shows me the symbol for B flat stamped on the handle in case I might be interested, which I'm not.

"Why's it doing that?" I ask.

"It's picking up the vibrations. Resonating. You can get a guitar string to do this with a piano."

He strikes it against the counter top. It rings again, the same note. The note fades. He hits it again. This time he touches the handle to the counter. The note is louder and lasts a little longer. Then he gets an idea.

"That's weird. Does he have any more of these?"

We look around and find none, but then, if Uncle Anthony had several tuning forks, they'd all be in the same place, arranged neatly by tone.

"What's weird?"

For a minute there I was spooked. I'm not sure what I am now.

"There are tuning forks for every note," he says. "Why does he only have a B flat? Mrs. Lewis told us once people mostly use a tuning fork that's an A, because that's a string on the violin. I don't think you'd just have a B flat hanging around."

"Don't look at me." I shake my head. I think I remember Mrs. Lewis saying something about tuning forks way back in elementary music class. Or am I making that up? I do remember her hitting one against the blackboard before we started singing 'Row, Row, Row Your Boat' once upon a time. Do they have any use besides getting a bunch of tone-deaf kids to howl on key?

"Calibrating things, I think," says PT Wood, "but I don't know much about it."

He glances around at all Uncle Anthony's 'things.' The room holds too many 'things' to take in. He takes things a step farther than I like.

"But there's no motive," he says. He's already made the leap. "I mean, why? And Little Anth... I mean, your uncle practically 'worshiped' Chief Dobbs."

"What are you talking about?" I growl, but I'm being disingenuous. I know what he's talking about. I just don't want to go there. "What's Chief Dobbs got to do with the national anthem?"

"When she hit the high note…"

"Screw the high note," I say. "This is stupid. Put it back."

He puts the tuning fork back in place exactly as he found it.

TouchDown Realty.

Four members marked for…

No.

No.

No, I will not go there. I hit Eject, remove the cassette. PT grabs it from me.

"It has our finger prints on it."

Our fingerprints??? I toss him a look of disgust Thomasine Épée could not deliver to better effect. He ignores me, stuffs the tape in his pants' pocket. His pants aren't tight this time. Gray wool slacks, a little high at the ankle, not too flood. I refuse to discuss his pants or his suppositions. I pick up the boombox and head for the stairs. I don't look back. I turn off the lights as I go by the switch and leave him to grope in the dark, leave him with Uncle Anthony's eyes.

In the living room, a white face stands out amidst the company. Everybody's favorite biology teacher Bill Corr has come from school. He's on one side of Georgina. Reverend Jake is on the other. They're of a height, they're of a weight. It could be fun. But they are both too much the gentlemen to do anything remotely entertaining, so they spend a few minutes trying not to get caught looking at each other, and then Bill Corr leaves. Reverend Jake wins the round. No race wars today.

Meanwhile, Sparky Manx finds a radio station that's not obtrusive and soon music without words is playing lamely in the background. She tells Woody it would probably be best if he went home now. If he needs someone to talk to, she'll be at the station and please don't hesitate. She knows how much Uncle Anthony meant to him. She puts an arm around his waist and escorts him to the door. He takes off his tie, stuffs it in the same pocket as the thing he and I would rather not know exists, and bikes home. When I pass him in the corridor at school next day, he's with Birnam and pretends not to see me.

Life is not rational.

It has betrayed us both.

ARTICLE 11

ALL TALK, NO ACTION in relation thereto

How did Charles Dickens do it? How does a person sit down with nothing but pen and paper and write volume after volume of classic literature while I can't string two sentences together using a computer and keyboard without getting a headache? Did his words flow like ink? He didn't use a feather, did he? Dear God, tell me he didn't use a feather! I dredge up memories that haven't seen daylight in thirty years. What did he say? What did I say? Did I really say that? Should I change it up a little so as not to embarrass myself? That slop I wrote in high school about star-crossed lovers and how they overcome racial prejudice only gets me so far. I wasn't entirely realistic in my writing back then, and I'm trying to be truthful now. I word process. I proofread and word process some more. I agonize. I'm awake half the night, struggling over sentence structure. I copy and paste, then I second guess, delete, re-type, insert, refer to an on-line thesaurus, find and replace. I had no idea choosing the right word could be so hard. I'm lucky if I make it through two pages a day (of course, I have other duties in the Town Clerk's office, and this story cannot be written wholly on the taxpayers' dime). I even get to take most of this from transcripts and newspaper articles, while he was pulling stories out of his own imagination. I never appreciated how much head-banging goes into writing a book. April Fool's Day, 2008, and I'm not close to done.

Am I?

I still think about that tuning fork and the B flat and wonder who was right, PT or me? Considering how things played out, he must have had a change of heart.

I still think about Number Forty-One, Tyler McVeigh and how things might have turned out differently if not for a joke we had going about women's liberation and burning bras. You can tell Birnam. He doesn't get bothered by that kind of thing.

Number Forty-One, Tyler McVeigh, does not come to dinner the following Saturday. A letter arrives in the mail on Thursday, speedy delivery for Jasper Lovell, sixteen-year-old illiterate learner's permit-only mailman. I can quote from it because I still have it. I am more sentimental than people give me credit for. It reads:

Dear Karen,

I am sorry I cannot come to dinner on Saturday as I have been marked AWOL (that's Away With Out Leave) for attending the funeral, and now I have two weeks of KP (that's Kitchen Patrol) as punishment. Please forgive me, and if you would like to write me a letter, I would very much appreciate it. I miss you and will see you in two weeks.

Yours very sincerely,
Number Forty-One, Tyler McVeigh

Naturally, I have no intention of writing him a letter, but then I relent, or better, compromise, and I make him a Halloween card in senior math with a chainsaw attacking a pumpkin. I don't exactly know what a chainsaw looks like, but I give it my best shot. It ends up a little like shark teeth on a machine gun. I put it in the mail next day and hope it will reach him before the end of the month, three weeks away, although you can't expect miracles, or Jasper Lovell, to strike twice.

That morning Petrified Wood hunts me down and asks, "When can we talk?"

"How about never?"

His wounded deer expression tells me I've cut him to the quick or at least poked a ventricle. He stalks away, then chases me down after lunch and says, "We've got to talk."

I know we do. I just don't want him to get the upper hand. One, he's only a junior, and juniors don't have the right to stiff a senior in the corridor by pretending not to see her. Two, he's a male, and much bigger than me, and white. And Three, I'm starting to respect him, and I don't want this relationship to go any farther than respect. He's already come up short with Arianna, screwed up big time, he and his hippie-dippy family and their small-town bigotry. I don't intend to make the same mistake she did.

Anyway, I have Number Forty-One, Tyler McVeigh, don't I?

PT Wood says, "I got a letter from Tyler McVeigh."

"What?"

He pulls it from his jeans' pocket, starts reading aloud: "Dear Woodrow—"

"Don't."

"He's on punishment for skipping school to go the funeral and he's missing us. I wrote him a letter back. He'll see us in a couple weeks, he says, when he's off punishment."

And just like that, without even trying, he's landed a perfect stomach punch. I feel my guts contract. Tyler asks me to write and I send him a stupid drawing, don't even color the pumpkin orange. PT Wood writes him a letter.

My attitude is not helping my cause, whatever cause that may be.

"I can give you his address," he says, stuffing it back in his pocket agreeably. "He'd probably like to hear from you. I think he's lonely."

Stonewall.

Admit nothing.

I lift my books in front of my chest to ward off further blows. Not as effective as Kevlar or body armor, but I have no other defense at hand.

"Yeah, whatever," I say. "How can he be lonely, all those people around him?"

"True, but they're all guys, you're a girl. And no one writes him letters. You do know he's an orphan, right?"

Oh, dear God! Shades of Oliver Twisted. Even without much knowledge of Dickens... we read *Tale of Two Cities* sophomore year, we're in *Great Expectations* now... I can see where this is leading. One of these two white boys is *Oliver!* and one's the Artful Dodger. Who's leading whom? And the only female in that movie ends up bludgeoned by her boyfriend.

Me and a snapping turtle, dead meat. And a newt.

I can hear Ma warning, 'Don't engage.'

"I mean," he continues, "he has a mother, but she lives in another state, and he almost killed his brother, so he doesn't go home except some holidays, and it's all pretty bad. He writes letters… they all do… but no one writes him, so it's like he's an orphan. Abandoned practically by his family, so it's like he's looking to find a family, and maybe he's got General Tarry as a kinda father figure, you know, and sort of a hundred and twenty brothers, but I think he's looking for someplace to belong and he likes our town and would like someone to make him welcome here, and maybe that could be you and me."

"This is why we need to talk?"

"Well, no, I mean, yeah, that too, but it's really about your uncle and the cigarettes… and the national anthem."

We meet after school in the music room. The marching band is out in the parking lot practicing for this weekend's football halftime, and we have the place to ourselves. Double room, sound-proofed, the sense of one big echo denied utterance. The blackboards are chalked with lines and arrows and dashes that suggest football plays but are evidently diagrams: trumpets go left, trombones break right, and the drill team will fake, split, and score. Bulletin boards are pinned with sheet music and love notes. I see notices for a bake sale and *My Fair Lady* tryouts. Someone's posted directions to a party. Band geeks may be more normal than I thought.

He's in shorts and a sleeveless T-shirt from afternoon gym class and his face is red but he doesn't smell sweaty. He has nice round shoulders. He could be a football player. Funny thing. He could almost be—

"Chief Dobbs…" PT leans in. "Chief Dobbs was an accident, I'm telling you. It wasn't intentional. Your uncle didn't mean to kill him," he says without introduction. "I mean, what motive did he have? None." I evade, read love notes: to Joey with Xs and Os doing something on a G clef; to Julia, Friday night at the mall(?), bring your sister; Yo, Ludwig, thanks for the sheet music, and he follows me, perturbed. "I never told you, but the night before Uncle Anthony died…?" *Uncle Anthony?* When did that happen? "Miss Makepeace brought us coffee. She was really supportive. She didn't blame him, I mean, running over Chief Dobbs, everyone knew it was an accident. Everyone knows he admired him. Knows how he looked up to him. I spent enough time at the station to know that. You saw how hard he was crying." A big pink arm comes out in front of my face and a pink hand leans into the bulletin board, stopping forward motion. I have to duck to get under it and keep avoiding. "That was real. And Miss Makepeace said Mr. Drummond's heart attack, it happens, and no one knows for sure what happened in the bathroom. She was on his side. She really likes Uncle Anthony. Everyone does. Sparky will tell you. So, I mean, if Mrs. Drummond had been killed singing the national anthem, like, seconds after her husband died, or if he died, like, somehow just when she hit the B flat, I mean, everyone would know something was up and they'd have postponed Town Meeting and everything. I mean, it doesn't make any sense. Would you just look at me when I'm talking?"

I give up my aimless perambulation through the hearts and flowers. I lean back against the bulletin board and look at him. His cheeks are rosy. His eyes are wide and, interestingly, wet. The hair under his armpit's blonde. He smells nice, clean. He's showered at least.

"He couldn't kill everyone in TouchDown Realty when Mr. and Mrs. Drummond start everything off and everyone would freak if they died within minutes of each other. Chief Dobbs wouldn't have stormed out and Mrs. Épée would never have made it to the bath-room and some teacher would get blown up next day instead and for what? You think maybe he left that tape in his boombox for us to find? Like, a message?"

At which point, making even less sense, he insists on digressing at the piano with a lesson on the high B flat over F that only Tara Drummond is supposedly able to reach, and the tuning fork which could be linked somehow to the metal thing in the cigarette pack and Tim Drummond's pacemaker. He sits on the piano bench, pok-ing keys and babbling. I stand, restless, go along for the ride, and don't argue. He's already sucker punched me with Tyler McVeigh. I'm not sure my head's on straight. He definitely ruined a whole senior math class thanks to his Goody-Two-Shoes Mother Theresa Sure-I'll-Write-You-a-Letter bit. But here's what I do know:

There's a funny metal device in a pack of cigarettes, and Uncle Anthony worked at Brate's packy selling cigarettes.

His wallet is missing, and PT Wood knew it, lied about it.

He was doing something with Tara Drummond's rendition of 'The Star-Spangled Banner' and a tuning fork.

He's killed himself.

All of these things might be random, unconnected, chance. Well, not the thing in the cigarette pack, that was pretty deliber-ate, showed purpose aforethought, and Uncle Anthony's suicide, which didn't come out of nowhere, which suggests these things cannot be coincidental. The death of two, almost three members of TD Realty, in the space of an hour-and-a-half cannot be coinciden-tal. And Uncle Anthony, Little Tony D, another TD. That can't be a coincidence. And why was I out in the swamp with two white boys looking for a "flaming, flying dead thing" that Tyler says may not be a coincidence either? Uncle Anthony's at the center of all this, I can feel it, but I'm not ready to verbalize. Putting it into words will make it too real. And we have to protect Arianna.

In the end we're no closer to an explanation than when we started. He's got me against the wall, his big hand palming the bulletin board behind my head, pink-blonde forearm at my cheek, and he's leaning in close, trying to drive home some obscure point, when the marching band comes straggling in to put away their instruments. They look at us funny. This is not our space. We are not what the love notes had in mind. We've been compromised.

I squirm my way from under his intensity, grab my books, and leave. I pass him going home on his bicycle. I almost don't stop, but conscience is quirky, so I have to pull over and wait for him to catch up and offer him a ride. We stash his bike in my trunk.

He slumps in the passenger seat and doesn't speak. He has nice shoulders. Plump pink football shoulders. Rosy cheeks, damp. And the Old Spice.

Unsettling.

It's my mother who points it out to me. "That boy," she says, "who came back to the house after the funeral. That boy you went down in the basement with?"

"What about him?" I ask, defensively.

"Don't get defensive," she says. "It was just your Aunt Rose mentioned he looked a little like Chief Dobbs when he was a kid, and once she said it, I could see the resemblance. He's big, and the blue-eyes, blonde hair. The shoulders. Don't get me wrong. It's no more than coincidence. He doesn't play football, does he?"

"No," I assure her. I almost laugh. Petrified Wood playing football? Boy, wouldn't that make his ducks squawk. "What are you trying to say?"

"I don't know I'm trying to say anything. Just what Aunt Rose noticed, and I saw it too when she said it. Isn't that the boy asked Arianna to the dance? The one who hangs out at the fire station?"

"Yes." I draw the 'yes' out, hoping to draw her out with it. Aunt Rose isn't an aunt but a cousin, and she went to school with Chief Dobbs, didn't like him much. She's also very perceptive. If Aunt Rose sees something, there's something to see.

"He the one did the sit-in? Is that Anthony's gold chain?"

"Yes. Is there a point to this?"

"We haven't seen chains enough without we pass 'em around?"

"Ma!"

"But of course, he's white, he wouldn't understand."

"We're Cape Verdean, Ma."

"Just be careful, that's all I'm saying."

"Ma!"

"Don't bite my head off. Just, if you're inviting him to dinner, I ought to know who it is I'm feeding."

"It's not him I invited to dinner."

"Who, then?" She winces. "Oh, no, not the boy at the wake with all the bullets."

"That's the one."

"I told you, No. I said, Don't engage." Her fingers crouch, ready to pounce. I still have the bruise. "That boy is no good."

"You don't even know him."

"I don't have to know him. Why do you think he's at that school?"

"The bullets are fake."

"What do I care the bullets are fake? That boy I wouldn't trust as far as I could throw him."

"Well, if you don't want to cook for him I'll take him to the diner."

"You will not take him to the diner. You'll bring him here and we'll see if I'm right."

"Ma, you're not gonna embarrass me?"

"When have I ever embarrassed you?"

The Wednesday following I'm on the evening shift at The Grub Pub when who strolls in but Number Forty-One, Tyler McVeigh.

"Miss me?" he asks. He's alone. His head's been shaved. He takes a corner booth some distance from the plate glass windows and yellow-checked curtains. He faces the door, alert for passing snipers. "Can't be too vigilant," he says and winks. Marge Botelho, who makes a mean meat loaf, gives me a surprised, or knowing, grin. She's our night manager, fifty-something, gray-hair tucked back in a net. Four children, all grown. None of them still in town. She's seen it all. She gets it all. Tyler orders the house special. His eyes follow me while I pass back and forth between kitchen and tables with orders. PT Wood comes in, sits down opposite Tyler. They start playing war games with the salt shakers and catsup bottles.

"I'll have what he's having," PT says when I come to the table to ask what he's doing here. "Ty says you invited him to supper Saturday. Can I come too?"

And then, nothing happens. Nothing related to Murder at Town Meeting, I mean. The investigation continues, one hears, there are rumors, speculation, whispered hunches about race and real estate that don't make it much past Hancock and East Hockomock, but no official word leaks. In small towns people talk. That doesn't mean we know what we're talking about. The police are mute. Sparky Manx is mum. PT and Tyler come for supper on Saturday, the first of several suppers we four share, all on our best behavior, careful to skirt the subject. It is bizarrely uncomfortable, but Tyler McVeigh is a completely charming psychopath, and even my mother is disarmed by his smile. "Maybe I was wrong," she admits when we clear the plates and meet at the sink. "Such nice teeth. Lucky he hasn't lost any to malnutrition. The other one—" She shakes her head, nods in the direction of the dining room. "Something funny there."

Tyler comes in and offers to wash dishes. My mother hands him a flowered apron. "KP I know," he says cheerfully, and goes heavy on the soap. Ma dries. He flirts, and she flirts back. I'm appalled. Parents are required by law to humiliate their children.

I go back to get the drink glasses. PT's studying the dining room like he's doing an appraisal. He doesn't offer to help but I hand him the salt and pepper shakers anyway. I eye the gold chain visible through open-necked polo and V-necked sweater vest. The gold

chain freaks me out, but the white boy inside it is becoming familiar. I'm starting to welcome the familiarity. He has a nice face, nothing that girls would swoon over, but nice. Comfortable. Good smile.
What does Mom mean, something funny there?

"You still have the thing?" I ask.

"Yes," he says. "Is that the Infant de Prague? I never understood
why they have the baby Jesus dressed like a girl."

Besides Wednesdays and Saturdays at the diner, I start taking
early dismissal from school on Thursdays and work at Town Hall,
filing old census forms. Miss Edith Ottick is seldom in attendance
although the piglet, Porky Doodles, no longer provides an excuse.
It's outgrown its welcome and returned to piggeries unknown or
unnamed at sister Kay's insistence. Kay's in negotiations with a new
real estate company to sell off a portion of the swamp, that's the
scuttlebutt anyway, the bogs and high ground around End Zone
Island, and spiteful Edie's throwing Wetlands Protection wrenches
in the machinery. Neither of them is getting enough Merlot. And the
Conservation Commission being stacked with conservationists, the
two surviving members, Woodchuck and Cher Wood, are shouting,
"Save the newts!" but as they've quietly turned several acres into
moonshine and marijuana production, not too loudly.

Mrs. Wood appears bi-weekly to turn in commission meeting
minutes. She regards me vaguely, smiles. If she recognizes my small
role in her son's life, she doesn't let on. She doesn't stop him coming
to dinner. I'm guessing he hasn't mentioned me to her, but I don't

ask. I smile vaguely and accept the minutes, scribbles torn from a sketch pad, as she says, "A shame about poor Mr. Drummond. So young, so young. Will Mrs. Drummond be back soon?"

She drifts away without waiting for an answer.

Tara Drummond will not be back soon. Our Town Clerk does not return to The Snake Pit. Nor does our Town Treasurer, Thomasine Épée, who is moved from hospital to rehabilitation facility in Lakeville. There's no word when she can resume her duties. General Tarry, meanwhile, is threatening to take out recall papers on Nigel Brate for sexually harassing the interim Town Clerk. He doesn't mean me.

Murder at Town Meeting sinks beneath the surface. I want to talk to Sparky Manx but I don't dare. We're withholding evidence, and I don't know what kind of trouble that could get us in if Sparky talks.

And Sparky talks.

PT gets a job working fall weekends with his father at "The Cranberry." At the height of the harvest Coastal Cranberries takes on extra workers to lug and load. Birnam is hired too and doesn't last a day. He's big enough that no one questions his age, but the overwhelming numbers of fresh berries packed into crates freak him out. He can't stop counting, and the crates hold too many to count. Woodchuck Wood brings him home, mumbling down from several thousand.

A failed experiment.

PT gets his learner's permit a couple of days before Halloween and I take him driving.

"Wait? What?" says my mother. "Not Tyler? Girl, you playing with fire, aren't you?"

Fire Wood, I think. There's an opportunity missed. Great name for a daughter someday.

PT's a good driver, but there's no status gained, me and a white nerd, him and a black bird. He does have a run-in with a mailbox (ours), shades of Jasper Lovell, our postal delinquent, who's hoping to trade his permit for a license (third times a charm) and all over the road. PT's a quick learner, despite a side mirror knocked loose backing out of the driveway. My cousin Joe Cabral works at Big Pauly Silvio's service station and re-attaches it for me, free of charge.

"Why don't you go out with Joe?" my mother asks. "He's a nice boy."

"Ma, he's my cousin."

"Third cousin. That's perfectly legal."

"He's pushing thirty! And he's missing a front tooth."

What Ma means is, Stick to your own kind.

But I refuse to *be* my own kind, or any kind but me. Not to mention, it's November, and I have senioritis. I'm liking the possibilities. Get me to high school graduation and then, look out! I will cut so loose I'll be unrecognizable. I will blow this little town and experience the world beyond its boggy borders. And who I take with me will be my choice, will meet no one's great expectations but my own.

I may have to flip a coin.

Wednesday nights and Saturday lunchtimes Tyler and PT are at the diner, making me wait on them. My own white boys' fan club, squandering their meager earnings on pub grub. They compete for my attention. That includes seeing who can leave the biggest tip which I do nothing to discourage. I'll be paying for college. They're free to subsidize. Marge Botelho makes fun of them to their faces. She's not bothered they're on the make for a bogscooper's daughter. They relish her wisecracks and rave about the meat loaf. Tyler talks ballistics and PT quotes musical theater. Sometimes he bursts into snatches of song. Tyler flirts and maneuvers the mustard and sugar packets into battle formation, blows up Brigadoon. I mop fake blood while they giggle.

(When PT gets his license in March, they'll bounce, squeal, and hug like schoolgirls.)

For Arianna's birthday Thanksgiving weekend, the four of us go out together to see the movie *Rocky,* about a small-time boxer in Philadelphia who fights a heavyweight champion and almost beats him. The champ is black, so no one roots for him.

It is not a double date, although I snark at PT beforehand, "Your mother's letting you go out with coloreds?"

"It wasn't my mother," he says cryptically, then hesitates to go on. He fingers the tiny winged figure on the gold chain.

"Who was it then?"

"Your uncle Anthony." He absently puts it in his mouth. I look at him aghast and, embarrassed, he spits it out. "That night in jail, he said it wasn't my parents, it was him didn't want me going out with Arianna. He said he was protecting me."

"Protecting you from what?"

But he doesn't know or says he doesn't. He gnaws at a hang nail. Maybe bullying? Maybe public comment? Did Uncle Anthony's nickname for him, Aryan Youth, raise a consciousness better left unacknowledged? Eventually I let it drop. I'm not ready to turn our whatever-relationship into a big discussion on race. It's nice just being whatever. Let's not spoil it yet.

Time enough for *yet* later.

In the dark theater I get pawned off on Tyler and his paws become exploratory and have to be put in their place. Later, when the two of us end up alone in my Ford Fairlane, I bring up Tourmaline Selsby. Embarrassing that a senior girl should be so bothered by a sophomore, but I can't let it go.

"I swear," he says, "nothing happened." His hands are on me again, and his mouth. "She's got nothin' but rolled-up toilet paper."

Well, that answers that question, doesn't it?

Which leads to a question he's had about women's liberation. Women's Lib. It keeps showing up in the newspapers. Specifically, he's heard about girls out there somewhere burning bras. Have I ever burned my bra to protest my objectification by males? Is he objectifying me? Do I mind being objectified? I have never burned a bra. Would I like to burn my bra? He likes strong women. He wouldn't object if I burned my bra. Do I like wearing bras? Are they comfortable? I like my bras. They offer support. But he finds them difficult to maneuver around. I have to do most of the heavy lifting. Next time can I just do without? Isn't that what Women's Lib is all about?

For a boy with absolutely no meat on him, he almost smothers me.

Come Christmas he visits the lingerie section in the JC Penney at the Taunton Mall and Women's Lib suffers a major setback. Fortunately, his present, a bare minimum of black lace, doesn't go under the tree or Ma would have a fit. He even gets the size right. I buy him good sun glasses and a book of movie passes. They're not cheap, but between Town Hall and the tips these boys are leaving at the diner, I'm doing all right. I'm returning their macho *largesse* in kind. Senior math suffers, but I can live with that.

Also, for Christmas, Police Chief Crockett gets his new cruiser, fully-loaded. I don't know what a 1976 fully-loaded police cruiser comes with, but he couldn't be happier, at least, that's the word at Town Hall. Makepeace gets the first ride. Is she objectified? She doesn't say. But she ends up with the handcuffs and next morning there's a little nip of something in our coffee.

We see *Rocky* again with the movie passes, the boys' decision, not ours. I'm hoping for *Carrie*, but it seems Tyler doesn't like scary movies. *Texas Chainsaw Massacre* gave him wicked nightmares. So we spend another evening with the Italian Stallion and his woman. In this less-than-pure form of democracy, the male vote outweighs the female. Afterward, Tyler runs around the empty parking lot, stripping off his shirt and shouting, "Yo, Arianna!" PT joins him. Even before the chain gets tangled in a button and almost chokes him, the contrast in body mass is striking. One's bone, one's flesh, both luminous beneath the halogen lights.

PT circles Arianna and me, says, "I could look like Rocky Balboa. Could you love me if I looked like Rocky Balboa?"

Yo, Arianna doesn't know how to respond to this. Aryan Youth? Italian Stallion? She's mortified. I'm amused. He attempts a kiss. I dodge, and he ends up bumping foreheads with Arianna, hard. Arianna retreats. As consolation Tyler gives his Woodrow a big, goofy smooch, then plants a professional one with tongue on me. Who's he been practicing on? When I come up for air, I am aware of Arianna at a distance watching PT watching me. Or PT watching Tyler? I should pull away. I plant both hands on Tyler's lank shoulders, start to push, and then don't. I go back in for seconds, it was that good. No one ends up kissing Arianna. She hangs back, a small, dark figure with a fist on the door handle. My cousin, my best friend is withdrawing from our world.

On the ride home, Arianna and PT uncomfortable in the back seat, she offers him Uncle Anthony's weight bench and weights. Maybe it's the unbuttoned shirt and not-insubstantial chest, maybe just a lame attempt at conversation, but the Sunday after Christmas we haul barbells and dumbbells from the basement and tie every-thing into the back of the military academy's Model A pickup. Thus begins the dismantling of Uncle Anthony. Thus begins the trans-formation of Petrified Wood. Thus begins the disappearance of Arianna DeBarros and the next act of Murder at Town Meeting.

I will miss Uncle Anthony. I will miss my cousin. I will miss PT.

I've moved beyond whatever for Aryan Youth wolf moon sweater white boy, but just when I start admitting it to myself, some-thing shifts and that boy's on his way to becoming someone else.

ARTICLE 12

BLACK ICE

Tuesday, January 11, 1977. 7:56 AM, end of first period. (Birnam pulled day and date out of thin air for me. I don't know how he does it. Freaky math recall.)

PT and Birnam come down the corridor, side by side. Birnam has grown since I saw him last which was probably back in October. He's taller than his brother, gained a couple of inches and more than a couple of pounds. He's big. He looks especially big this morning because he's wearing several layers of clothing. We're going on a field trip with Mr. Corr, he and I and one hundred-and-one other kids (not PT), and Birnam is dressed for a polar expedition. He's wearing the wolf moon sweater over everything, a hand-me-down that, in this case, is more like a hand-me-up. It's tighter on Birnam than it was on PT and riding high on his hips. The woolly wolves are stretched like greyhounds over bubble chest. They gaze gauntly at the white vinyl moon and howl their longing for the cold, wide wilds. Birnam is still a baby, but a freakishly large one. He looks like the Stay-Puff Marshmallow Man. This is not the beginning of some true romance. Not even close. But I do have to say, he dominates the corridor just by being in it. While PT and I make plans to see *King Kong* with Tyler, who's hoping it isn't too scary, Birnam counts floor tiles. Arianna's expressing doubts, but maybe we can talk her around by Saturday.

"Take care of Birnam," PT says as we part. "Don't let him fall through the ice."

The whole sophomore class and one senior class of advanced biology are loading two buses. We're heading for Little Quagmire Swamp, five minutes from school. (Birnam says, eight. About 1.4 miles.) We, Mr. Corr, and three sophomore teachers, math, Spanish, and Miss DeBarros, also two special needs aides, the school nurse, and four parents, are off to study biodiversity. We seniors are too cool to be excited, and this winter morning is well below cool, but breaking free from the classroom for a few hours is a pleasure, and Mr. Corr is always fun.

Biodiversity.

Miss Katherine Ottick wants to know if that's something like saludinity, or saltiness, or whatever-it-is. She has her faults, but she believes in education and is unperturbed letting one hundred-and-three high school students out on her bogs to get bitten by sharks. Biodiversity is a new concept and Mr. Corr is happy to explain.

When man turns the environment into lawns and crops, what is lost? What happens to the red-winged blackbirds, snapping turtles, and black-bottomed newts as we alter habitat for housing, golf courses, and cranberry bogs? In September Mr. Corr took us to Narragansett Bay where we made counts of invasive species in an estuary that drains our watershed. In October we learned we weren't the only creatures lost in a corn maze (we scared the shit out of a deer, literally!). And now we have, says Mr. Corr, a singular opportunity. For days after Christmas the temperature hovers around freezing before plunging into single digits, and Little Quagmire Swamp has a lot of black ice. It hasn't snowed since December 17 (thank you, Birnam) and the ice is bare. Our biology classes should take advantage of this meteorological singularity. It's not often you get to see so much black ice or, more specifically, what's underneath it.

Black ice isn't black. It's transparent, and the black is the water underneath, and everything that dwells therein. Normally ponds look white when frozen over, but ice isn't white either. That's the air bubbles trapped when the ice freezes so quickly air molecules have no chance to escape the surface. If the pond or flooded bog or irrigation reservoir freezes slowly, however, the bubbles rise and dissipate in the atmosphere and the ice becomes see-through. This also happens, he tells us, when there's heat generated under the water: low heat, heat from decomposing swans, bog bodies, and rotting mats of vegetation that produce methane and other poopy gases. Tendrils of black ice spread from decayed tree stumps in patterns imitating the veins of leaves, dark dendrites, and through the ice we'll be able to study and count life below. There won't be turtles, They'll be buried in the mud, hibernating. There may be fish, leeches, the plucky hydrophilid. There will be plant life. And after a week of near zero temperatures, the ice is thick.

Safe.

I have no intention of looking after Birnam.

We split into groups, each quartet armed with four meter-long pieces of white PVC pipe epoxied into a neat square. The sophomores are assigned partners because of their immaturity, but we twenty-two seniors get to pick our friends. My group is all female, three Cape Verdeans, one Filipino. Even here we self-segregate.

We lay our square of PVC on the black ice, get down on our hands and knees, and count the different species of life we see in that one square meter. (Birnam is in his glory.) We start on the cranberry bogs where we have transparency blooms in several places. We come up with nothing more than *Vaccinium macrocarpon*, the common cranberry, and fingers that grow numb fast when we take off our gloves to record data on clipboards (11 degrees Fahrenheit at 10:20 AM, Birnam Standard Time). One group hits pay dirt over an irrigation ditch where the weeds are thick, but they're an outlier and the irrigation ditch is cheating.

Next we hike into the woods along the narrow trail Tyler took PT and me in October. The slower pace allows us ample time to dodge low branches, and no one gets slapped in the face, except deliberately, by friends. We hypothesize there'll be more diversity where the land is untended, but there's not a lot. We count club mosses, lycopods, a dead fern, then cluck over the neighboring sophomores who are too silly to take the project seriously. They're grubbing dead leaves and twigs from outside the square and putting them in to boost their body count. They think life's a contest that someone wins.

So young, so foolish.

We hike further to the edge of the reservoir and venture onto the ice, white ice fractured into yawning crevasses of transparency. Some of us are nervous. I am nervous. Is it really safe? We can almost see our fear reflected in the black seams. Every charred tree poking from the ice has its own web of black ice reaching out from the base in slick, dark tentacles that probe, grope, hint of leech-y ends. This is not a world we're used to. It's disconcerting. Slippery. Like walking on glass. Toeing the void. But, a football field away, Nigel Brate's helicopter beckons. It's lying on its side, imprisoned in winter's grip. One rotor blade sticks skyward in Aryan salute.

The other's crumpled beneath the surface. While some of us debate whether or not Mr. Corr is out of his mind, he grabs Miss DeBarros and says, "Let's go take a closer look." The love birds start off across the ice toward the downed craft, underbelly exposed, a black insect partly encased in milky amber. Their enthusiasm is all it takes us to overcome hesitation, and a century of students braves its first hesitant step. The ice holds, not even a safety crack heard. I guess we're good. My friends giggle nervously, shiver, express reservations. It's cold. Are we crazy? My boots aren't waterproof. I should have worn Jimmy's mad bomber hat. Don't let go of my hand. If I go under, you're coming with me. The crowd fans out, though the majority weaves its way slowly in the direction of the 'copter. We're sticking with Mr. Corr. He's a teacher. He must know what he's doing. Besides, who wouldn't prefer an embalmed 'copter to a square meter's worth of muck? Birnam's group however has Birnam, and he will not be distracted from his task by mob mentality or enticed by aerial disaster. They separate from the pack and head toward End Zone Island.

Birnam's group has four students in it: besides Birnam, there's a conscientious, unassuming girl named Sue who carries the clipboard, and Krystal Tull and Jet Lovell, cigarette-rolling Rocks. Krystal's a pill and not much interested in today's activity. She's more concerned over the whereabouts of Tourmaline and Ruby and is only going easy on Turd Man because the special needs aide is hovering close by, eyes on Birnam, accustomed to his fragility, and besides, Krystal has Jet Lovell to drag around by his thick, black hair. That's how Jet got his name. He was born with a black mop on his head that so tickled his mother she decided against Skyler Byron and went for Jet Black instead. Jet Black Lovell. He's a tough guy, a wise ass. He could be trouble, but luckily for us his brother Jasper's not here today (suspended for smoking in the boys' room, and probably out on Bill Early's mail run, knocking down mailboxes) and, as it turns out, Jet's a decent student and likes Mr. Corr. He's also intrigued by black ice and hopes to see a fish swimming under his knees or, better, a great white shark. In 1976 I consider Jet Lovell, if I consider him at all, a hoodlum and a bully, but Jet, it turns out, will go to college, become an occupational therapist, quit smoking, raise a family, and turn out the All-American Husband and Father. He shows up in 1998 for South Quagmire's Sesquicentennial, its 150th birthday celebration, and greets Birnam and me like we're old friends. He's married a Haitian girl he met in college and has two lovely daughters. He and I partner in the water balloon-tossing contest and we both get soaked.

It's funny how names can define you. One time it's T.D. initials and you gain access to the coolest kids under Friday night lights and end up in real estate and dead. Another time, you're a Rock, and your parents never even planned it that way, just liked your hair color. Or your name is Birnam Wood and whenever Mr. Corr taps his chest and says, "Dunsinane," you come, a trained bear, Shakespeare's fatal forest on the move. It's a signal Mr. Corr has worked out with you when you're about to freak, and supposedly, about as effective as counting down from one hundred.

But for now, Dunsinane is checking out the 'copter with Georgina and a cohort of distractees, while Birnam and partners are far afield (or a-ice), seeking a likely spot to set down their square meter and look for life. The 'copter is cool, a prop from a war movie dumped in our own personal low-rent water park. One of the senior boys has actually crawled into the cabin and is lying on his side, making everyone laugh as he pretends to work the controls, doing a decent imitation of Nigel Brate in crash mode, minus the obscenities, when we hear a distant, high-pitched scream, the scream you hope never to hear in life.

Mr. Corr takes off at a run in the direction of the scream, and we follow like Thomasine Épée's lemmings, swarming after him over a frozen field of burnt trees and bruised hummocks, less concerned than intrigued as we skirt the island, heading toward Indian Cove. The scream holds more promise than a square meter of PVC. Let's hope it betokens funny, not fatal. I'm not much behind Mr. Corr, well ahead of Georgina, and the screaming gets louder as we approach the island. It doesn't let up. Krystal Tull is having a meltdown. She's a puffy pink wad of inflated bubble gum insulation clinging to Jet Lovell, wailing like a banshee, which it turns out is appropriate to the situation this once. A few feet away, submerged to his wolf pack, Birnam looks up from a gaping rent of splintered ice. The water's not deep. He's fallen backwards, bum first, broken through, and is sitting on the bottom. He's sunk in, but the situation hasn't, not yet. He's too cold to meltdown. He's leaving that to fashionably insulated Krystal Tull who's got hysteria covered. His eyes are glassy and his face drained of color. The aide is telling him to take her hand, although she's scared about her footing too. Evidently the ice isn't thick enough to support his weight, and maybe not hers. Mr. Corr shouts, "Dunsinane!" which triggers a response, and slowly Birnam begins to wallow, trying to work himself onto his knees. The math and Spanish teachers are herding everyone away, onto the island, onto solid ground. Time lurches. The world slips gears and drops into slow motion. I'm with Mr. Corr. I am my whatever's brother's keeper. For PT I grab at a tree trunk. One foot goes through and I almost lose my balance, but it hits the bottom, I catch myself, hold the tree with one hand and grab Birnam's hand with the other. Mr. Corr's in behind him and also through the ice. He gets him under the armpits. The aide joins us and together we haul.

Birnam doesn't know what's hit him, but now that we have him upright and barely knee deep, the screams of Krystal Tull shift time back into high gear. Georgina has the puffy pinkness sticky in her arms now, talking, reassuring, cooing. It's all right. It's all right. You're OK. We're OK. Everyone's OK.

Safe.

Birnam's safe. See? They've got him.

Safe? Bird Brain? What's this got to do with Bird Brain?

Krystal Tull breaks free of Miss DeBarros's embrace. It's not OK! It's not safe! Between gasps and shrieks, she lets everyone know it's not about Birnam, and it's horrible! Horrible! There's a body under the ice, a dead body, a bog monster, a face, a skull, a thing with big black eyeballs, or no eyeballs at all, looking up through the ice at her. It's right there! Right there! Inside the square meter of PVC. Don't look! No, don't look! I can't look! You have to look! Where's Tourmaline? She has to see this!

Jet Lovell says it's true. He's taken off his knitted Bruins' hat and his black hair stands on end.

Mr. Corr strips Birnam of sweater, fleece, flannel shirt, thermal underwear, T-shirt, all soaked, all scant degrees above hypothermic. Birnam doesn't protest, doesn't blubber. He's revealed for bare seconds in neon pink baby fat before Jet Lovell's pulling off his own hooded sweatshirt and Mr. Corr his ski jacket. We have trouble zipping Birnam up, he's so much bigger than his rescuers, but Birnam's drier from the waist up in under a minute.

The school nurse is on her walkie-talkie, calling the buses. "Hawkes Ave entrance," she's saying. "Drive in as far as you can."

Georgina drops to her knees and looks through the PVC square, through the ice. She stares. Her gaze is frozen to the surface like tongue to metal.

"OK," says the nurse, the image of calm, competent authority. "The buses are on their way. Let's get everybody back to the road. You, you, lead. That way."

She points. The students move. Jet Lovell finds Krystal Tull in his arms, to have and to hold, but he's having second thoughts about her hold on him. She deflates as he guides her away. Where's Tourmaline? Tourmaline needs to see what Krystal's found! No, wait, we've got to show Ruby. Does Ruby have her camera? Does anyone? It's horrible. Horrible. We've got to tell the newspapers.

The math and Spanish teachers gather PVC squares that have been dropped in the confusion.

"Good job, Birnam," says Mr. Corr. "Good job. We've got you. You're OK. We'll get you back to school, into dry clothes. Dunsinane, man. Dunsinane. It's all good. Lay on, MacDuff."

Our Stay-Puff Marshmallow Man, the fatal forest, shambles over the ice with difficulty and Dunsinane's help, managing not to break through again. It must have been the force of the fall, the impact when Krystal's screams flung him backwards in surprise, that broke the ice under him, because nowhere else does ice give way. Water sloshes from sodden pants and swollen boots as he trudges toward the road with his aide under one armpit, pretending to hold him steady. Mr. Corr looks back to Georgina. She's looking down through the one square meter.

I'm on my knees beside her. I can't believe my eyes. If only PT and Tyler were here now. They must have passed within feet of him.

It.

Him.

Georgina looks at me.

"You knew," I say. "You suspected. I mean— the plaque was—?"

She cuts me off without explaining. "We've gotta go. The buses."

"But—" My wet knees are already freezing to the ice. I have to twist and jimmy to free them. "We're skipping school. Tomorrow. We need something to mark the spot."

The sodden wolf moon sweater is lying abandoned on the ice. I grab the closest tree and tie the sweater around it, waist high. My fingers are so cold they can barely knot the sleeves.

We will come back. Not all the heavily armed inmates of the South Quagmire Military Academy can keep us away. Not the police, nor the county coroner, nor Paleo-Indian archaeologists, nor the despicable Thomasine Épée who's somehow incriminated in all this, I feel certain of it:

"And we bore no responsibility for the death of his half-baked brother, that loser. He drowned himself. It had nothing to do with us!"

The face is rotted, there's scant flesh on the skull, nothing left to identify it lying there, inches below the magic mirror, no longer in flames, no longer in flight, but I'm convinced of its identity, and Georgina is too, I know it.

We load the buses, go back to school where PT empties his gym locker to get his brother into dry clothes.

"Thank you," he says after his father's come and taken Birnam home.

"For what?"

"Saving Birnam."

"He wasn't drowning."

"Everyone says you went right in and got him, so thanks. Thanks for looking out for him."

"Whatever," I say. But I'm gratified by his obvious gratitude.

He grabs me by a shoulder as I turn to leave. "You're going back out tomorrow? You and Miss DeBarros." He doesn't wait for me to confirm. "I'm coming too."

"You can't."

"Why not?"

"Just can't."

He looks suddenly pained.

"It's a race thing, isn't it."

He makes it a statement, not a question.

"No. What?"

"Because I'm white."

"What are you talking about? It's not about that."

Is it?

Is it a gender thing? All I know is Georgina and I are doing this alone. Arianna doesn't even cross my mind, and when she does later, I shrug her off. I don't intend to share Georgina with anyone.

PT follows me to my car. "Is Tyler going?"

"Why would Tyler be going?" Now he's pissing me off. I move to throw my books in the passenger seat, but he's climbing in without invitation. "Stop being stupid. You just can't come. Change the subject."

He looks up at the sky. "Cirrus clouds," he says. Wispy white tails fan across a field of blue. "If you're gonna do it, you better do it now. Snow's coming."

Night falls early in January. The wind strengthens, the snow comes down. By morning there's a foot of snow on South Quagmire. Georgina and I go back out. I half expect to find PT waiting for us, offended Eskimo hip deep in drifts, but he's honored my injunction. The black ice is buried. The wolf sweater is gone. All charred tree trunks look alike.

We shovel and scrape.

We crawl on hands and knees.

Nothing. I hold her when she cries, and after a while I cry too, for her, for Arianna, for Uncle Anthony, for all that's lost along the way.

"We'll come back," I say, "when the snow clears. We'll find him."

The wind bites and tears away our tears. Two small dark figures in a vast, arctic flat. The sun goes down. We go home.

We never do come back, although PT insists and goes out with Tyler and several of Tyler's grunts. Their comb-and-seek mission returns empty-handed. Georgina leaves town at the close of the school year. Arianna leaves with her. No one ever finds Albert DeBarros or the wolf sweater, enfolded in fen. They pass from memory, local footnote into lore and, at last, darkness. Together they bed in peat dreams, one faint cry, outcast embraced in death by pack, howling to a white, vinyl moon.

ARTICLE 13

THE TDs

Albert Thomas DeBarros.

Clearly we have found and lost the body of Albert Thomas DeBarros, sixteen-years-old, drowned in a quarry.

Not.

But why the swamp, and why the lie?

I want to ask Georgina, who was only five at the time, but I feel like I have to be patient until she's ready to talk. I am not a patient person.

My patience is taxed further when the official transcript for the October 4 Special Town Meeting is delivered to Town Hall and I spend a Thursday afternoon reliving events. Articles Three and Four, specifically. The Town has a chance to buy three thousand acres of swamp before TouchDown Realty scoffs it up. Georgina wants to dedicate the new swimming pool to the memory of her brother, twenty-years dead.

Why? It feels self-serving, and Georgina is not a self-serving person. The plaque is about Uncle Anthony, isn't it?

There's Thomasine Épée's vehement denial of anything of value in the swamp. There's Tara Drummond's stammering support, or is it an apology, for the plaque? Uncle Anthony makes an oblique reference to letting Albert rest in peace in the quarry, a quarry that stopped working thirty years before, granite for monuments and Boston bank facades, mostly, then filled with spring water and become a favorite swimming hole. They found Rocky Mackiewicz's body easy enough in August, but never a sign of Albert's. There's a "flaming, flying dead thing in the swamp" that traumatized a middle school delinquent. There's a dead thing under the ice in the swamp that's got me plenty freaked, not to mention Krystal Tull, who refuses to recant, and Jet Black Lovell, who's not as certain now. Maybe it was a hollowed-out log. He can't be sure.

Wilhelmina Makepeace has made me a coffee mug. I'm flattered. More, I'm touched. This means something, I'm not sure what. People are starting to see me now. People who come in for dog licenses, marriage licenses, to get copies of birth certificates, register to vote, they look at me, talk to me, ask questions, recognize me as someone who knows something, has value. I'm not so invisible anymore. I'm becoming a real person. It starts as a strange feeling, becomes less so. Commission members submit minutes of meetings. They share gossip. They accept me as part of the furniture. I'm getting paid to be part of the furniture. I like it.

Miss Makepeace invites me into her office to christen the mug. We sit and talk, town employee to town employee, woman to woman. She asks how the family is doing, asks for Arianna. Is there anything she can do to help? Offers advice. "Steer clear of the Conservation Agent and Town Planner," she cautions. "The engagement's off. He got a little frisky with the Zoning Board chairman and, unfortunately, the car took out a guard rail on 95. They made the evening news." She asks about my plans for the future. We talk colleges. At some point I get up the nerve to mention, "PT says you were with them in jail the night before Uncle Anthony died."

She acknowledges, says how much she enjoyed Uncle Anthony's company, admired him for everything he'd overcome. I don't know quite what she means by 'everything.' She says, "I don't really know anything Sparky Manx hasn't already told you. It was before my time."

Sparky Manx hasn't told me anything because I haven't gotten the courage to ask. I take a big risk.

"Do you think he… killed… anyone besides Chief Dobbs?"

She politely breaks eye contact, moves a file folder from one side of the desk to the other. "Things went missing. The pack of cigarettes. His wallet." Now she looks back at me. "There were plenty of people who had issues with TouchDown Realty." Her smile seems genuine. "And, of course, it could just as easily be a series of unfortunate coincidences."

When Sparky Manx comes in to renew her dog's license (she keeps a golden lab named Spot for company), I take a deep breath and ask, "Please, can we talk?"

"You still have it?" she asks, writing out the check.

I am stunned speechless with guilt. She knows. Of course, she knows. Sparky Manx knows everything that goes on in this town. Miss Makepeace suggested as much. Which means, she knows PT and I know and trusts us not to do anything with it, to make it public. Is that what 'it' means? The metal device in the pack of Marlboros? She trusts us? Makepeace too?

Of course, they trust us. They know we'll do anything to protect Uncle Anthony. Does Chief Crockett know this? How close are he and Makepeace? Are we all involved in some mutual protection racket and I'm only just figuring it out now?

I nod. It takes another deep breath and less courage to throw my accomplice under the bus. "PT has it."

She nods.

"Come down to the station when you get a chance and we'll talk."

I go. We talk.

I say, "I don't understand Aunt Georgie's motive for Article Four."

"The plaque? You haven't asked her?"

"I don't know how to bring it up. It seems like it's none of my business."

Sparky nods.

"She was little when Albert died. She wouldn't remember much herself. I don't suppose you heard Chief Crockett found a small transmitter in Thomasine Épée's purse the night of the explosion in the bathroom."

I'm confused. "A transmitter?"

"A little keypad that sent a signal. No one's sure what the signal went to. No fingerprints but hers. It muddied the water. Which it was meant to do."

"They never found his wallet?"

"And they won't."

I draw out my long, "O… K." But I'm having a hard time following the thrust of her hints. Is she telling me she has his wallet? How and why? Or suggesting that someone planted something, a transmitter, in Thomasine Épée's purse? That she, Sparky, planted it there?

'Meant to do?'

Who and when?

Is Thomasine Épée implicated? And if so, implicated in what?

Sparky asks me, "Georgina never talked about her brother, Albert?"

"No. I mean, clearly he didn't drown in the quarry."

"No, clearly he didn't. That's common knowledge. The quarry's not so deep or... cluttered. They found Robby Mackiewicz's body in a few minutes. There's only so many places down there you can look. People knew... I mean, the ones who cared... knew there was something wrong with the story. But your Uncle Anthony was there, and he swore by it. Twelve-years-old, and he refused to change his story. The boy was more loyal to his friends than to his brother."

"So Albert died out by End Zone Island."

"So it would seem."

That's what Sparky Manx thinks anyway, and I trust Sparky Manx.

Sparky Manx, Reverend Jake, PT, Ma: eventually I gather enough bits from one source and another to piece together a story. Dickens could do it better, but I'm what you've got:

July, 1957. Albert Thomas DeBarros, sometimes Al, sometimes Tom, has seizures. They're frequent enough and severe enough that he doesn't play sports. He wants to, but there's always the possibility he'll have one in the middle of a game and cause a scene, humiliate

himself. He envies his little brother Tony who's a football phenom-
enon, who's traveling with the coolest kids at the high school, the
football players and the cheerleaders, Albert's classmates. Little
Tony D's on the bench with the high school basketball team, Dobbs,
Drummond teaching him how to foul shoot, everyone's favorite
water boy. He's in the dugout, batboy for the baseball team. They've
got him in the batter's cage, strengthening his swing. He goes to parties Aunt Flora doesn't know about and wouldn't approve if she did.
He's the TD's mascot. Little Tony D is Albert's ticket into the TDs.

And his older brother Albert would give anything, do anything
to be part of that scene.

They could bend the rules, after all. He could go by Tommy
DeBarros if that makes a difference. Not everyone in the gang shares
initials: Rufus Paul, quarterback, Cissy Loughlin, Brandy Hines.
Yes, Ted Dickson and Tiffany Dowd add to one of those Dickensian
convergences where T.D. becomes the byword for the End Zone
Island clique. But there's no compelling reason to exclude Albert
Thomas DeBarros besides the obvious. One, he's too big to be their
pet, and two, he's epileptic, has fits, is weird. He's embarrassing. And
he's colored. So, no, they don't want him in their gang. One cute
little pet monkey's enough.

The cute little pet monkey begs, however. He loves his brother.
He wants him to be happy. He entreats his heroes to give Albert
a chance. The kid's relentless. Eventually they surrender. On a hot
afternoon in July they all go out to End Zone Island for a party. I don't
know who 'they all' are, but thanks to Murder at Town Meeting and
what came later, I can be sure about some of them. They dare the
stupid colored kid to do something, I guess we'll never know what.
Prove himself worthy, tough, cool enough to be let in. Albert's out in

the water. Has a seizure. Drowns. Do they try to save him? Are they drunk? Do they watch and snicker until it's too late?

Thomasine DeAngelis Épée says he drowned himself. It had nothing to do with her... or them! So, does she see him disappear under the water and not attempt a rescue herself? Does she prevent her friends from doing so? Is she complicit? Guilty by association, or neglect, or...

Then they invent a story about the quarry and have Little Tony D swear by it. Which he does. And carries the guilt for twenty years. A lie which the others can shrug off as none of their concern and with which he alone has to live. But never alone because now he has to be kept close. They have to make sure he doesn't betray them. They don't need a youthful indiscretion damaging their reputation. Toby Dobbs will handle it. Fire Chief Tubby Dobbs will handle it to the bitter end.

Motive enough? Maybe? Was the chief pushed or was Uncle Anthony waiting for him?

The years pass. They all grow up. Tiffany Dowd marries a college sweetheart and relocates to the Carolinas. Ted Dickson moves to Texas, starts a restaurant chain. Tara Darsch marries Tim Drummond. Together with Tobias Dobbs and Thomasine DeAngelis, they start a real estate company, TouchDown Realty. They build a lot of houses and make a lot of money. And one day they make an offer to buy three thousand acres of land from Miss Katherine Ottick, and develop the high ground around End Zone Island, where their joint secret has been decomposing for twenty years. They make no effort to consult Little Anthony, include him in their plans, elicit his blessing. He hears about it as others do, second or third hand. He's not important enough to let in on their plans.

Uncle Anthony grows distant, has strange mood swings. He spends too much time alone in his basement lair. Shuns Georgina, shuns Arianna. Somehow Georgina works it out, but I never do learn when or what clicked. She guesses they're going to desecrate the final resting place of the brother Little Tony D let die. Bulldozers will chew on his remains, unearth the secret.

And the TDs don't care. Albert Thomas DeBarros, the 'half-baked brother,' meant nothing to them. Little Anthony means nothing to them either, evidently. Motive enough?

Before he can do something crazy, Georgina comes up with the idea of the plaque. She's hoping to distract him, use a vote of the Town memorializing Albert to assuage Anthony's anger, cool him down before he implodes. The Rocks wreck her plan, Town Meeting votes it down, and the effort is moot, because two members of TouchDown Realty die and the remaining two are sidelined before the vote's even taken. Two days later, he's dead.

"I think people knew," PT says.

We're in my bedroom. The door's open. Ma is doing laundry.

"Knew what?" I ask.

"I think people knew," he says. "They knew when Uncle Anthony ran over Chief Dobbs. They knew when they voted down the swamp. They knew when they voted down your aunt's plaque. They just didn't want to say anything. No one wanted to admit they knew. They've known for years."

"What are you talking about?"

"You knew. You had to know."

I have the urge to kill him.

"What did I have to know?"

But he's waiting for me to tell him. He's accusing me, but he won't say of what. He has something to say and he won't say it. Just provokes, then backs away, words unspoken, secrets withheld. Typical male behavior to poke and duck. We argue, and I don't even know what we're arguing about, and then he stalks out and takes off on his bike.

I don't believe I knew then. I'm pretty sure I know now. The pain was always there in the dark behind Uncle Anthony's eyes. I guess I recognized its presence even as a child. I may not have understood it, but I saw it. Why his girlfriend ditched him and their baby. Why his football career withered. I just didn't know what it was I was looking at. It was out of context. It was home and not the fire station.

Murder at Town Meeting. Does PT, despite protests and sullen silences, believe what I believe? How about Sparky Manx, Wilhelmina Makepeace, Chief Crockett, who are missing key pieces of evidence? What do they believe?

It works for me, and yet, something's missing. By daylight I'm convinced Uncle Anthony's a cold-blooded murderer, a skilled technician who sought revenge on those he blamed for his brother's death, but sometimes after dark I'm not so sure. Maybe it's something else PT says Uncle Anthony told him the night before he died.

"He said he was protecting me." I see him fingering the gold chain.

Protecting him?

Protecting him from what?

Or from whom?

MONDAY, APRIL 4, 1977, ANNUAL TOWN MEETING

7:32 PM

PT Wood here, back in the non-voters' section, this time for the Annual Town Meeting. I'm still sixteen, I won't be seventeen until August, so I'm stuck here in the balcony. At least there are no Rocks this time. They don't have any article to present they can screw up, and anyway, Krystal and Tourmaline just got in this massive fight in the corridor over some freshman boy who moved in from Rhode Island and it looks like The Rocks are on the rocks. Wouldn't that be nice? The mean kids always turn on each other in the end.

Anyway, it's Monday, April 4, 1977, 7:32 P.M., and this is the Annual Town Meeting for the Town of South Quagmire (just north of East Quagmire). We're waiting for a quorum, which is one hundred people. I count 98.

Actually, it's Birnam who just counted 98. Thank you, Birnam.

This is not good because Article Fourteen on the warrant is asking to reduce the quorum to seventy-five. It was proposed by our last Town Moderator, Mr. Drummond, at the Special Town Meeting in October because it's always a struggle getting a hundred people to turn out on a Monday night to vote, but then Mr. Drummond died and it was passed over. It's back now because two of our Selectmen, Nigel Brate and Katherine Ottick, want it passed. Miss Ottick says,

"If they don't show up and vote, they don't get to whine." She has a point, but still...

All the usual suspects are here. The three selectmen are onstage, Miss Ottick, Mr. Brate, and General Tarry. So's Miss Makepeace, our executive secretary, Mrs. Épée, the hippo, and Town Counsel, whose name I forget. There are five Finance Committee members onstage too. I don't know any of their names except Mrs. Perkins who coaches girls' softball. Police Chief Crockett's in the front row. So is Fire Chief Biff Larsen, who doesn't have a temper and should make it through all thirty-eight articles, and Sparky Manx and Reverend Jake are over by the exit. Everyone's hoping there'll be no casualties tonight.

I'm here with Tyler McVeigh and my brother Birnam.

Birnam, quit punching.

Arianna didn't want to come and not Miss DeBarros either. Karen Pina's down below with our new Town Clerk, Mrs. Botelho, who used to work at The Grub Pub. Or, she still does, but only nights. Now she works days at Town Hall, which Karen calls The Snake Pit because the Health Agent has a war going with the Assessors and the secretary for the Planning Board has it in for the Building Inspector, and Karen is getting paid as her assistant. There's also a woman sitting with them who'll talk everything into the dictam-ask, so we have a record if Mrs. Botelho screws up. She's never done this before.

The other new person is our new Town Moderator, Mr. Baresel, who's been appointed by the selectmen until the Town Election next Saturday. He'll get it because no one else is running.

And, oh, good, here comes more people. Three, four...

We have a quorum. It's 7:34 PM. Better than in October.

Mr. Baresel's at the podium. He's banging his gavel.

One, two, three.

Good, he's still standing. He's calling the meeting to order. We are all standing for the pledge of allegiance.

I pledge allegiance to the flag of the United States of America...

Hey, he knows all the words. That's cool.

Good, he's still standing. He's asking for a Moment of Silence for those devoted town citizens who are no longer with us:

Moderator Mr. Timothy Drummond

Fire Chief Tobias Dobbs.

Postmistress Carmen Selsby.

Former Town Clerk Theobald Doppelmeier.

Firefighter Anthony DeBarros.

And now, he says, in their honor, we will have 'The Star-Spangled Banner' sung by Mrs. Tara Drummond, as she has for nineteen years. Unfortunately, Mrs. Drummond could not be with us tonight, but she is in our thoughts, so we will please remain standing. Will her friend Mrs. Épée do the honors?

That's a laugh. Mrs. Épée, anyone's friend? The tape deck's set up in the middle of the stage. Karen says they wanted to play the tape of Mrs. Drummond singing in her honor, so I loaned them my mother's tape. The hippo's getting up. She still looks mean. She's coming to the front. Check out those ruby red shoes. So creepy. She's turning on the tape. We're all waiting. She sounded so nasty last October about Mrs. Drummond singing, I never thought anyone could convince her to do this, but I guess Miss Makepeace or someone is persuasive. Miss Makepeace can draw sweat from a cactus. Here we go.

"Oh, say can you see..."

Ya da da da da dum…

Uncle Anthony.

Tuning fork. Did he know I'd be the one to find that tape? Like he was telling me…?

Anyway…

Da da dum dum da dum dum.

Arianna.

TouchDown Realty.

"Through the perilous fight…"

Ramparts. All that cannon fire and smoke. Hard to see. Hard to be sure.

Francis Scott Key.

Was it Fort McHenry? Baltimore? It's been over a year since U.S. History sophomore year. I'm getting old and senile.

"The bombs bursting in air…"

She really does have a nice singing voice. Wish I could have heard her sing it live just once. Well, there's a last time for everything.

"Oh, say does that star-spangled banner yet wave…"

A thousand years from now? A hundred, even? Uncertainty, but maybe hopeful too.

Hold your breath. Here it comes.

"O'er the land of the free…"

And that effortless jump from F to B flat.

Beautiful.

That's so—

(*Metallic screech!*)

Huh?

What?

(*CRASH!*)

(Sound of splintering wood as the stage floor gives way.)

What the...!

Omigod, what is that?

It's just crushed the tape deck and the hippo!

Holy shit!

It's a safe!

A safe's fallen from the overhead onto Mrs. Épée. A safe's just landed smack on Mrs. Épée! Everyone's jumping up. People screaming. Holy shit! There goes Sparky Manx and Reverend Jake. General Tarry's pulled out his gun. Bambi Saville's running down the aisle. She's shouting, "I got this!" Chief Crockett clotheslines her, yells for everyone to sit down.

Everyone's running for the exits. The cops can't stop them.

This has gotta be the end of democracy as we know it!

All you can see is two ruby red shoes sticking out from under the safe.

How did...?

Who...?

Whoa, baby! All this time?

Wait. What?

Holy shit! There's words on the front of the safe. It says...

It says... Hard to see... I got this...

'The Albert Thomas DeBarros Burial Account.'

You gotta be kidding me.

"The Albert Thomas DeBarros Burial Account."

Talk about just desserts. I wish he were here to see this!

Karen, can you believe this?

"Cry havoc, and let slip the dogs of war!"

Revenge!

APRIL 4, 1977,
ANNUAL TOWN MEETING

OK, I just made that up. If Charles Dickens could do it, why not me? Sadly, this doesn't happen. Annual Town Meeting goes on for three nights. No one gets killed. The Woods, in exchange for an easement through their property to the town wells, want a parcel of equal acreage carved from adjoining conservation land as compensation. A two-thirds vote is not achieved, and Woodchuck ends night one with a paper bag over his head again. The changeover from town dump to transfer station takes the entirety of night two. We talk trash for hours. It's boring as hell. On night three we vote to accept Martin Luther King Day as a holiday, only a little slow on the uptake. The state voted it such in 1974.

I serve as assistant Town Clerk to Marge Botelho, who has, in fact, been hired as Tara Drummond's replacement. We share some good laughs as we cross the street between menus and amendments.

Thomasine Épée isn't at Town Meeting. She never comes back to Town Hall. She does make it home from rehab, but her lungs are badly fried and, on July 3, 1977, she dies, age 37. *Cause of death,* Heart failure. Too much weight, too little oxygen. At the wake I see photos of her as a teenager. You'd never recognize her. She was beautiful. I mean, truly beautiful. I guess life was not kind to her and she gave back in kind. TouchDown Realty is left in the sole hands of

Tara Drummond who sells her home to a family from Dorchester and moves to Florida near a sister in Orlando.

She's set for life. Set for life, but not happy.

Four years later she's dead, supposedly by her own hand. They say she sees a ghost just before she kills herself.

Murder at Town Meeting claims two more victims.

ARTICLE 14

———

To see if the Town will vote to amend Article 1, Section 6 of the Town By-Laws to read as follows: "Section 6: No article involving sums of monies shall be acted upon at any Town Meeting unless there are present at least seventy-five registered voters of the Town," or take any other action in relation thereto.

Interestingly, the article to reduce the quorum fails. The hundred and twelve people present decide to keep democracy alive a little longer by a large margin. (95 – 17, Birnam says.) I'm pleased, but my mother, who never attends Town Meeting, thinks it's only a matter of time. The town is growing. People get busier and busier. It'll be harder to coax people away from their televisions, and eventually we'll turn Town Meeting over to a handful of elected representatives from each voting precinct, like they already do in the cities, and that'll end the only pure form of democracy left in the United States. I think this is terrible. My mother says I'm young and idealistic, and this too shall pass. Democracy is messy and unfair. Forty-nine percent of the people lose. We share a cigarette as compromise although I'm trying to quit. PT's introduced Tyler and me to his parents' weed. It helps the spring go by.

ARTICLE 15

FLIGHT OF THE VALKYRIES

"I'm not graduating in May," says Number Forty-One, Tyler McVeigh.

"Wait. What?"

"I'm flunking pre-calc," he says, "and Weimar Republic. I don't have enough credits. So I'm gonna be here another year."

He waits for me to break out in joyous Hallelujahs, but that isn't happening.

"You can't, I mean, pull your grades up?" I'm incredulous. "Do extra work?"

"I don't want to," he grins. "I'm gonna stay here with you."

"But I'm going to college. I'm not staying here."

I've been accepted at Northeastern and UMass/Dartmouth. This town's too small for the three of us. I plan on getting out of Dodge. But Tyler will have none of it.

"Go to community for two years and commute," he says. "Save money. Then we don't have to split. Anyway, the general says I can do a postgrad year. Do a project. He's a wonderful man, the general. I'll go to college after that."

I feel the circle of life constrict. It never enlarges or opens. No matter the wider world, no matter the experiences that saturate the barrel staves, the hoops close tighter as the staves strive to expand. We're bound in metal bands. We strain against them, long to grow, but the more we grow, the tighter the bands. The fuller our lives, the more unbearable the limitations. Barrel makers use this knowledge to their advantage. The rest of us resist, surrender, endure.

Why does Tyler's vote count more than mine? I have plans. I don't intend to be stuck in South Quagmire forever. I have a political future. In America I can do anything, be anything I want. President, even. That's what democracy means. Black, Cape Verdean, female: I will not be defined by someone else's words. Yet, as Ma said, democracy is messy and unfair. While I was distracted by my studies, PT Wood relinquished claim to Tyler McVeigh without my notice, without giving me voice. Tyler's a fighter and PT's not, and now Tyler's got the upper hand and I'm in it, fingers, lips, and tongue.

I am weak. Defined.

"It's all good," Tyler says. "When I'm done with my project, I'll take you for a ride."

"Will it have windshields. Doors?"

Why do I have to be the one taken?

"Seatbelts, even."

"No over-turned milk crates?"

Why can't I be the one who takes?

"Not a one."

"Well, that's a relief."

Truth to tell, I've grown fond of the Model A pickup. We've had good times in it, he and I (and PT or, as Tyler bills him when we hit thirty-five miles per hour, Woodrow). But for comfort, my Ford Fairlane's bench seats are easier on the back.

Porky Doodles is the last collateral damage of Murder at Town Meeting, though not the last death. He lies on his side in Nigel Brate's postage-stamp-sized parking lot, pink and cream head blown off by Brate's double-barrel shotgun. Where did he come from? His curly, black-tipped tail hasn't been seen in town since Miss Edie sent him away to an exclusive swine haven, the name of which she's forgotten. Lakeville, wasn't it? Maybe Stoughton. There are no licensed piggeries closer. Tragically, he's broken free and come home to Miss Edie, an incredible journey that ends here on a small patch of dirt, weeds, and empty nip bottles. Butchered and dressed, Porky Doodles weighs in about 170 pounds. He's been well-fed. The Grub Pub's dumpster has seen to that.

"Pig roast," cackles Nigel Brate. He blows smoke from both barrels. It was an easy shot. The hog never saw it coming, let Brate get close and personal. "Sunday afternoon. My parking lot. Whole town's invited. All you can eat!"

He's in an expansive mood. One down, who knows how many more fat pork loins lurking in the bulrushes, just begging to become ham? This'll show General Tarry and his floozy not to break faith with Nigel Brate. Right to Farm, indeed! Ha!

A year's gone by, May, 1978. I've just finished my second semester at community college. Tyler graduated last Friday, PT next week. The academy's closing down for the summer and Tyler's hanging around for PT's ceremony. That's his excuse for staying anyway.

Besides, he has nowhere else pressing to go. ROTC doesn't want him until next month.

Not everyone in town will show for Nigel's pig roast. Sale of the swamp has bogged down without TouchDown Realty's deft hand at moving things along. Miss Kay has cut Miss Edie out of her will for contacting the state's conservation agencies. Miss Edie's been protecting her boyfriend's interests, and, of course, her boyfriend knows nothing about any pig. He has nothing to confess. There's no illegal piggery at South Quagmire Military Academy. His students eat kosher!

Miss Edie's grief is but a sideshow to our fractured spring. The two Protestant churches have enjoyed a recent spat over competing Lenten services. Easter's come and gone, but there's still grumbling in the congregations about the passion play that sidled into torture porn and the Easter egg hunt that came up short on chocolate bunnies. Also, environmentalists, led by those obnoxious Woods, have forced the Board of Selectmen by a two-to-one vote to issue a cease and desist order for the motorboat races on Cushing Pond Two. Big Pauly Silvio and his mechanics storm a Board of Selectmen's meeting. What's Memorial Day without an oil slick and the roar of gas-powered engines? A wet May has raised the three brooks near to flooding their banks, stopping just short, but the six Cushing Ponds are full to capacity, and half the basements in town have sump pumps running twenty-four hours.

People are cranky. [18]

---

18 Isaiah Cushing, 1694 – 1756, miller, dammed two brooks to make six ponds and named them all after himself: Upper Cushing, Lower Cushing (now Cushing Pond Two; there is no Cushing Pond One), the Big and Little Cushings, Cushing Major, and Muddy, which was Cushing Minor on early maps, but no one calls it that now. Whatever works to keep your name in the town histories.

Still, the Friday and Saturday before the festivities are sunny, and things dry out enough to be pleasant. Nigel and Big Pauly have built a wooden frame and strung Porky Doodles onto it with baling wire. They've got a nice fire going in half a 55-gallon metal drum. It's taken a bottle of Jack Daniels to convince Big Pauly he can't catch swine flu from a pig roast. The Grub Pub's closed for the afternoon in a gesture of community goodwill. I'm helping Marge Botelho give the place a well-deserved spring cleaning while opportunity lasts. The smell of smoldering fat coming in through open windows is intoxicating. I feel sick.

PT appears. "Tyler's gonna pick you up in twenty minutes," he says. "He'll meet you here. Be out front on the deck."

You wouldn't recognize PT. His yearbook picture was taken almost a year ago. He looks nothing like that now.

The first time I paid any attention to Petrified Wood (and I didn't pay much) he was a sophomore, I was a junior, and he was singing '*Younger Than Springtime*' to Arianna on a South Pacific island under high school theater lights. He was tallish, blondish. Nothing much else registered.

May, 1977, *My Fair Lady*. My 'whatever' plays the lovesick guy who wanders '*On the Street Where You Live*,' looking tall, blonde, fit and dapper in his three-piece suit as he moons over the girl. He makes me film him on Super 8 at dress rehearsal. It strikes me how easily he inhabits a persona not so unlike, but also not so like, his own. Tyler and I give him flowers after the show. He blushes to the pink tips of his baby-face roots and hands them off to his little brother Woodstock who's cranking out pressed flower arrangements with his mother.

I think PT had his yearbook photograph taken in that three-piece suit.

May, 1978. (For the first time, Birnam isn't quoting me dates. He was never much interested in his brother's theatricals.) The high school puts on *Joseph and the Amazing Technicolor Dreamcoat*, a pop musical retelling of the Bible story. PT's cast as the Elvis impersonator, Pharaoh, to whom the hero is summoned to interpret dreams. PT makes his entrance perched on a *papier-mâché* recreation of the Sphinx at Giza. The applause is tremendous. No one's cheering the Sphinx. In the audience, Tyler shakes his head and asks, "Do we know that black kid?"

That black kid overwhelms the Sphinx, the pyramids, a scenic assortment of crepe paper palm trees, his gold *lamé* shirt open to reveal chiseled brawny tawny brown torso draped in gaudy gold chains. But for adjacent signage indicating the Nile River, he might be a Mardi Gras pimp or the spoiled son of a Central American drug lord. He gyrates for Joseph, thrusts hips provocatively at a chorus of mummies, flirts with the appreciative females in the front row of the auditorium, and sings with enough raw abandon to waken any number of Memphis Kings in their sarcophagi. He's dripping sweat, hottest thing onstage, all sheen and glisten. His final high school performance and he's funny and sexy, almost popular. He steals the show. At curtain call the girls in the cast strip him to the waist and towel him down. The applause is crazy, a strange strain of idolatry usually reserved for football heroes.

Sparky Manx takes me aside afterwards. "What's up with Woody?" she wants to know.

"Nothing," I say, defensive. They read *Black Like Me* in senior English and he's been pretending it didn't get him thinking. "The Pharaoh's Egyptian."

"The other Egyptians didn't look like him."

"He gets into his character."

"And which character is that?"

I won't admit to her I'm unsettled too. He's spent three months in a tanning bed at the racquetball club, preparation for his role, he says, and he's almost darker than me. That's taken some getting used to, his transition from baby-faced pink rosy-cheeked to brawny tawny brown. It feels like misappropriation of racial identity. It feels like a come-on.

"Why are you doing this?" I ask. The smell of lilac is strong in the spring breeze and overwhelms the Old Spice.

He's showing off the new, used Willy's Jeep he's bought with his cranberry money: five-on-the-floor, open-topped canvas, doors removed, big, muscle tires, and fully-loaded, courtesy of Arianna's parting gift, with this new, improved body in the driver's seat, equally jacked and running on adrenaline. He's so over-proud of both it's comical. A skin-tight powder blue T-shirt hugs the cleavage he's carved himself from Uncle Anthony's weight bench. The single gold chain dances in the cleft.

"I'm doing this for you," he says and honks gaily at his brother Birnam who's puffing up High Street hill on PT's hand-me-down bicycle. If Birnam recognizes us he makes no sign and PT doesn't stop to offer him a lift.

"Not for me, you're not," I retort, but I'm not as resistant to the transformation as I should be. He's come a long way this past year, and fast, but still he's a child, young enough to think he's impressing me with his jock physique and driving skills, skills I taught him, by the way. He's a senior in high school. I'm on the Dean's List at college. I'm holding down two jobs. This past winter Miss Makepeace hinted that Town Hall's running much smoother with me in it. He's the one should be impressed, impressed with me. He could at least notice I'm wearing my hair short these days. But, no, he's into himself. The rest of us are extras in his stage show fantasia, groupies and hangers-on. He doesn't get that neither his body nor his sharp left-hand turns are of lasting interest to any but himself and the shallowest of females, and even then the Tourmaline Selsbys and Krystal Tulls of the world will not remain long impressed by a guy who isn't even more impressed by them.

And tells them so on a regular basis.

He shrugs. Short sleeves bulge with too-much shoulder as he lightly palms the steering wheel. "OK, the play then. When they told me about the gold *lamé* shirt, they said I needed to look good in it."

The play's not the thing either, and as we pull into the Town Hall parking lot and distress the brake pads with a grinding squeal, I joke we may have to alter his birth certificate in the Town Clerk's office. He's pretty much the color of his name now, or darker. He jumps out, leaving the key on in the ignition, sprints around the front, and, with a mock, sweeping, gentlemanly bow, mimes opening the door for me, the door that isn't there. His burly arm's toned and toasted to a smoky buff somewhere between me and the Little Bighorn. He's not a white boy anymore. That appears to be the plan, anyway.

And we've yet to see the best (or worst, or at least most startling) of it. The afternoon before dress rehearsal he goes to Bambi's Beauty Salon and comes out with bushy hair and eyebrows dyed black. He's unrecognizable as PT Wood. Bambi Saville is taken aback by her handiwork. She makes a comment about Lazarus rising from the dead. Thank God Arianna has moved to New Bedford. The sight of him would break her heart.

Nor would my Aunt Rose note any resemblance to our late fire chief. With his bodybuilder physique and choice of jewelry he looks uncomfortably like—

"Tyler's gonna pick you up in twenty minutes," he says. "He'll meet you here. Be out back on the loading dock."

"Whatever," I grunt. He and Tyler have been scarce for most of April while I'm in class and final exams. Now comes this make-believe black dude in tight T-shirt, muscles popping out all over the place, single gold chain nestled in the cleft of his chest muscles, telling me I'm going for a ride with Number Forty-One, Tyler McVeigh.

"It'll be great," he says as he checks himself out in the rear-view mirror. He adjusts his baseball cap to just the right sideways angle. It perches jauntily atop his bushy black hair. "See you in twenty minutes."

"This thing's gonna have a windshield, right? Seat belts?"

"You betcha," he assures me. He drives off someone else.

Sunday afternoon in a small New England town in late May peers out at me through the detritus of lost worlds and dreams deferred, the day ripe with every nostalgia-laden cliché New England towns claim to inspire. Main Street hums with excitement. The center is full of people. The afternoon warms, the buds on the trees burst into leaf. Birds skim the maple tree tops in front of the library slash senior center, catch a rising thermal off the pavement, and spin off into pines. The world smells green. Green and greasy. The odor of hot pork permeates everything. Dogs circle, salivate. Their tongues hang out in hope. The crowd in and around Brate's parking lot spills into the road, which has been blocked off between Bridge Street and High with the two police cruisers. Chief Crockett's in the new one, listening to the game. The Red Sox are ahead by two runs. (It's been thirty years and, admittedly, I'm making some of this up, but you'll forgive me if I embroider a little. It's the nostalgia kicking in.) The whole place feels like a party, one big All-American picnic, festive, and if some of our finest citizens are not in attendance from personal or political animosity, plenty are here to partake in the feasting. Folding tables line the sidewalk. The Grub Pub's baked fifty pies for the occasion. Makepeace has spent the morning stringing brightly colored banners from the telephone poles. They rustle like prayer flags in the light breeze. Kids run around, laughing and chasing. Some have woven red, white, and blue streamers through their bicycle spokes. You'd think it was the Fourth of July. The ice cream man shows up in his truck and is doing a whopping business in creamsicles and sherbet bars. Cher Wood has her own table in front of the post office and is selling hand-made trinkets. The Lovell brothers, Jasper and Jet, lounge on top of the mail van, catching rays, open bottles of Pabst Blue Ribbon in full view of anyone who cares. No one cares. Brate's got one of his remaining helicopters in Big Pauly's parking lot. He's offering free rides to the lucky raffle winners. Two of his cashiers float around, selling tickets, beer, wine, and soft drinks at today's special discount prices.

I'm inside the restaurant, cleaning the exhaust hood above the fryolator. It hasn't been touched since before Christmas. It takes a good hour and a lot of whining. When I'm done I pull off my greasy bandana, scrub myself down in the industrial sink, and go over to the plate glass windows, drying arms with a towel. Through the yellow-checked curtains I have a clear view of the festivities.

And something odd.

There's a trickle of water running down Main Street. A few of the littlest kids have discovered it and are splashing in it as it makes its way to a storm drain. Then something odder happens. It doesn't disappear down the storm drain. Instead, water comes bubbling up through the storm drain. A large, creeping puddle moves across the road.

"Marge, check this out," I call, and head for the back door which is unlocked.

"Check what out?" she asks. She sets down the coffee pot she's scouring and follows.

From the rear loading dock we have no view of Main Street and Brate's Liquor Emporium. What we do have is a clear view of the two brooks that sandwich town center. Stump Brook seems high but Bim's Brook is overflowing its banks. Water's running through the sumac trees and grape vines and thorn bushes that secure the embankment. It wriggles over the scrub grass, running across our packed dirt parking area. It's not taking its time either. It moves right along, catches a soda can in the bushes, and takes it for a ride.

Marge sees the water swirling around the side of the restaurant. "The dam's let go," she says. "Cushing Pond Two."

"Oh, no." I step back as it advances. We're three feet above the ground but is that safe? "What do we do?"

"I didn't wear my L.L. Beans," she says.

All at once there's a dull rumble from upstream like something in a hurry to get somewhere. We turn to the sound. Between the skinny sumac trunks and twisting brambles we see water cresting in a small but insistent wave higher than the brook itself. Suddenly, there's water pouring into our parking lot. We run back into the restaurant, thread our way through tables and booths to the front door. Out we come onto the deck. In the street, a light but certain current races around ankles. People are scrambling for higher ground. There isn't any. Several run up the handicapped ramp onto the deck with us. One lady's pushing a baby carriage. The baby's crying.

"What is it?" she wants to know. "What's happening?"

Across the street a dozen or more rush up the six concrete steps of Brate's packy. They cling to each other and the wiggly metal railing. Kids splash through the rising tide on their bikes. There's laughter. There are screams. The ice cream truck tries to back up and bumps into the new police cruiser, busting a headlight and interrupting the game. Chief Crockett flings open the door and steps into ankle deep water. Curses ensue. Tables overturn. Fifty pies disappear *en masse* into the current. "Not the pies!" Marge gasps. "I baked for two days!" The water flows from the street into Brate's postage-stamp parking lot. It picks up speed on the decline and washes over the 55-gallon firepit. A great cloud of steam rises with a hiss we can hear half-a-football field away. Brate and Big Pauly and others are scalded and shoved backward. Porky Doodle's cloven hooves go under. The town has turned into a clamor of confusion.

There's another sound too.

Faint, in the distance. we hear a rumble, a beat, music. It grows louder, accompanied by a low roar that grows louder too.

"What the heck?" I ask.

Marge squints, listens intently. *"Flight of the Valkyries,"* she says.

We look at each other in recognition. Nigel Brate!?

By now Main Street is under an inch or two of water. Brate's parking lot is under a foot or two of water. Paper plates and plastic cups and wilted flowers ride the surge. A hundred empty nip bottles bob and duck. A millstream of litter races over the postage stamp, flushing into the swamp. And coming from the swamp, up over the trees at the rear of the parking lot, swelling as it nears, music blasts over loudspeakers. Wagner! It *is* Wagner! Marge's right. We know that martial strain from our cartoon days. The whir of rotors slices the air in furious circles. The treetops whip frantically, bend and thrash. The rotors ascend and then, to our astonishment, beneath them a fiery red helicopter materializes. It gleams, sun at its tail, showering sparkles, shards of glitter, a Chinese parade dragon with great, black cockpit eyes, an angry red dragonfly primed for assault. Its landing skids part the highest tree branches. Foliage is flung. A surge and billow of humanity scatters as the chopper thunders in above the parking lot, the fury of its rotation driving air and steam and water and smell in all directions. I see Brate fall on his back, disappear beneath the torrent, come up spitting. Big Pauly Silvio crawls over the tailgate into the bed of his pickup truck. He's cussing loud enough to be heard above the clamor. He shakes an angry fist. The 'copter moves into position over the wooden frame and pauses in midflight. Some people continue running up Main Street, fearful of turning into pillars of salt, spray pelting them from behind.

Others turn back in mid-slosh, hands held high to shield faces, "Look! Look!" they're shouting. Fathers are tossing young children onto their shoulders. Mothers clutch infants to their chests. They see a rope ladder drop from the cockpit, a tumble of rung and cord linking sky to earth. Down the ladder scrambles a figure, a dark figure in camo gear. A broad, dark figure, holding (but it's hard to tell through steam and spray) what looks to be a hook on a rope. The crowd watches as the tall, broad, dark figure snags the wooden frame with the hook, shouts something unintelligible above the din, and Porky Doodles, what's left of him, is hoisted to the underbelly of the beast where he spins in circles on his wooden frame. A momentary lurch sends 'copter, ladder, figure, pig swinging sideways. Below, screams and gasps. Then the beast rights itself and roars forward over Main Street. Shrieks and whoops erupt from every side as the crowd flees to safety (if safety is possible), although the water on the street is still not higher than ankles. The ladder swings wildly. The tall, broad, dark (and well-muscled) figure on the rope ladder hangs on. He swings toward me. Marge Botelho stumbles back against the building in fright. Others do too. A few terrified souls fling themselves through the front door for refuge within. The music cuts off, stopped in mid-measure. Pharaoh in camo clings to the ladder with one hand, stretches out the other to me. From above a voice booms over the loudspeaker, God talking, or maybe Rambo:

"Hey, lady, want a lift?"

About that 'copter.

So, back in November, 1976, a month after Murder at Town Meeting, Selectwoman Katherine Ottick snaps at Selectman Nigel Brate during a special session convened to replace Fire Chief Dobbs, "When exactly are you planning to remove your helicopter from my swamp?"

Brate stubs out a cigarette in the ash tray behind his name plate. It'll happen, he suggests, about the time she agrees to sell him that quarter-acre of land to expand his postage-stamp-sized parking lot. She promised. He's getting tired of waiting.

She counters that not only did she not promise anything but that she's not subdividing her property until assured of a buyer for the remaining three thousand acres. She will not pick away so that its value decreases. At least twenty people witness the exchange.

The helicopter sits through the winter, frozen in fen. We see it the day we go field tripping with Mr. Corr and discover the body under the ice. Then one day in early spring, not long after the big thaw, Brate drives out in his Hummer to see what's possible and finds to his surprise that the 'copter is gone. He's pretty sure he knows where he left it. It'd be hard to lose. But there's nothing there except water and charred tree stumps. Bad Bertha has disappeared.

"Hell and damnation," he says to Big Pauly Silvio. "Quicksand."

Well, that takes care of that, doesn't it? He goes up in another helicopter (he owns three or four) and hovers over End Zone Island and environs, peering down through binoculars. Not a trace can be seen. The swamp has swallowed Bad Bertha whole. Next time Selectwoman Ottick snipes, he snipes back, "Done."

No one thinks more about it. Memories run short in South Quagmire.

Now go back a few weeks. Over the course of several days in February, 1977, fifty or so students in winter combat gear spill out of ten surplus Army jeeps, dump trucks, and trailers, armed with socket wrenches, crowbars, and WD-40. I picture them racing across the ice and swarming the helicopter like busy little maggots on a carcass. They disassemble the entire helicopter as part of Number Forty-One, Tyler McVeigh's special postgraduate project. They break it into its components and cart the whole thing piecemeal back to their campus in the woods. For the next year, Tyler and his minions consult their teachers, pore over manuals, clean away muck and char, scour rust, re-tool engine parts, scavenge from junk yards and military depots near and far, all to re-assemble Brate's 'copter, good as new, even better. They sand and paint, gloss it to a photo finish, cherry red, Chinese red, fire dragon red. Bad Bertha, never a beauty, has become a work of art.

And no one outside the academy's the wiser, certainly not Nigel Brate who lacks imagination. If he's heard occasional engine noises deep inside the expanse of Little Quagmire Swamp as Tyler teaches himself to fly the thing with none but a couple of instructors and, eventually, PT, to witness, the sound doesn't register as familiar. Bad Bertha's humming a different tune. The covert mission has been a complete success.

In the movie version there will be no telephone poles and wires. The chopper will fly over the front steps, the ladder brush by, PT's arm extend, and I'll be swept into the action sequence. Even the awning over the deck will be removed so there's no chance of getting tangled in it. Life is not a movie, however, but a circle tightly constricted, hemming us in with iron bands of obligation and phone lines. Tyler is not an experienced pilot. We're lucky we're not electrocuted. The 'copter pauses over the middle of Main Street. That's the closest he can get to me without turning the center of town high voltage. The ladder's dragging in the water. PT's climbed a couple of rungs to avoid the flood. He steps down into the current and wades to the front steps. The air's churning. Spray fans out in a huge circle. We're pelted and pummeled. From above a voice booms over the loudspeaker, God talking, or Number Forty-One, Tyler McVeigh:

"Hey, lady, want a lift?"

PT hollers in my ear, "Live!"

He doesn't give me a chance to protest. I'm scooped up and carried back through the water to the ladder. Over his shoulder I see Marge watching us go, horrified. She's shouting something, but I can't hear her. Later, people will remember how the big black dude snatched the black girl right off the front deck of the restaurant and hauled her off in a blinding burst of sunlight and rainbows. The audience may even applaud, who knows? But I'm totally stupefied, barely able to catch my breath, and I don't get to beat him senseless before he's physically pressing my hands to the rungs.

"Hang on!" PT bellows, smile broad enough to ingest a roast pig whole. He's got some kind of earphones and mouthpiece under his baseball cap. He speaks into it. I can't hear anything above the din. The ladder begins to rise. We lift from the surface of the flowing street. Water froths and boils. The ground falls away. "Don't look down," he says. I look up. The helicopter's holding steady. The ladder retracts in fits and jerks. I look down. We're several feet in the air.

I'm hanging on with both hands. I don't know that I've ever been afraid of heights. As a child I climbed a lot of trees, but I've never been in a plane and certainly never dangled midair on a rope ladder that's waling crazily like a pendulum gone three-dimensional. We're higher than the telephone wires. I see people beneath forming a great ring beyond the spray zone. Marge's got a hand on her heart. There's Chief Crockett yelling at Lieutenant Watson, who's pointing at us with wide-eyed impotence. Everyone's ankle deep in water. Rooftops become islands in the flood. The ladder whips around, laundry on a clothesline in gale wind. There's Nigel Brate, screaming as he slogs the incline from his postage-stamp-sized parking lot, more and more postage-stamp-sized by the second. He's waving a big knife and shouting, "That's my pig! Give me back my pig!" along with many colorful vocabulary words, none of which I can actually hear above the roar of the engine, the thunder of rotors. The ladder whips back. The Lovell brothers on top of the mail van clutch each other with laughter to keep from falling off. Now Jet's holding out his thumb, asking if he can hitch a ride. The ladder whips again. I find myself nose to snout with the pig.

"Have you met Porky Doodles?" yells PT.

The three of us, plus ladder and wooden frame, meet in hurricane collision. A piece of wooden frame knocks loose and falls. I don't look down. I pray it doesn't hit anyone. I pray a lot of things. I'm hanging on like my life depends on it.

It does. It surely does. Am I breathing? I don't know.

We're up to the open cockpit door. Several hands reach out, arms in camo shirts.

"Careful, now, careful!" and "We've got you!" and "You can let go, it's OK!"

I'm hauled inside. I land hard on my knees. PT clambers in behind me, tries to step over me and sprawls. My head's spinning. I may have vertigo, I don't know. I've never had vertigo before. I've never been in an open helicopter before. I feel drunk, limp. Someone's got me under the armpits. I'm manhandled to a seat in the front, the copilot's seat. Tyler's in the seat beside me, talking into his headset.

"Buckle in," he says.

I don't have to because PT is hanging over me, securing straps and latches.

"You'll be great. This is awesome. Wait'll you see. Bell Jet Ranger. All the military use 'em. Brate has no clue. The general said paint it black but I thought red would make more of a statement, and Tyler said OK, and it's his baby, so—"

"Hang on," Tyler says. "We're going up. Don't touch the foot pedals."

The whole thing lurches. PT almost front flips into my lap. We're going up. Through the cockpit windshield I see the world widen, expand around me. I never knew that was possible. The sky looms. The horizon spreads and spreads. Everything is blue and bright and green and blue and bright and green. We turn, a violent turn. The world careens below. Three white church steeples swoop and bow.

The sun's blinding, but Tyler's already got a pair of sunglasses in hand which he holds out to me without looking. "You'll need these."

I do. I'm squinting hard against the glare. I put them on. PT's behind, pressing something over my head. Not until I hear voices do I understand it's a headset, and I'm part of the operation. He jiggers it into place, flips a mouthpiece in front of my lips. His hands clutch my shoulders. I'm pinned to the seat by his big brown paws. The pine trees at the bottom of Brate's parking lot rush us and I don't scream as they fling headlong at the glass. Then we're up and over, only a crazy shake from beneath as our landing skids shave the topmost branches. Before us, Little Quagmire Swamp opens wide, a great, vast plain of blue and green and the vibrant red of cranberry bogs laid out in tidy patchworks.

Windshield. Seat belts. No over-turned milk crates. I'm overwhelmed. I've never experienced this much life squeezed into mere minutes, seconds, moments. The barrel's full to bursting, every bit of wonder straining against the hoops and miraculously, the hoops seem willing to allow expansion. They grow wider to accommodate the surge of adrenaline. They've never done that before. I can't speak I'm so caught up by the feeling of fullness. Only the crush of PT's hands on my shoulders keeps me from exploding.

Live!

Beneath, the swamp! Beneath, several people in camouflage hacking at a sand pile, a big earthen something. Water's behind it in a small pond. Tyler swings the helicopter around, over their heads. They wave at us. Shovels and pick axes.

I hear PT through the earphones. "We dammed the brook, backed it up. Two weeks and a front-end loader and we did most of it at night. I got to help. The night of the big rain storm we almost lost it. Almost washed away. We had to—"

Under the sleek muscle and dark skin our garrulous Petrified Wood lingers. He's just harder to distinguish behind his cool shades. The 'copter rocks and he staggers.

"Porky Doodles secure?" Tyler asks into his mouthpiece.

"I'll check," PT says. He releases me. He shifts, leans over the top of Tyler's head, grabs both cheeks between large brown hands, and tilts his face to him. "Bro, this is the greatest day of my life," he says. "I love you, man!"

He plants a big kiss on Tyler's forehead.

Tyler lets go some lever stick and without a word smashes a fist into PT's chin. I can't hear the impact, but I feel it. PT falls backward. His sunglasses are tossed against the ceiling. I hear the thud, boots clattering, confusion through my headset. Tyler grabs the stick, jerks around in his seat, and snarls, "Don't you ever do that again in front of my men, you perv."

First there's nothing, a stunned, engine-drowned silence, then all at once a fluster of low voices, interspersed with mumbles, gasps, and exhalations. The consternation's palpable. My lungs are squeezed by the circle of life. It was a kiss, for Heaven's sake, a kiss. I've seen Tyler kiss PT a hundred times. (I exaggerate. Maybe twice.) Seen PT kiss Tyler. Watched them hug and squeal and giggle like schoolgirls, poke and punch and slap each other on the backs, arms, faces, horseplay that speaks of budding bromance. Only difference now is the audience, an all-male audience in army fatigues and headsets. God forbid machismo be compromised in front of his precious grunts. My fingers ball into a fist. The nails dig into my palm. I want to punch him, punch him hard, punch him for PT who'd never think of punching back in anger, but discretion stays my hand. The ground is a long way down. Tyler fights to regain balance, expression stone. The 'copter seesaws and we're moving forward. Beneath, the earthen dam gives way and a gout of water pours through the break into the swamp.

Tyler growls, inscrutable behind dark lenses. "Going down."

We drop. My stomach drops too, or leaps, or turns somersaults. I've been on a roller-coaster. It's a lot like that. I unclench my fist, glare at Tyler. He glares at me. Our glares are hidden behind shades and carry no weight. Only the set of our mouths speaks displeasure. Petrified Wood's committed the unspeakable sin of male-on-male endearment, and for this breach of manhood, my brief intoxication's done. The town's behind us, behind the trees. Everything familiar's gone. Smug complacency, the mundane everyday, home and safety, all blown away in an instant on a sunny Sunday afternoon in May. One kiss, and we descend, star-crossed, into dangerous miles of trees and pond where thin, snake-like waterways slither though fields of grass. It's strange. It's scary. People die here. I've never seen the world from above. I've never imagined it. The world's a map laid out in violent colors, a writhing unknown seen through 3-D glasses. I find no visible landmarks by which to orient myself. I can't pick out the burn at End Zone Island. Two springs and a summer and the swamp has greened again, only faded spines of tree trunks jutting from new-blossoming snot-colored foliage to hint where, once, callous, calculated evil was done. The thought's fleeting, gone almost before it comes to mind. I don't know if I'm in trouble with Tyler or not. Guilt by association? Am I allowed divided loyalties?

Tyler brings us down over a pond I have probably never seen before. We hover a few feet above its surface. On the far horizon, a water tower pokes the sky. Maybe a Bridgewater? I wish I'd paid more attention to maps.

"Can we pull it in?" he asks his mouthpiece. He sounds calm, in perfect control.

I turn, try to see what's behind me. Three or four bodies, boys in camo, bob and weave in the cramped space between flanking open doors. How they haven't been tossed out by now I can't explain. A couple of them are on their bellies on the floor, hanging out over the churning water. They appear to be attached by ropes clipped to the 'copters innards. I can't make out PT. Maybe he's one of them. They're trying to reach something, grab hold of something. One boy's holding another by the ankles.

"Almost."

"Can't quite—"

"Here, you—?"

"Wait, hold—"

"Grab onto—"

"Hey! Who stole my Oreos?"

"Got it, got it! Nope!"

Suddenly I'm angry, defensive, bold. Tyler's machismo galls. I'm not his bit of overhead décor, my purpose here to complement the testosterone flooding the cockpit. I'm not the girl candy at Tyler's elbow nor the maiden in repose. They hauled me into this outlaw band. Didn't ask, just presumed.

I want to make sure PT's OK.

"Let me help!" I shout.

I start to fumble for the seatbelt latch.

Another boy crouches in the opposite doorway, looking out. The kid with the eyepatch, Nondescript Someone Number Forty-Three, holds an enormous pair of black binoculars, strap around his neck. He's staring into the distance. A loud bark. He drops the binoculars, points. They're so big they almost drag him out the door. A deafening shout rattles my ear drums. I wince, forget the latch, try to pull the earmuffs away.

"What?" asks Tyler into his mouthpiece. "Who? Oh, shit!"

His legs shift and the cockpit bounces. I grab his arm, my momentary resolve sapped by nausea. His hand's hard on a lever stick. [19]

"What?" I ask, almost a choke.

He flicks the mouthpiece aside, leans at me.

"Brate. He's coming after us." He pushes the mouthpiece back with a forefinger, says with calm authority, "We're being followed. Secure yourselves."

I'm twisting myself into a pretzel to see what's going on behind me. Bodies are up, down, back against walls. The engine roars. Slowly the helicopter makes a quarter turn. Sure enough, a black helicopter's sidling into view over the trees. It looks like the one Brate had sitting in Big Pauly's parking lot. Shouts spew from several headsets. I want to block my ears but can't. The headset's too tight. My stomach's doing flips.

"No time for the pig now," says Number Forty-One, Tyler McVeigh, pilot. "Gotta beat it home. Everybody clipped in?"

He doesn't wait for affirmatives. The pond sinks, not by much. We start forward into a broad, flat stretch of marsh.

"Stump Brook!" he shouts. "Hang on."

I'm hanging on, but a voice I know well shouts in my earphones, "I'm not—! Shit, there goes my hat!"

Another: "Three-Fifty-Two's on the landing skid. He's not—!"

And another: "He's—not—hang on, hang on! Oh, fuck!"

Time does one of its inexplicable loop-de-loops and everything slows down and speeds up together and I understand that Three-Fifty-Two is PT Wood, honorary member of the platoon, status

---

19 I now know it's called a cyclic and controls direction of flight. Back then I was clueless.

now in doubt, and he's under the helicopter. I picture arms and legs wrapped around a landing skid.

"Keep going, keep going!" Three-Fifty-Two shouts through the earphones. "I'm good! I got this!"

He sounds giddy. I expect to hear hysterical laughter. Surely the next bit in the movie will involve someone riding a bomb to earth. Instead, a loud ping provides an exclamation point to his giddy "got this!" and someone yells, "Shit! They're shooting at us!"

Two loud pings in quick succession.

And another.

Someone shouts, "Forty-Three, get your head in!"

And another.

Tyler says, ever-so-coolly, "I knew we shouldn't'a shot out his tires."

Big Pauly Silvio. Oh, jeez, we got Brunhilde and the Bloody Red Baron after us.

"What's going on? Who's shooting?"

This from PT somewhere beneath me.

"Still clipped in?" asks Tyler.

"Can you give me a little height? I'm scraping grass."

Tyler says nothing, but instead of going up, he veers onto the brook, surface lower than the marsh. The brook winds. Tyler winds with it, twisting over the watercourse. Bodies pitch right, then left, then right again. Our horizontal waterslide leans into hairpin turns and bullets.

A bullet evidently zings through one side door and out the other. Screams and obscenities rebound off ear drums. We're so low I'd swear we're leaving a wake.

"Tyler!" I shout. "PT! He can't! You'll kill him—!"

"Reinforcements ahead, Three-Fifty-Two," he says without emotion. "Almost there."

Through the windshield I watch the ground blur below, scant feet below, water and grass racing at us, swallowed in our wake. Ahead, a long, straight embankment looms. Beyond it, the plush red carpet of Bog 19. Along the embankment three open-topped Jeeps and a dump truck are tearing toward us in a rapidly narrowing acute angle. A cloud of dust billows behind them. Someone rises in the lead Jeep, swings a giant black gun in our direction. Damn! They've got a cannon!

"Tyler! No!"

Before I can give further warning, a flash of light from the muzzle, a second later a blast of sound that outblasts the sound of engine and rotors. The world shakes. I scream.

Tyler reaches over and grabs me by the shoulder, forces me back against the seat. "General Tarry. He's not shooting at us. They're scaring off Brate. Hang on, I'm taking us in. Woodrow, unclip! Repeat, unclip! Now! Everyone, heads between your legs."

He's pulling back on the control. The nose pitches and I see sky. My body strains against the barrel hoops. The road comes at us, less, less urgency. Another blast from the big gun shakes the cockpit.

"Brace for impact," Tyler says.

"Guys!" A voice I know well through the earphones: "Wee-ee-e-e're gonna nee-e-ed a bigger boat!"

The brook's below us. The road's straight ahead. The windshield's mostly sky.

"Hey!"

"Omigod!"

"Mayday, mayday!"

"Commander, up, up!"

The 'copter tilts forty-five degrees. I watch a body in slow motion sail out the door. Time becomes relative to the edge of stop.

Number Three-Fifty-Two, Petrified Wood, Woodrow, calls out in syllables stretching toward infinity, "JAA-AA-A-AWS... has... got... the... pig... Hee-ee-ee-e-ee's—!"

We hit the brook.

Later, after we've retrieved Nondescript Someone Number Forty-Three (but not his Oreos) and Three-Fifty-Two (but not the pig) from the quagmire, climbed the embankment twenty extra pounds sodden, been cheered and back-slapped by the entire faculty of the South Quagmire Military Academy for our part in a success-ful postgraduate project (they've provided anti-aircraft cover for the operation), I find myself sitting on the side of the road in a blanket, cold, wet, staring at the Chinese dragon submerged almost to its fiery wingtips in the swamp, while Tyler's swilling champagne with his crew, promising General Tarry he'll be forever grateful. Forever will be two years, Christmas, 1979. An argument over a *Victoria's Secret* catalog ends with barracks burned, the General dead, and Tyler in prison. Tyler dies in prison. I'll hear the news third-hand, blame myself.

I could have surrendered my bras when he asked.

But that's the future and, fortunately, I am no oracle, have no crystal ball. For now, I'm grateful to be alive, marveling that Tyler has crash-landed his 'copter with no loss of life. Brate's gone. He and

Big Pauly have retreated before superior firepower. There's no sign of a dorsal fin slicing the water There's no scary music thumping in the soundtrack. Only my heart, which gradually regains its own mundane rhythm. I've had enough excitement in the past twenty minutes to last a lifetime.

PT sits down beside me on the roadside. He too has a blanket over his shoulders but he's careful to make sure the wet powder blue T-shirt is exposed, clinging to him like a coat of cheap paint, leaving no sinew to my imagination. The single gold chain is plastered inside the cleft of his chest muscles. He unlaces a military style boot and dumps water from it into the grass. Yes, even his feet are tawny brawny brown.

The adrenaline's only now beginning to recede. "You OK?" I ask. "For a minute there I thought we lost you. Was there really a great white shark?"

He grins. "A punch is nothing. He means well. I was looking forward to that pig," and drapes a big arm over my shoulders, pulling me close. I let myself be pulled close. He feels good. Warm seeps through the wet. I reach back and put a hand on that arm. I want to spend my life within reach of that arm. Even if I'm just a stand-in for Arianna who's out of our lives, although we don't admit that yet, or Tyler, who's into me, but probably more into making out, yeah, and weaponry (not necessarily in that order), PT's arm says we belong to each other. We're something together. I don't know what. It's a cinch the arm doesn't. Only time will tell, and time has no plan for letting us in on its secrets. Thirty years will pass. Uncertainty will remain. I'll write about it, him, us, try to set down in words what I felt. What we felt. What I think we felt.

I won't get it right.

PT's fracturing *My Fair Lady,* changing lyrics to *'In the Swamp Where We Live'* (he does have a pleasant singing voice) when a shout, a screech of brakes, and the mail van grinds to a halt behind us, not before colliding with the bumper of the lead Jeep. Jasper Lovell flings himself out of the driver's side door, Jet the passenger's.

"Dudes!" shouts Jet. "That was awesomeness like I never seen awesomeness! Hey, man, you got the town buzzin' like a nest o' hornets. You guys bust the dam? Can you give us a ride?"

A commotion follows with General Tarry yelling angrily and a swarm of males making a major production out of unlocking bumpers, but the Lovell brothers pay the militants no heed. They scramble down the slope to check out the drowned chopper up close. Then, laughing, they clamber back and throw themselves on the verge beside us. PT drapes his spare arm over Jet's shoulder, Jet reciprocates, and they burst into a chorus from *Joseph and the Amazing Technicolor Dreamcoat* that goes off on some breathless, giddy riff about reds and yellows and browns and a bunch of other colors.

I guess we're all included in there somewhere.

"Or maybe we can give you a ride," says Jasper, who's no singer. He's all eyes for PT's wet powder blue T-shirt chest muscles. "Crazy you never played football, man. You'd rock. Need help getting that thing outa the water? I got an uncle with a tow truck. We can give you two a lift home. They'll never think to look for you in the mail van." [20]

20 I mentioned earlier that Jet Black Lovell turns out well. PT's junior year, the drama coach drafts the entire football team and cheerleading squad to be in the Ascot Race scene in *My Fair Lady*. This casting coup so ensnares Jet that the next year he tries out for and gets the lead in *Joseph*. He turns out to have a really good singing voice, and for the remainder of their time at Quagmire Regional, he and PT are friends. As for Jasper, he looks good in that fancy English morning suit (and has beautiful teeth, damn!), but musical theater isn't his thing. Today, Jasper, now Jazz, is our town's postmaster, of course. You saw that coming, didn't you? He's got a barn behind his house with the craziest collection of mailboxes you'll ever see. Some look like trucks, lobsters, covered wagons, large-mouth bass, doll houses. All of them look worse for wear. No one in town has a mailbox anymore. We pick up our mail at the post office. It's not as convenient, but it does save money on bruised mailboxes and fosters a sense of community. If you ever get a chance, you should ask Jazz to see them. He'll make it worth your while.

ARTICLE 16

———

DUNSINANE

October, 2007, a month before I begin to write our tale. The Town Accountant's Office, Town Hall, South Quagmire (just north of East Quagmire). Birnam Wood is crying, dry-eyed but with breath that's short and ragged. I stop in the doorway, hesitant to intrude. After eight years of marriage, we seldom communicate in words of more than single syllables and never with blatant emotion. We do some of our best work nonverbally.

"What's up?" I ask. Emotion in the Town Accountant's office is unusual at best. He runs town finances so smoothly now there's barely a hiccup. Town Meetings are finished in a night. The vipers in The Snake Pit seldom bite these days. They've been de-fanged by his competence.

And, although I don't like to brag, mine.

He acknowledges my presence by a big hand to the receding hairline where the blonde mixes almost imperceptibly with threads of gray. He's forty-five, still the baby face, the chubby pink white boy cheeks, but sheer volume makes him look older. He's making sounds somewhere between sputter and gasp. His desk's a mess. His desk is never a mess, but today books and papers are piled in a disorderly central pyramid of ledgers and spread sheets.

"I found it," he says, though the words come out blurred, and I'm not sure I hear what I think I hear.

"Found what?"

"The Albert Thomas DeBarros Burial Account," he says. "I found it."

At first I don't register. Instinctively I move in and press his head to me. I have no need of rolled-up toilet paper. My heart and other assets have proven easily as effective as counting down from one hundred. Once I get him calm I translate his mumble-blurt into words that may have meaning. Thirty-one years have passed, almost to the day, since Murder at Town Meeting. I've forgotten. What was it Georgina said that night about a burial account? Something about her grandfather and five hundred dollars? I'm not sure I ever believed such a thing existed.

He takes me through a convoluted trail of money laundering that hasn't been opened since Thomasine Épée was blown from the bathroom and never made it back to Town Hall to cover her tracks. Skimmed BINGO profits. Diverted postage. Embezzled funds from TouchDown Realty. There's over seven million dollars stashed in a secret account that's remained outside the purview of the state auditors and unseen since 1957 when a sixteen-year-old boy drowned in a swamp, when a clique of cool, beautiful high school kids concocted an alibi and let a twelve-year-old carry it to their graves. Birnam hasn't been looking for this. He's stumbled on it in his meticulously obsessive travels through the Town's fiscal history.

This is not the beginning of true romance. Birnam and I will never bother with the accoutrements of true romance. I've had my share of romance. It turns out badly. For the last decade (almost) we've settled for something true-ish.

True-ish begins with a meltdown nine or so years before his discovery. I forget the cause. Birnam could tell you, but why bring it up now? He's only been the interim Town Accountant for a couple of months. The books are a mess. He goes by my office banging his fist against the bulletin boards. I recall the utility of numbers and get him breathing again, then invite him across the street to what used to be The Grub Pub but is now Aunt Marge's Diner. There's absolutely no thought of romance on my mind. I'm just doing my civic duty for a provisional town employee. After dinner I drive him home. Isn't this where we began twenty years ago? He doesn't drive, never got his license. He lives in a trailer on Elm Street, an acre of land bought from his parents in the eighties. He walks or bicycles everywhere, but tonight rain threatens, and I insist. He gets in the car without protest. He's a big boy. The meat loaf's done him good. Marge Botelho still makes a mean meat loaf.

There's a meeting of town accountants in Boston and he's required to go, but he's unnerved by the thought of taking the newly-commissioned train in-town. Thirty-five, and Birnam doesn't venture anywhere he can't walk. I volunteer to accompany him, questioning my motives. We ride the line from Middleboro, spend a long day at the State House. I treat him to Italian in the North End. He counts the shrimp in the scampi. He probably counts the noodles. A little wine, and then a little more, and he becomes almost sociable. He's smiling and garrulous when we leave the restaurant. Reminds me of some guy long ago, the plump shoulders and rosy cheeks, smelling of Old Spice.

We walk back to South Station in the dark, but I'm not afraid, not in the company of this six-foot-four, three hundred twenty-pound behemoth. There's a 10:23 to Lakeville about to depart.

We're on the platform when a guy jogs out of the dark and grabs my purse. Before I can react, Birnam's got him by the wrist and pulling him in close. Birnam doesn't say a word. He squeezes the guy's hand so hard I hear bones crack. The guy howls in pain. He drops the purse. Birnam releases and the guy runs off, clutching his hand, and disappears into the terminal.

"Thanks," I say as he stoops to retrieve my purse.

"It's OK, OK," he says. He hands it to me with a little, nervous scowl. "You're welcome." We get on the train.

Next day he closes his office door and doesn't come out, but the day after he appears at my office window, noon exact.

"My turn," he says. I forgo my chicken salad sandwich. We head to lunch at Aunt Marge's Diner, and he treats. "Meat loaf for two," he says, and Marge grins. Is there anyone who doesn't take comfort in meat loaf?

It takes time. It's like coaxing a wild bird to eat from your hand. Eventually he can look me in the eye without hyperventilating. He learns breath control. He learns the gratitude of flesh. He comes when I say, "Dunsinane." I don't ask him. He asks me. We marry June 23, 1999, a simple civil service. His younger brother Woodstock runs the local flower shop (you may remember he loved flowers, especially funeral arrangements) and does the bouquets for us. Roses. Lots of roses. His niece Fire is flower girl. She's only two and in the course of the day eats my corsage.

PT is best man. Birnam only punches him once (well, maybe twice) and PT hugs him until he whimpers, then turns him over to me with a questioning grin and one raised, black eyebrow. "That time I asked you to take care of him? I didn't mean you had to go to these lengths."

PT's always good at taking punches and not holding a grudge. He's happy, if not quite real. He's spent years far from home and Little Quagmire Swamp, first to a college in Ohio where he double majors in theater and visual arts, then on to Mexico, the Caribbean, any tropical beach where the sun is strong and skin bakes bronze. His bushy black hair and Pioneers baseball cap worn sideways and the open shirt and single gold chain will always bother me, but he says he's good keeping alive a life that never reached its potential and ended young. He paints, landscapes and portraits mostly (and ducks, which are oddly marketable), retro-Impressionism, he calls it (I think it translates into Monet with buttocks), and he's not bad.

"Come," he says. "I want to see Italy and maybe we can check out Cape Verde on the way," and he says 'Verd' without the extra 'e,' a nice touch, very un-white boy, but our mothers have both been diagnosed with breast cancer within a month of each other, and I can't leave mine just when she's starting chemotherapy. He's unconcerned about leaving his. She's got Woodchuck. She's got Birnam. She'll be fine.

He spends a year backpacking Europe, lives Mediterraneanly for most of another. The Grand Tour, he tells me, was once the provenance of the rich and restless. He's penniless and gets by on looks and personality instead. Mostly looks. I visit him between marriages (mine). A little island off the coast of Tuscany called Giglio, picturesque beyond words, where he's an ornament in the villa of a handsome Italian count who patronizes him on both sides of the canvas. By now he's earned a modest reputation for his work. He exhibits in galleries in Milan and Manhattan. He becomes a minor celebrity in the art scene as painter and model. Poses nude. He goes by Tony D. He looks more like a Tony D than a Petrified Wood with his bodybuilder's chest and gold chain and sunglasses. He got tired of clever people referring to his favorite part as Scared Stiff.

"Live!" he says.

And he does. He works on cruise ships, whipping off likenesses for the tourists by day, taking chorus parts in the onstage entertainment at night. For our wedding, his Flavor-of-the-Month is Bartt from Jamaica who attends in a mango-colored wifebeater and a kilt and flip-flops. One Christmas, we have Lin-Lin in magenta, who's held his interest for a couple of years and (apparently) a couple of kids, another, Max in Ross Hunting plaid and ear muffs. PT or Tony, his appetite holds no regard for race or gender. There are women. There are men. There are gender-fluid. Black, white, Asian. We don't peek up their kilts. They don't peek up ours. They're all physically attractive. He's visual and can't get enough of beautiful things. While he revels in the sensual and the sublime, the rest of us settle for lives and lovers more pedestrian. Sometimes I think we wanted too much, too hard, too thoughtlessly in our teens, and who can live up to those first infatuations? We were children. Dear God, we were children playing at passions we didn't understand.

I will never understand what hunger drove Petrified Wood, what lay beneath the artificial surface, infecting the core. (Then again, I don't suppose we ever understand anybody when we can't understand ourselves, and here I am.) Even with my basement full of his letters, journals, paintings, theater programs, who knows what else (I've yet to open most of those boxes), he remains unknowable, as do Arianna, Uncle Anthony, Tyler....

No one will replace him. Or them.

Or miss Tara Drummond, who's in line for the Haunted Mansion at Disneyworld, spring break, 1981, with her sister's grandchildren when a black man pauses on his way by, says, "Hi, Tara, long time, no see. Hey, don't get spooked in there." The children remember later he was a big guy in a blue T-shirt and sunglasses, and after he was gone, Aunt Tara freaked out and had to leave the park.

The next day she overdoses. She leaves no note.

That July Sparky Manx says some guy named Rufus Paul's drowned off his houseboat in the Carolinas. Dead drunk, falls overboard at night. He's a graduate of Quagmire Regional, played quarterback. Then a Ted Dickson has a heart attack on a golf course. Texas, maybe, or is it Georgia, a year or two after?

The word gets around town. PT was right. People know, or think they know. They're just not willing to say what they know because, in the end, can anyone ever really know for sure what they think they know for certain? Even in a small town where people claim to know everything about everybody, the truth eludes.

The quarries are drained and filled to build a golf course. A body is found, in fact, but it's not Albert DeBarros. It's a guy who went missing in 1948. Only took fifty years to solve that mystery.

Little Quagmire Swamp is sold to Massachusetts Fish and Wildlife. No one goes looking. There's a tacit agreement around town: Let sleeping things sleep.

At a retirement party for Chief Crockett Sparky wonders aloud if the Aryan Youth adopted Little Tony D, or if Anthony DeBarros appropriated PT Wood? When Uncle Anthony looked at Petrified those lazy summer mornings in lounge chairs, who did he see? What did he feel? Was the single gold chain with winged figure talisman or curse? What went down that night in the police station jail PT's never told us? He shows up in South Quagmire for holidays and occasions, his parents' funerals, donates two of his paintings to our local library, another to a Parent-Teacher raffle, a russet swampscape with a V of geese heading south. Summertime, he'll spend a few hours with Sparky Manx taking sun on the fire station lawn. He wants to know everything that's happening in town, who Tourmaline Selsby's harassing this week, how we offer tax incentives to maintain a quorum. He's the dark, beautiful, shirtless one with the gold chain nestled in the cleft of his chest muscles, a new Flavor-of-the-Month cuddled in his arm.

Before he dies of HIV in 2004, PT Wood has sampled life's banquet to its fullest. I'm sole beneficiary of his will. The cellar's full of boxes I've yet to open, his leftovers. Maybe someday, when I'm feeling hungry. Hungry for what, you ask? Hungry for whom?

Birnam and I move in together with my mother who's getting on and needs company. The circle of life constricts.

"Wait. Who?" she asks when I tell her we're engaged. She doesn't understand, but after all these years my straining against the barrel hoops, she's given up hope of understanding, and simply says, "Congratulations. Maybe this one'll work out better than the last. I told you he'd be trouble." The last was my third cousin Joe Cabral for whom my mother played matchmaker. I smile. I fill out the marriage certificate. The Commonwealth of Massachusetts removed the Color question back in 1968, so there's no need to speculate, but on a honeymoon visit to the local paint store, the groom matches himself to Sherwin Williams VF 62 Softer Tan SW 6141 and his bride to Benjamin Moore Brown Teepee 2102-40. We check each other out against paint chips. So now we know. We laugh. We laugh more and easily as the years go by. And on PT's burial certificate (the Color line remains on burial certificates in 2004, as if waiting to close a generational chapter of our nation's history) we write in Pittsburgh Paints Hot Chocolate 420-5, our own little rebellion.

(And, to this day I've yet to find a box of crayons that includes Portuguese.)

As for the barrel hoops, no, they do not protect against scarring. Together Ma and I will cook a big pot of *canja* in PT's memory. The surviving aunties will come and offer advice about the garlic and say, "Wasn't he that nice boy came to Anthony's funeral?"

Aunt Rose whispers, "I never noticed how much he looked like Anthony. I thought he looked like Toby Dobbs. The skin color threw me off."

I've gone through all three birth certificates, but there's nothing there. In the end you've got to believe in coincidence. Or in Birnam, who shakes his head with pity when I mention the resemblance and says, "Do the math!"

ARTICLE 17

———

NOVEMBER 1956, POSTSCRIPT

There's one person deserves the last word.

Sunday afternoon before Thanksgiving, the days are short and the sun's low. The oaks cling to their leaves but the maples and birch have let theirs go. A few skitter across the field in a brisk November breeze. East Quagmire has the ball at the forty-seven-yard line, and the South Quagmire Warriors are down by three. The quarterback's a good-sized twelve-year-old and he's got the ball. He takes aim and throws, a well-aimed shot to his receiver, who's wide open. The ball flies straight, the receiver's hands are there, and a second before he lands it, out of nowhere comes Little Tony D and intercepts. The crowd leaps to its feet.

Little Tony D runs and runs and runs. There's a moment when he's almost taken out by the opposing tackle. He loses his footing and then, with a miracle pivot, is twisting sideways and running again. He runs seventy-two yards. The last twenty there's no one within a million miles of him. The crowd is screaming.

Touchdown!

His teammates rush him (it takes a while for them to reach him) and hurl each other into a big group hug and pig pile. After that, Leo Bushnell kicks a field goal, and thus ends the last and best victory of the season for South Quagmire's first-ever PAL football heroes. Little Tony D is carried off the field in triumph. His arm is nearly shaken off by friends, parents, spectators. It's the best, man! It's the best!

Then the team goes off to the Athletic Association to celebrate its win, and Little Tony D can't go. He's colored. He knows he can't attend the party, no matter the game's outcome. He's been prepped by his dad beforehand. No matter that an eleven-year-old doesn't honestly understand what the issue is.

"Tell you what," says Toby Dobbs, high school god, fingering the tiny winged figure on his gold chain. "Next Friday a bunch of us are going out to End Zone Island for a party. High school football team, y'know? You can come too, honorary Quarryman. No one's gonna keep you outa there, little man. You're a TD. You're our guest."

Little Tony D looks at his hero wide-eyed. "Really?"

"Really. Whaddya drink? Coke? Mountain Dew? You look like a Mountain Dew man to me, buddy! I'm treating. You're the greatest, Tony D!"

The team goes off in many cars to the Athletic Association for pizza, and Little Tony D climbs back into his father's 1949 Ford Tudor.

Uncle Manny says, "Hot dogs or pizza? We're proud of you, son."

Of course, Aunt Flora won't hear of her boy going anywhere near a bunch of high school football players. She's no fool. Everyone knows what goes on out there at those parties in the swamp. When Little Tony D appeals to his father, Uncle Manny says, "What your mother says."

End of story.

But Little Tony D is nothing if not headstrong. He's barely aware that Thanksgiving passes because he can't think of anything but Friday night. The high school Thanksgiving Day game is unremarkable. South Quagmire loses even though Toby Dobbs makes a couple good blocks and Tim Drummond gets three first downs. Friday evening Little Tony D goes to bed early, tired, and then he's out the bedroom window. He runs and runs and runs, a good four miles from his house to End Zone Island, but the moon's up, it's not too cold, and the air's a stimulant. He runs the dirt road, a straight-away through flat, open landscape of low bog, recently harvested and flooded for the winter. The narrow ridge of sand drops down on both sides to water. The water's black, and once or twice something splashes in it. He feels a little scared of swamp monsters, but nothing's gonna stop him, and before long he can see light off to his right, over the water and through the ghostly spines of limbless, leafless trees. Firelight shimmers off the ripples.

Now, far ahead he sees headlights, tiny at first, growing brighter as they approach. Oncoming car, and he's a little, dark boy on a long, dark road. But before it reaches him, hits him, it turns off the straightaway into the trees, and Little Tony D sees it flickering through the cedars as the sound of the engine fades.

Soon enough he turns off after it into the woods, where the trees close in and the night gets deep, and he's breathing hard, but nothing's gonna stop him. Nothing! There could be mountain lions. There could be wolves. An owl swoops past on silent wings, a shadow in a shadow. At last the trees open and the flicker of firelight beckons not so far ahead. The bogs have been flooded and the water level's low in the reservoirs. He wades the shallows for twenty or thirty yards. There's lots of noise, hollering, music getting louder as he splashes forward, heart pumping fast. Someone's wailing Elvis Presley's *'Long Tall Sally'* on a guitar. Bodies writhe in the bushes, broken bottles glitter the base of trees. Little Tony D crashes the party.

Toby Dobbs and Tim Drummond are stretched out by a roaring camp fire with a couple of cheerleaders. They look surprised.

"Hey, boy," they greet him, slow on the uptake, and then, to everyone else, "Look who's here! Our new football legend, future Quagmire Quarryman! It's Little Tony D!"

There are cheers and slaps on the back and drunken congratulations. There is no Coke or Mountain Dew or anything non-alcoholic. The team plies him with Ballantine Ale and Carling Black Label. It tastes awful, but it's worth it to be accepted by the coolest guys in town, to be a TD.

The camp fire burns low. The moon is down.

"You can sleep in my tent tonight," says Toby Dobbs.

"Really?" asks Little Tony D, groggy in the presence of his varsity god.

"Really," say Toby Dobbs. "Go ahead. Climb in. Use my sleeping bag."

So Little Tony D climbs in and falls asleep in Toby Dobbs's tent. Toby Dobbs grins at Tim Drummond. Across the fire, Tara Darsch glances at Thomasine DeAngelis who rolls her eyes and stalks off to relieve herself in the bushes. Tara shrinks back, uncertain, too timid to interfere, then follows.

There are other nights.

There are other tents.

There's love and hate and self-loathing and plenty of guilt to go around.

There's always scarring.

At least, that's the way I imagine it.

I offer the last word to Sparky Manx, but Sparky Manx isn't saying.

THANKS!

So many people built the town of South Quagmire (just north of East Quagmire) in so many crazy, humorous, meaningful ways, their contributions could be entire stories in themselves:

Arlene Dias, classmate, collaborator, and friend since first grade, also, Lorraine and Wendy Deas, who taught me attitude early on, and class valedictorian Judy Berry, whom I was not allowed to take to the Senior Prom;

Beth Sloan and Jean Kelly, Hanson Town Clerks, who made sure we got the Birth, Marriage, and Burial Certificates right; Stephanie Blackman, editor, publisher of Riverhaven Books, for her insight; Lt. Cmdr. Amanda and Cmdr. Jeremy Denning, USCG, helicopter pilots and flight instructors; and Joe Warren, USMC, my weapons expert;

Mark and Helen Vess, and Bruce Young, Town Meeting provocateurs;

Laura Dunkum, John, Claire, Tori, and Dani Seamans, Jim Hickey, Hal Marshman, Barb Tirrell, Ray and Cindy Fish, Al and Carolyn Galambos, Ruth Stoddard, Corey, Debbie, Mary, Nathaniel, Sue, and Tim Blauss, Edna Howland, Scott Ripley, Jack, Heather, Jess, and Peg Weydt, Kathy Fuller, Steff, Scott, Al, and Mike Sayce, Chris, Kevin, and Paige Cameron, Peggy Comerford, Jeff Sironi, John, Marie, and Yon Hanlon, Kip Florence, Emily and Mike

McLeod, Chloe and Jeff Wilson, Chris, Corey, Al, and Gordon King, Lil Dignan, John Dexter, Paul Bouzan, Laurelle Christian, Jim and Kelly Armstrong, CJ King, James Siegel, Cole Fountain, Jon Gillis, Mike Drewniak, Dot and Karl Baresel, Bennett Childs, Rob O'Brien, Britney Siereveld, Madi Storey, Debbie and Steve Dennison, Audrey and Jim Flanagan, Neil Fortin, Pam Cohen, Rick Teague, Brian Wilson, Amara Robinson, E Spencer, Joe and John Gannon, Julia Pendrak, Melody Young, Carol Polio, Matt Hickey, Nick Merritt, Kristen Clifford, John Mahoney, Steve Melisi, Chris Leonard, Jonas Gaffey, Jason Bannon, Mary and Lauren Bain, and the many, many others who brought these characters to life onstage; also, Steve Capellini and Matt Dyer, for moments of perfect slapstick,

Annette Wilson, Ellen Galambos, and Laurie Bianchi, fearless editors;

Joanne Blauss, intuitive, impatient, and a force to be reckoned with; and 45 years of Annual and Special Town Meetings in the almost-fictional town of Hanson, Massachusetts, without whose inspirational characters this story would not have been possible.